COURTNEY
CAN'T
Decide

H. L. MACFARLANE

Copyright

Content Warnings

For Cara, who knows what it's like

COURTNEY
CAN'T
Decide

H. L. MACFARLANE

"Could I interest you in everything all of the time?"

Welcome to the Internet (Bo Burnham: 2021)

Chapter One

COURTNEY

THE MAN WHO'D TAKEN THE LAST two sausage rolls from Greggs, stolen my taxi when I was late for work and slammed a door in my face on my way *in* to work was currently standing before me, and all I could do was smile.

In geography there's this concept of a shrinking world affecting space and place. For example, there are 8,598 miles between Glasgow, Scotland and Darwin, Australia. That distance is constant in the grand scheme of things. But in the good old days a person could never fathom travelling from Glasgow to Darwin, nor meet a person who lived half a world away. Those 8,598 miles may well have been infinite. But then we developed ships, then planes, and suddenly that distance had grown smaller relative to how far a person could now travel.

Here's an example: you could, say, flee the city you were born and raised in to live with a hot Aussie guitarist you met through a friend – thus avoiding your mother constantly pressing you to get a 'real' job – for a solid three years straight out of university.

But after ships and planes came the phone and the Internet, and instead of having to travel those 8,598 miles to visit someone on the other side of the world you could instantaneously contact them. You could have a fulfilling relationship with them without ever being in the same place as them.

Or you could relentlessly bother them, instead.

Following my previous example: when you return to Glasgow with your tail between your legs after catching said hot Aussie guitarist cheating on you with not one but three of his band-mates, rather than flying out to beg for your forgiveness all they do is constantly send you messages, and call you, and generally virtually hound you until you block them on absolutely everything.

For better or worse, in the span of a few hundred years Glasgow, Scotland and Darwin, Australia went from being impossible to connect to immediate. The *space* between the *places* had grown smaller, even though the physical distance hadn't.

Anyway, both my space and my place were feeling pretty fucking small right now.

"I'm sorry to bother you," the sausage roll and taxi thief said, "but I think there's something wrong with my room."

I took a long moment to scan my new nemesis as I pretended to type up something on the reception computer. He was inordinately well dressed – was that charcoal grey suit *Armani?* – with hair styled perfectly away from his face that was gracefully going grey at the temples. Grey into glossy black. But he wasn't that old; looking at his face – grey *eyes*, too – he was maybe in his mid-thirties. He couldn't be much more than five years older than me. God, it took one hell of a secure man to rock the silver fox look in his thirties. Peeking down I saw he had on the most pristine pair of wing-tip Oxfords I had ever seen. Money doesn't buy taste but clearly this man was wealthy in more ways than one.

All in all the guy looked way too rich to be nicking the last sausage rolls from a fucking Greggs. I'd been the only person in the queue behind him, anyway; why couldn't he have taken *one* and left me the final, delicious baked good? Who the hell ever wanted the cream of chicken bakes? Nobody, that's who. Everyone wanted the sausage rolls.

Including Mr 'I Look Like I Could *Buy* Greggs', who was no doubt about to complain about how his room wasn't up-to-scratch. It would be just my luck.

Satisfied with my assessment of his entire person I fixed him my usual bland-but-cheery receptionist smile. "It's not a bother at all. What seems to be the problem with your room?"

"There appears to be a couple having sex inside it."

I choked on a laugh. Come on, who wouldn't? Of all the things for Mr Fancy to say I certainly hadn't expected it to be that. Thankfully the man took my unprofessional response with as much grace as his greying temples, and he smiled. "I imagine they weren't a 'welcome to the Plaza' perk of the room, then?"

"No, I'd wager they weren't. Can I have your room key, please?" Mister Fancy dutifully handed it over. When I swiped it the resultant ID attached to the room popped up on the computer screen: that of a woman with an overly severe pixie cut and a pair of lips that looked way too large to be natural. I coughed softly into my hand. "Unless you've gone through some *seriously great* gender reassignment surgery, or your girlfriend booked the room for you, I think you may have gotten the wrong key."

The man fished through his inner suit pocket for his wallet, then handed me his driver's license. "Definitely still a guy last time I checked," he said. "Still single, too."

I ignored his comments. "Simon Saint," I murmured, typing his name into the computer whilst also taking account of all the rest of the personal info the license gave me. Born on the tenth of June. Age thirty-six. Registered address down in London with a very expensive postcode.

That would explain the wanker London accent, then.

"Ah, you're meant to be in...oh, the penthouse," I exclaimed, though why the fuck this would surprise me given all of the prior information I had about Simon Saint was beyond my understanding. "For three months?"

He nodded. "I'm overseeing a new restaurant opening in the city centre. A friend offered to let me stay with them but I prefer having my privacy...and a view of the river."

I hadn't asked for the explanation but it satisfied my burning curiosity nonetheless. "I wonder how Samantha got your room key so wrong..." I mumbled, more to myself than to Simon.

"Forgive me for saying this but she was too busy flirting with the security guard to take much notice of me," he said, sounding genuinely apologetic for ratting out Sam. I didn't care. I didn't get paid enough to care.

Which might have been why the next words out of my mouth were, "I wish they'd do us all a favour and bang it out already."

"If they look inside room 501 I'm sure they'll pick up a trick or two."

Damn it, that was funny. Stupid, stunning Simon Saint was funny. I proffered him the correct key card but when he reached out to take it his hand paused, hovering over mine. A frown cast his eyes in confused shadow. "Have we met?" he asked, cocking his head to the side to regard me curiously.

It's funny what five minutes of rushed make-up, changing clothes and tearing a brush through your hair can do to alter how a man perceives a woman. I was about to tell him we'd never met before – he was an arsehole, but I'd rather let my grudge burn in private thank you very much – when his gaze locked on the faint red mark on my forehead. "Fuck, I hit you with the door on my way in," he said, grimacing as he did so. "I'm really sorry. I didn't realise it was automatic and I used *way* too much force to haul it open."

"It's okay," I reassured him, because I guess the fact he had both correctly identified who I was and apologised was a point in his favour, "just don't go stealing the last sausage roll *and* my taxi to work next time and we'll get along fine."

It took Simon a few seconds to process this. Then something clicked in his brain, and he sheepishly took his key card from me. "I guess I won't be your favourite guest, then."

"I guess we have three months to find out."

"Do you always work the evening shift?" I didn't know if Simon was asking to be polite or if he was genuinely interested. Either way, there was someone tutting impatiently behind him for us to wrap up our conversation.

"Only Wednesday through Sunday," I ended up telling him, which was the truth. "I hope you enjoy your stay, Mr Saint."

Simon, to his credit, took this as the dismissal that it was. He flashed me a winning smile of perfect white teeth and pointy canines. God, I loved pointy canines. "I'm sure I will. Have a good evening, Miss...?"

"Courtney," I said, pointing towards my name tag.

"Of course. Court—"

"*Ahem,*" the disgruntled woman standing behind Simon let out. He offered her the same smile he'd given me, and she visibly shied away from how handsome he was.

"I'm so sorry for taking up her time," he apologised, running an awkward hand through his perfect hair even though not a single strand was out of place. Pointy canines *and* a nervous tic? Simon was getting more attractive with every passing second. Then he turned to me and said, "When my luggage arrives can you make sure it comes up to my room? I'm afraid Samantha might have directed it to 501."

"Of course." And with that Simon left for the stairs – the *stairs,* not the lift – and I was left to deal with the frustrated woman who had resumed tapping her foot, even though the only person who could hear her do so was me and I was now available to hear her complaint.

"What can I help you with this evening?" I asked, my perfectly bland smile back in place. Until that moment I hadn't realised I'd changed it to a genuine one for Simon.

"There are only three towels in my bathroom. I want four."

Ah. Great. Simon Saint had, of course, been an anomaly. Interesting guests always were. Tonight would be just the same as any other night.

I hoped he'd come down to reception asking for more towels.

Chapter Two

SIMON

Sometimes you just want a Gregg's sausage roll. Even when you run an award-winning bakery in London. Even when you grew up with renowned gourmet pastry chefs cooking for you. Sometimes, just sometimes, you get an urge that only your favourite childhood junk food will fulfil.

I shouldn't have bought the last *two*, though. I hadn't even wanted two, but it felt like the right thing to do when there were only two remaining. Had I not been so absorbed in the call I was taking through my earphones I'd have noticed the fact there was a woman behind me and it was ten minutes to closing so no more damn sausage rolls were going to be made.

Perhaps, had I taken five minutes away from my phone, I'd have also realised said woman was the one who flagged down the taxi I so arrogantly hopped into, and I wouldn't have also strong-armed the door into the Crowne Plaza when I arrived there, thus hitting the aforementioned woman in the face.

All in all, I'd made a series of stupid choices that had ultimately made someone else's life worse.

At least, by the end of our conversation, the funny,

charming, gorgeous receptionist I'd accidentally screwed over three times that evening (in a bad way) didn't seem to hate me. Considering I was going to be staying in the Plaza for three months I considered that a good thing.

A very good thing.

Unfortunately, the penthouse suite was absolutely perfect. I say 'unfortunately' because I was already looking for an excuse to bother Courtney No-Last-Name to help me out again. But the bed was crisp and pristine, with a perfectly crease-free duvet folded around the mattress in a manner I'd never been able to replicate at home. The glass wall with an uninterrupted view of the River Clyde was faultless, the bar was fully stocked, all of the furniture in the room was clean and new, and the massive bathroom was practically sparkling. On a small table between two armchairs, overlooking the Clyde, was an ice bucket with a bottle of champagne and eight German beers inside.

"Fun night for one," I said, amused at the excessive volume of alcohol as I took up a bottle opener to crack open one of the beers. I didn't have anything to do until tomorrow: my head chef had arrived the week before as a request from Tom, who'd asked if he could steal Kei for a private meal he wanted made for his girlfriend's thirtieth birthday. Ever the romantic, I'd said yes. Kei had met Tom before, anyway, and liked him enough to do him a favour. But it meant that the first couple of days of restaurant prep had already been completed ahead of my arrival. It was Thursday now, so I'd probably have nothing to do until Monday.

Since I'd gone to uni in Glasgow I hardly wanted to piss away my free time sight-seeing. It was so rare that I had a full weekend free, after all. Deciding that it was worth bothering Tom for something decent to do I picked up my phone to call him, only to be met with an incoming call from my grandmother.

"What's up?" I asked the moment I accepted the call. I was met with a familiar tut-tutting.

"Who taught you to answer the phone like that? Not me or your grandfather, that's for certain."

"I'm sorry, I wasn't aware this was a business call."

She didn't laugh. "How's your room at the hotel? It *is* the penthouse Rupert booked for you, correct? I told him he should go for the Hilton but—"

"It's wonderful, Nan. I promise." I knew fine well she'd have found something to criticise about any hotel I stayed in, so ultimately it didn't matter if my grandfather had booked the Plaza or the Hilton or even a Premier Inn.

"Do you really have to spend three months in Glasgow?" Nan protested, dissatisfied that I'd closed the door to complaining about the hotel too early. Lord only knew she'd blow off her head if I told her about the couple humping like rabbits in Room 501. "Can't your chef, Kai whathaveyou—"

"Kei Nakamura."

"Can't he handle everything? You have a business to run down here, Simon. Not to mention the bakery. I thought *that* was your passion project? So what's this restaurant all about?"

I could only sigh good-naturedly, taking a swig of beer before plonking myself down in one of the armchairs to look out over the Clyde. It had a stiff newness to it, like it would take another few years to wear in, but it was still inordinately comfortable. In the last five minutes it had begun raining: big, fat water droplets ran down the glass wall as if they were racing each other. This was Glasgow, after all. Rain was part of the deal. "I told you I didn't want to oversee the catering company forever," I said to my grandmother, after I ran through several possible lines I could feed her before landing on the least complicated one.

One that she'd ignored a million times before.

"But it's so lucrative! I thought that was the point in me and your grandfather investing in—"

"I'm so sorry, Nan, but I have another call coming through."

This wasn't a lie, though the timing was impossibly convenient. Tom was calling. I could simply call him back later but since I'd been planning to contact him anyway it seemed like a good excuse. "Call you later?"

"Hmm, you better," my grandmother said. "I don't like you being away from home for so long."

"I know, and I love you for it. Make sure Papa takes his meds, okay?"

"As if I needed reminding. I love you, Simon."

"You too. Have a lovely weekend."

I hung up and answered Tom's call, which had come through on Whatsapp. "The hell are you doing calling me on an app, you fossil?" I teased. "I wasn't aware you even *knew* what an app was."

"I'm four years older than you, bastard," came Tom's reply. In the background I heard his girlfriend, Liz, snort at the comment. I'd met Tom through the whisky club at the University of Glasgow, when I was a baby undergrad studying economics and he'd just begun his PhD in some area of biology I couldn't pretend to understand. Despite the age and experience gap we'd quickly become close friends. "Have you landed in Glasgow yet?"

"About an hour ago." I loosened my tie and undid the top two buttons of my shirt before continuing, "I'm in the hotel. Just waiting for my luggage."

"I can't believe you rejected living with me."

"With you *and* Liz," I amended. "No offence but the two of you are nauseating."

"Says the hopeless romantic."

"The single hopeless romantic."

"As it transpires, Si, I may have a potential solution for that."

I leaned forward, intrigued despite myself. Tom hadn't attempted to play matchmaker for me since our university days.

"Who's the unlucky lady, then?"

"Not a lady."

"God, we've been through this before. I banged *one* guy then knew it wasn't for m—"

Tom's cackle cut me off. "I forgot about Steve. Steve and Simon. It was cute."

"Tom—"

"It's not a dude, either. Liz and I are hosting her friend Chloë's thirtieth up at the townhouse. You remember Chloë, right?"

"Smoking hot redhead with a girlfriend named Harry?"

"Harriet, yeah."

"So what are you telling me about it for?"

"It's on Saturday. A costume party with a film theme. You should come along and socialise."

And here was my dilemma. Tom had just given me a perfect opportunity to *do* something with my weekend, yet I found myself shaking my head at the invitation. Because as we'd been talking about my romantic failures my mind invariably wandered back down to Courtney in reception. She said she worked nights Wednesday through Saturday, but that meant she could be free during the day on Saturday - or might be up for grabbing a drink after work.

That sounded far more preferable to a costume party for someone I barely knew.

Tom took my silence as the rejection it was. "I know you're going to say no but let me appeal to your better nature. I *need* you there. The party is going to be full of musical theatre nerds. Lord help me, Liz'll be screeching all night to - *ow*, Liz - well, you get the picture. Keep me company."

"We both know you'll get two tequilas down you and you'll be singing along just as loudly as her. Louder, even. And letting your already inflated ego get bigger when everyone tells you how wonderful your singing is."

It was Liz's laughter I heard down the phone; it made *me* laugh just to hear it. Over the last two years we'd become comrades-in-arms when it came to insulting Thomas Henderson.

"In any case," Tom huffed through our laughter, "at least think about it before saying no. It's not for another two days."

"Okay, let's compromise and say I'll promise to pretend to think about it."

"Bitch. I'll see you Saturday." Tom hung up before I could fire another rebuttal his way. Feeling refreshed from having an actual conversation with an actual friend rather than the days and days of business meetings I'd had all week, I necked back the rest of my beer and stood up, flinging off my suit jacket as I did so. Then I headed down to reception.

At first Courtney was nowhere to be seen, but then her blonde head bobbed up from behind the reception desk, her arms laden with presumably dropped folders. She looked *ruffled*, for lack of a better word – and somehow all the more gorgeous for it. Perhaps it was the rosy tint to her cheeks.

"Miss Courtney the Receptionist," I said softly. I say softly but I may as well have shouted it going by the way she jumped half out of her skin and dropped the folders once more. I cringed at the mess I'd made, but didn't want to make things more awkward by going around the desk to help her. So instead I leaned on the desk and said, "Sorry. I didn't mean to startle you."

"Oh, it isn't your fault," she replied from the floor, sweeping up the folders before dumping them on her desk. When she straightened to give me her full attention she offered me a slightly crooked smile. "I'm easily startled."

"Regardless, I'm sorry."

"What can I help you with, Mr Saint?"

"Simon is fine, if you'll give me your last name."

That crooked smile grew wider. "Miller. But if I'm calling you Simon you can call me Courtney."

"Courtney it is, then. Are you free before your shift on Saturday?"

There was a beat of silence where Courtney took in my words for what they were – a request for a date – before she said, "I'm sorry, I'm so behind on housework and my flat mate will quite literally flay me if I dunk out on it this time." Courtney looked genuinely apologetic; I took this as a sign she was telling the truth, and that I was free to try again.

"What about after your shift? I'm sure a Greggs will still be open somewhere."

Courtney's eyebrow twitched, and I thought she would burst out laughing, but – like earlier when I made the joke about Samantha and the bouncer taking sex tips from room 501 – she stayed silent. "I'm not actually working this Saturday," she said after a pause. "I have plans with the aforementioned flat mate."

I wasn't one to strike out after three attempts; two would do. I hardly wanted to harass a woman whilst she was working, anyway. "It was worth a try," I relented, swiping a hand through my hair. Nan always chastised me for doing this, calling it an unsightly nervous tic, but I'd never grown out of it. "Thank you for very kindly rejecting me."

This was what finally caused Courtney to laugh. "Being busy isn't rejecting you."

"I was trying to gracefully leave. Why would you call me out like this?"

Another laugh. "I'm off Monday night. If you want to do something that isn't buying a Greggs, that is."

I felt like whooping in the air like Judd Nelson at the end of *The Breakfast Club.* "I'll take it. Know any good places to eat?"

"I wouldn't be a very good receptionist if I didn't. Here" – she held out her hand – "give me your phone." I unlocked it then gave it over; Courtney stuck her tongue out very slightly as she tapped in her number. "Send me a text or whatever and we can get something organised."

"Excuse me, I've been waiting over ten minutes!" cried a grumpy old man to my left who had definitely only just shown up.

I didn't bother suppressing the grimace I felt my face desperately want to make. "It seems we must always be interrupted."

"That's what you get for flirting with me at work." Courtney flashed me a smile then, with a swish of her hair, turned from me to help the grouch.

I found myself grinning from ear to ear as I made my way back up to my suite – taking the lift this time, because I'd already gotten my steps in for the day – then, grabbing another beer, I sent Courtney a text that read:

> Simon says this is his number. Don't hate the joke.

Two minutes later she replied:

> I can hate the one who made it, though, right? ;)

Taking that as a very good sign I sent another text, this time to Tom. I was in a good mood, after all, and with my Saturday now free as a bird I could do with helping my friend out.

> Dressing as someone from Office Space counts as fancy dress, right?

Under a minute later he said:

> It'll do.

Satisfied, I sat back down in front of the glass wall and watched the rain get steadily heavier. God, it was good to be back in Glasgow.

I wish I'd never left.

Chapter Three

COURTNEY

"And I'm telling you, Court, she knows fine well she's not paid for the last three weeks!"

"And I'm telling you to tell *her* to pay her damn bill."

Rich, my boss slash best friend, sighed enormously: wrangling money out of Mrs Campbell was one of the most difficult parts of his job. "You know what she's like," he said, shaking curls of sandy brown hair out of his eyes as he sorted through the list of dogs meant to be coming in that morning. "She pulls in here ten minutes late, apologising for the roads being too busy or her kids refusing to get ready for school or—"

"Or a plane has come crashing down on her house, or the whole of Glasgow has gone up in flames, or—"

"You know what I mean," Rich complained, nonetheless sniggering at my increasingly exaggerated excuses. "She pulls in here, drops off her damn labradoodle and dissolves into the ether before I can do anything about it. And it's even worse at pick-up!"

This is where I came in handy. I was the proverbial muscle of our two-man team at Blake's Dog Day Care. "Leave it to me.

Even if I have to barricade the door she is *not* leaving without settling that bill." I flexed my (pitiful) biceps to prove my point. "Happy?"

"I could only be happier if we didn't have to resort to intimidation in the first place."

Whilst I worked reception in the Crowne Plaza every Wednesday through Sunday 6-11pm, with my hair perfectly washed, my face made up, and my uniform ironed to perfection, on Monday through Friday 9-1pm (except Tuesdays) I worked with Rich at his day care. Sometimes I worked afternoons, too, especially on Wednesdays when my favourite dog in the entire universe was in all day. It made it difficult to get to the Plaza on time but it was so, so worth it. After all, pretty much no one else in Glasgow had a Tibetan Mastiff other than Tom Henderson and Liz Maclean.

Rich and I were currently waiting for the Friday morning dogs to arrive, including Mrs Campbell's very spoiled, very aloof labradoodle. The creature only ate raw, organic, non-processed food. To be honest I wanted to punch some sense into Mrs Campbell – did she even know what 'processed' meant? How did she think the mince she fed her precious dog came to be? It certainly didn't come out of the fucking cow looking like that. It would serve her well to look in a dictionary sometime, then maybe she would understand how stupid she was.

Anyway.

The doorbell rang, and when Rich opened the door not one, not two, not three but *four* French bulldogs barrelled their way inside, followed by a gust of bitter January air. A full-body shudder ran through me whilst Rich chatted to the owners and double-checked the pick-up times for their respective terrors. I don't have anything against bulldogs (aside from the obvious pedigree breeding atrocities) but they were definitely my least favourite dogs to babysit. They were by far and away the messiest of the lot, whose sole life purpose seemed to be drooling all over my favourite jumper whenever I naïvely wore it to work.

Next came a labradoodle – not Mrs Campbell's – and a cockapoo. About seventy percent of the dogs Rich and I looked after fell into the Bulldog, pug or poodle-cross category; personally I thought it was bloody weird how certain types of dogs went in and out of fashion. They were animals, not watches or bags. That's why I loved Wednesdays when we mostly just had the big dogs in, including a half-dozen absolutely ridiculous mongrels whose owners couldn't for the life of them tell you what breeds made up their beautiful idiots.

"Can you hang the leads up for me, Court?" Rich asked, barely sidestepping out of the way when a pug and two dachshunds waddled through the door. Wordlessly I complied, steeling myself for what promised to be a very busy morning. We were at full capacity, which was the usual story on a Friday.

Ten minutes later and all we were waiting for was my favourite dog (Mrs Campbell had called to inform Rich that she was *so sorry* but precious Benjamin had a cold so she wouldn't be bringing him in today). It wasn't like Tom to drop Ludo off this late; he was usually the first one here before he ran (yes, actually ran) the half an hour from the day care to his lab at Glasgow Uni. With a chuckle I wondered if he'd give me one of Mrs Campbell's many ridiculous excuses for his tardiness.

Then Tom and Liz showed up, arm-in-arm, giggling and grinning and so ridiculously in love that I felt like burning my eyes out with a red-hot iron poker. It was easy to conclude why they were late when they were looking at each other like that.

God, I wanted what they had. A love that you didn't want to leave your bed for because you'd rather face the consequences of being late to work in order to screw the morning away. But because it was Tom and Liz who had the love and the regular, active sex life (rather than me) I hated them for it.

Just joking. I loved the pair of them. Almost as much as I loved their giant bear of a dog.

"Ludo!" I cried in glee, letting the Tibetan Mastiff full-on bowl me over to the floor. He was actually an incredibly docile dog, with impeccable manners and the patience of a saint, but for me he acted like a giant puppy. I wasn't smug about this in the slightest. Not at all.

"Someone's running late today," Rich greeted Tom and Liz, either blissfully oblivious to the reason for their glowing skin and general lateness or very professionally ignoring it. He had one of those faces that was great for service work: pleasant, pretty and non-threatening. If he wasn't my best friend I'd have hated Rich for having the longest, thickest eyelashes known to man framing his damn Bambi eyes. Actually, scrap that, I *did* hate him for it, but he was bullied so much as a kid for looking like a girl that I didn't have the heart to neg him for it.

Liz blushed entirely un-self-consciously. "All the students in the lab were at a lecture this morning."

"So I made the executive decision that Liz and I should go for brunch," Tom explained, giving Ludo a generous head rub when he came back over to whine for attention.

"How awful for you," I said, extending them both a middle finger. "Must be great being your own boss."

Tom waved an emphatic hand at Rich. "What is Mr Blake here if not his own boss?"

"Yeah, and if I showed up late because I spent the morning having sex before going to brunch you can bet your exceptional arse he'd yell at me about it." If I made such a comment at the Plaza in front of guests I'd have almost certainly been fired, but the same comment made in front of Rich, Tom and Liz? The cavernous, echoey room that was the dog day care boomed with their collective laughter.

Actually, that's sort of a lie. I'd been joking like this was Simon Saint only last night. But that wasn't normal Courtney-the-receptionist behaviour. I never had guests like that. I mean okay, yeah, there had been some lewd comments thrown my way from guests in the past, as well as a few dating requests, but not from anyone I was mutually interested in. Usually they were all dirty old men.

Proverbial butterflies fluttered through my stomach, my face warming just a little as I thought of my impending date with Simon on Monday.

Liz, ever the perceptive one, noticed my change in demeanour immediately. "What's on your mind? Did you have to skip out on having sex in order to get to work on time?"

I snorted. "If only. I got asked out at the Plaza by a new guest yesterday, though."

"Is he fit?"

"Extremely."

Liz cooed in excitement. "Is he a sugar daddy?"

"Definitely wealthy, but only four years older than me."

"You seem to know an awful lot about this hotel guest that you apparently only met yesterday," Liz said, eyeing me suspiciously. "Did you stalk him online?"

I baulked at the suggestion. "Stalking a man's social media is inappropriate, Elizabeth." But I was grinning, and so was Liz, because if I hadn't gained Simon's personal information whilst working I almost definitely would have looked him up online already. "All information I have on him I gleaned from his driver's license and his very expensive suit."

"Makes sense. Did you say yes?"

"I did, actually."

To my left Rich dropped the wad of cash Tom had only just handed him. He scrambled to pick up the notes before running to his tiny office to store them in the safe.

"That's a shame," Tom said, which was the exact opposite of what I'd expected him to say. When I raised an eyebrow in his direction he elaborated, "I have a friend in town who I thought might be a good match for you."

"Sorry, I don't think any blind date could live up to the

reality of this guy." I didn't know why I was so sure of Simon, to be honest, especially because my taste in guys was usually – to put it bluntly – fucking atrocious. Yes, Simon was handsome and yes, he was staying in the penthouse suite for three months and yes, his suit probably cost more than I made in a year, but I didn't know anything about *him*. Well, he had a nervous tic and he was very polite. And he wasn't above making a filthy joke. I supposed that was something.

But I knew nothing, really.

After Tom and Liz bid us good-bye – Liz promising to send me more photos of her new kitten and Tom insisting I tell him if my date got cancelled so he could set me up with his friend – Rich finally closed the door to the outside world, and we settled into our usual morning routine. But even through the hectic mania of running around after a pack of dogs, I could tell my friend was quieter than usual.

"Right, what's up?" I asked an hour later, when I caught Rich cleaning the same section of the floor for the third time in a row even though there was nothing to mop up. And he *hated* mopping. "Spill."

Rich glanced up at me through his damnable eyelashes, a grimace plastered to his face that he seemed to believe he was hiding. "Nothing. This place is just extra filthy this morning. Ruby keeps peeing."

"Bull shit. Tell me what's wrong, you big baby."

It took Rich long enough to reply that I stopped throwing tennis balls for the dogs in order to give him my full attention. Only once he realised he couldn't get away with saying nothing did he mumble, "You're going on a date."

"Yes?" I went on dates all the time; it shouldn't have come to a surprise to Rich that I had one lined up. Well, I had a lot of *first* dates, at least. Australian ex-boyfriend aside – someone Rich himself introduced me to when we were working on an apple orchard together – I was notoriously bad at getting past a first date. I was far more of an expert in the 'casual hook-up' sphere of human relationships.

"And you don't think he might be a serial killer?" Rich asked, when it became clear I wasn't going to elaborate.

"Have you ever met a serial killer who pays to stay in the penthouse of the Plaza for three months?"

"No, but I don't know any serial killers to compare him to."

I chucked a tennis ball at his head, satisfied when it bounced off his curly hair with a *thump*. "That you know of."

"Touché."

"Seriously, what's up?"

"It's nothing. I swear it. Hey, your phone's buzzing. It's probably your dad. You should answer it."

I wish I could have called Rich out on his deflection but it was true: Dad was calling me. I glanced at the screen then gasped in horror. "What day is it today?"

Rich stared at me incredulously. The way anyone looked at me when I asked a question anyone with a brain knew the answer to. "Friday."

Shit. Yeah. Of course. That's why we had a full house this morning. I ran off to Rich's office in order to accept the call. "Dad, I'm so sorry – I meant to call you before work this morning!" I forced out before my dad could say a single word. "How did it go? Do you qualify? You must have – your back's been fucked for months now, there's no way you can keep working removals—"

"I didn't go, dove."

"*What*? Why not?" Dad said nothing for even longer than Rich when he found out about my date, so I added, "Please tell me you didn't forget about the appointment."

When my dad sighed I could practically see him rubbing a tired hand over his face. "It wasn't that – not this time. It's just... there are probably a whole lot of people more deserving of Universal Credit than I am. Who need it more."

"*You* need it, Dad. At least until your back gets better."

"I can work through it. I've done it before."

"Damn it, stop acting like you're going to fail the interview. You're injured. You can't work. It's as simple as that."

A long, long pause, then he said, "You know it isn't as simple as that." It hurt because Dad was right. We were both painfully aware that the idea of potentially failing an interaction – be it for work or personal reasons – was paralysing enough to stop either from us from even trying.

It was something I wanted to change about myself.

It was something I knew Dad wanted to change about himself, too.

Moving behind Rich's desk I flicked through his calendar. "Can you make a new appointment for next...Thursday? That way I can go along with you." If the appointment was *for* me then there was no way in hell I'd ever be able to remember to go, but for someone else? For my Dad? It would be the only thing on my mind for the next week.

Aside from my date with Simon Saint.

This time when my dad sighed it was with relief. "I can do that. Thank you, dove. You know it means a lot."

"Any time, Dad. Right" – I snuck a glance through the dusty window in the office door, catching Rich just as he fell dramatically to the floor to allow the pugs and then the bulldogs to pile on top of him – "I better go before Rich suffocates under fifteen dogs."

My dad huffed out a laugh. "Of course. Love you, Courtney."

"You too."

When I returned to the fray I briefly relayed my conversation to Rich. His face twisted in sympathy; at this point he was basically a surrogate son to Graham Miller. Dad would never admit out loud that he wanted a son – my sister and I were more than enough trouble for him growing up - but I knew he adored Rich with every fibre of his being.

"He's going to hurt his back even more if he tries to work through it," Rich said from beneath a pile of dogs.

I picked up one of the pugs - Ruby, the one who kept peeing everywhere - and chucked her onto his face. She squealed in delight. "I know. I told him that. Won't change anything for him, though."

"Like father, like daughter, I guess."

"Shut up, bitch."

Finally Rich sat up despite the whines of complaints from his loyal dog followers. His hair was an adorable mess, but Rich didn't care. It was one of the things I loved about him: he was extremely secure in his own skin. "Are we still on for Monday, by the way?"

"Monday?" We always hung out at his place on Monday night once the day care closed. I almost said yes, but then I remembered that I couldn't. Rich could see from the way I frowned that the answer was *no*. "I can't. My date's on Monday."

A shadow crossed his face, then Rich was up on his feet and throwing the abandoned tennis balls for the dogs. All of them went wild, save for Ludo, who padded over to my side for a head scratch. "That's fine, I guess," Rich mumbled. I could barely hear him beneath the cacophony of barks that followed the tennis balls.

A twinge of something like guilt twisted my stomach. "I've had to cancel before. We—"

"I said it's fine," Rich cut in, sounding anything *but* fine. I valued our Monday nights just as much as he did, but it was also one of my two precious nights off a week. Sometimes I needed that time to do something fun and impulsive.

Like having a date with Simon Saint with the greying hair and the nervous tic and the posh London postcode.

Despite Rich's bad mood I headed to the Crowne Plaza that night absurdly looking forward to my shift. There was a first time for everything, I guess.

Maybe tonight would be the night Simon asked for more towels.

Chapter four

SIMON

"THINGS ARE LOOKING GOOD IN HERE!"

"That's a lie. Things are a fucking mess in here."

"I was trying to spare your feelings." It was true; the location for my future ramen restaurant was stuffed full of boxes covered in paint dust. Not a single sheet was protecting said boxes, or the floor, or the windows. I leaned against the door frame and gave Kei, my chef and business partner, a resigned smile. "What happened?"

Kei, as usual, was a whirlwind of activity, abandoning the broom in his hand to pick up a box and plonking it down on the bar with little regard for the rattling of half-pint glasses inside it. It covered the bar top in even more dust, but we were replacing it with a brand new surface next month so I didn't care. It was only after he put it down that he turned to me and said, "Whoever you hired to paint the walls did a shit job, that's what happened."

"At least the walls *look* good," I murmured, investigating the smooth, calming, perfectly sage green colour that adorned them with approval. "So there's that."

"And now I need to clean every fucking inch of this place and a hundred glasses, too!" Kei swore more than anyone else I knew, and I loved him for it. He once told me that his main goal with excelling at English back when he was an angry teenager in Japan was so he could curse fluently. It was just as well; if he hadn't been so fluent he'd have never come over to London to work as a sous-chef, and eventually work with me.

And so it was that I picked up the broom from where Kei had dropped it on the floor and resumed his forgotten sweeping job. "It won't take long to clean up if there's two of us doing it."

Kei clucked his tongue. "Get Tom to do it as thanks for me cooking for his girlfriend's birthday."

"I'm sure he'll appreciate being interrupted halfway through a protein purification to sweep a floor."

"The fuck is a protein purification?"

I shrugged my shoulders. "Hell if I know. I was just repeating something he said on the phone. If you really want we can delay cleaning until tomorrow, then we can rope him in."

But Kei, as expected, shook his head and carried on cleaning. He was always one for getting something done *now,* not *later.* Which was why I wasn't surprised in the slightest when he said, "Have you told your grandparents you're leaving the firm?"

"You know fine well I haven't."

"The longer you wait the worse it'll get. And I can't take another fucking minute of them getting my name wrong because they don't respect me, or what we're doing."

Kei was right and we both knew it. I loved my grandparents – they'd been raising me since I was ten, and I owed them everything – but they were hardly the warmest people in the world. Well, that was putting it lightly. They hadn't gotten to where they were in the world of investment banking by being nice.

"Look," Kei continued, jumping up to sit on the now-clean bar top when I didn't respond. He pulled out a half-pint glass from a box and began cleaning it of dust. "I know they think *they* know what's best for you. And I know it's hard to get them to listen to you. But the clock is ticking, Simon. We open in three months, and you and I both know you aren't going back to London come April."

Once again my friend and business partner was right. I had my bakery in London but I didn't need to be in London permanently to run it. *Saintly Pastries* – named by my puntastic pastry chef Nicola – was more than professionally run by said pastry chef and her team of very capable staff. I hand-picked them myself: the best and the brightest service people who'd ever worked an event for my catering business. But like I had, in fact, already told my grandmother, I didn't *want* to oversee the financials for a catering company, let alone run an entire investment firm.

Studying economics and finance had taught me two things. One: I was good at it. Two: it didn't matter that I was good at it. I wanted to do something else.

And that 'something else' was running a restaurant or two in my favourite city in the world, Glasgow. The only reason I'd even been able to open *Saintly Pastries* was because it was in a bougie area of London: something my grandparents could approve of. But Glasgow, and the affordable food I actually wanted to sell in a restaurant, was a step too far for them to accept.

Yet at the end of the day it was my responsibility to make Rupert and Maria Saint see exactly what I wanted out of my own life. I was an adult; it was about bloody time I made all of the important decisions pertaining to that life on my own.

I was still mulling over how I was supposed to get my grandparents to listen to me hours later, even when I took advantage of the Plaza's gym to take my mind off of things. The problem was that I enjoyed lifting weights and working my core and even practising yoga too much for any of them to really help when I needed a break from my head, but if there's one thing I despise more than overthinking, it's cardio.

Just this once I was willing to slog it out on the treadmill in the hope that the roar of lactic acid in my muscles would drown out my brain.

And it did, but it was awful. I really was an abominable runner. To make things worse the walls of the gym were all made of glass, one of them overlooking the swimming pool whilst another one overlooked the gym reception and, just off from that, the very corner of the hotel reception proper. The last thing I wanted was for people to see me, red-faced, sweating and out of breath, running at half the speed of the man next to me.

And by people I mean Courtney Miller.

But to my blessed relief, for the next ten minutes of agonised running I didn't spy a single blonde hair upon her head, even though it was after six o'clock so she'd have started her shift already. By minute fourteen I thought I might finally be getting the hang of the treadmill, and my head began to clear of all my troubled thoughts. All I could focus on was the pounding of my feet, the distance on the display slowly but surely ticking up, and the burning in my lungs.

Until Courtney was suddenly *right there,* standing by the gym reception desk and staring straight at me. A coy smile twisted her lips, arms crossed over her chest and hip cocked to one side as if she had been watching me for a while.

And I tripped. I tripped over my own feet and went face-down onto the treadmill.

"Holy shit, mate, are you okay?!" the marathon-running-man on my left exclaimed in concern, pausing his own treadmill and leaping off the damn torture device like a gazelle to help me back to my feet. But I couldn't hear anything but Courtney's guffaws of laughter from the gym reception, clear as a bell and full of glee.

I'd made a fool of myself, sure, but I'd always been taught to make a fool of myself with grace. "I'm alright, thanks," I told the very helpful man, allowing him to set me back upright before offering him a smile. "I just got distracted."

He looked me up and down in understanding. "You're a weights man."

"Guilty."

"Slow your speed and increase the incline on the treadmill next time. Easier workout but the benefits are just as good. You can work on your speed once you've built up more endurance."

I thanked the man once more then – swallowing my pride – walked over to the gym reception and the still-laughing Courtney. She had her hair up in the most impeccable ponytail I'd ever seen, pairing it with cherry red lips and just a hint of mascara on her eyelashes. A classic, bombshell look that she absolutely rocked despite the demure black uniform she was wearing.

Damn it, this was not the time nor the place for a boner.

"Nice fall, Forrest Gump," Courtney said once she finally stopped laughing. She looked me up and down with entirely different intentions than the man on the treadmill, which did nothing to help me out with my impending erection. "Are you training for anything?"

"I had something on my mind that I wanted to forget."

"So you, what, dropped the thought on the floor?"

It was my turn to laugh. There was no circumstance under which I could look cool right now; all I *could* do was laugh at myself. "If the thought wants to stay there, I would welcome it. Do you want to grab a drink after work today?" The question flew from my lips before I could stop it, but I didn't regret it.

Courtney's eyes lit up, and I thought she'd say yes, but then she shook her perfect ponytail and I knew the answer was *no.* "I'm drinking tomorrow," she explained, "and I'm trying to cut back. I'm a bit of a...manic drinker."

It warmed my heart that she was willing to share something with me that wasn't entirely flattering, especially after the fool I'd just made of myself. "Then I'll wait for Monday," I said, grinning as I headed back into the gym. "Be sure to watch me do my tricep dips. I swear I'm better at those."

Courtney waved me off with that crooked smile of hers, and sure enough she *did* hang around to watch me do a set of dips. But then she had to return to her desk and I was left, regrettably, without an audience.

God, Monday couldn't come quick enough. All I had to do was get through the party tomorrow night and I could spend all of Sunday impatiently planning our date.

Chapter five

COURTNEY

I'D LIVED WITH REBECCA EVER SINCE I moved back from Australia. Since then we'd spent eight glorious years living as perfect flat mates. Well, not perfect in the general sense, but perfect for each *other*. Quite frankly I couldn't imagine living with anyone else, and I didn't want to.

"More prosecco, Court?" Becca called from the kitchen, her voice echoing off the high tenement ceiling and booming through the nineties house music I was playing on the TV by virtue of Youtube Premium. It was the only subscription service I'd ever committed to...namely because Becca paid for all the others. But that was because she couldn't live without constant reruns of *The Office, Supernatural* and *Modern Family*. She was a stickler for her favourite shows, and who was I to make fun of her when I got free streaming services out of it?

At least I paid for the music and the silly Youtube commentary videos.

"When is the answer to that question ever 'no', Becca?" I hollered back, returning my attention to the floor-length mirror I was currently knelt in front of in order to finish my make-up. A minute later my flatmate appeared and dutifully placed a very generously filled glass of prosecco by my side, taking away my old glass before throwing herself on my bed to inspect my costume prep for the night.

"Who are you going as again?" she asked. I saw her reflection frown at the green-and-white striped polo shirt on my bed, along with the dark braces covered with exactly fifteen pins and badges.

"I swear to god, If I have to remind you *again* then you'll never remember. Speaking of costumes, I can't believe you're actually wearing a wig tonight. Heaven forbid a single hair on your head is out of place!"

Becca gave me the finger then primly sipped on her own prosecco. Rebecca Luton was the kind of woman you thought only existed in films. She was twenty-nine but looked as if she'd simply transcend ageing for the rest of her life and look forever twenty-two. She was five-foot-seven, model thin, with big brown eyes and the shiniest, healthiest brown hair I'd ever seen in my damn life. Even after eight years of living together she still wouldn't let me use her haircare products.

She never left the house without her pale skin covered in factor fifty, nor her face made up to perfection. Her insanely ethereal image and professional manner was why she'd been promoted to manager at the best vegetarian pizza and cocktail bar in Glasgow, *Cornstar Martini,* last year, and also why I was fairly certain she would one day take over the world.

A lesser person would feel inferior in her presence. Instead I felt blessed to call her my friend, and thanked my lucky stars that I had someone like Becca fighting in my corner. She was my ride or die, and I was hers.

Then she started dating Peter Fisher and all that went to shit.

Just kidding. Peter was great. When Becca first slept with him when helping out at a fancy winter wedding two years ago she'd told me it was a spontaneous decision. A one-off event. But I could tell she was smitten. That it had taken another year before the two of them happened to cross paths again and make things serious was ridiculous.

It was because of Peter that we were heading to a film-themed party tonight. One of his best friends was turning thirty so he'd invited Becca along. Becca, being a little anxious when faced with the prospect of socialising with dozens of strangers without her service work face on, had asked if she could bring me along. I was always one for a party. Of course I said yes.

So here we were, Becca readjusting her blonde wig for the millionth time in fifteen minutes as I finished my make-up and plonked myself on the bed beside her. She made an amazing Spider-Gwen: a character she knew nothing about before Peter had her watch *Spiderverse* with him. Peter was Miles Morales, which I found hilarious given his actual name. Apparently he was a mega nerd.

I loved that for her.

"Love makes us do mysterious things," Becca said. She picked up my braces and inspected the shiny badges adorning it. "Seriously, what is this?"

"It's from *Office Space*."

"Never heard of it."

"I know you haven't. Because you only watch the same handful of shows on repeat. It has Jen Aniston in it, though."

Her eyes lit up in recognition. "Is that who you're going as, then?"

"I'm hardly going as fucking Milton." The blank look she gave me was all I needed to see to stop talking about it. "So what are Peter's friends like, then?" I asked, rolling onto my front before chugging a generous gulp of prosecco. "Will I like them?"

"Oh, you definitely will. Well, some of them are huge anime nerds—"

"Blergh."

"And some of them definitely think they belong on

Broadway—"

"And yet you think I'll *like* them?"

Becca laughed graciously. "In spite of everything aforementioned I swear you will. Speaking of friends" – she narrowed her eyes at me – "I thought you'd invite Rich along."

"He's busy," I lied, because in truth I hadn't asked him at all. He was still being weird with me because of my date with Simon, even when I sent him my usual deluge of funny animal TikToks this morning. The mere passing thought of Simon Saint, tripping on the treadmill because he noticed me watching, caused my face to heat up before I could stop it.

Becca shuffled over to my side immediately. "Oh my god, are you two finally dating?!"

"Me and who?"

"You and Rich, you bloody airhead!"

"Oh."

"*Oh*? We were just talking about him!"

"You know what I'm like," I said, because she did. Sometimes it took me minutes or even hours to remember what someone had said to me, by which point it was far too late to respond. "Why do you ask?"

"What do you mean 'why do I ask'? You stay over at his every Monday. You hook up all the time—"

"We hooked up *once,* when we got back from Australia," I amended. "Kissing when I sleep over doesn't count."

Becca rolled her eyes. "You're hopeless. He's so obviously into you."

"And just like you, Rich knows what I'm like. He knows where we stand. I'm no good at the whole 'relationship' thing. We're better as friends."

"Friends who do everything together, and sleep in the same bed together, and—"

"Can we move on?" I protested. A moment later I felt my phone buzzing inside my bra and almost laughed at the convenient timing. There was not nearly enough space for it in there – I missed the days of Moto Razrs – but habit dictated that I kept it there when I wasn't at work so I didn't misplace it.

"Who is it?" Becca asked curiously, peering over my shoulder to read the text my dad had sent me. "He forgot when your *sister's* birthday is?!" she cried, scandalised on Ailish's behalf.

"Don't hold it against him. His brain is like a sieve." I told him that it was on the thirteenth of February, not the twenty-third, before unceremoniously shoving my flat-mate off my shoulder. "It would help if Ailish spoke to him more often."

"Yeah, and it would help even more if *you* didn't keep avoiding her and your mum, too."

I made a face. This was ground Becca and I had covered far too often already. "I don't avoid Ailish. She lives in London; it's hard to stay in touch."

"And your mum?"

"You and I both know she's a different story entirely."

Becca fiddled with an artificial stand of blonde hair. "Speaking of stressful situations you don't like talking about... have you had a call yet?"

I flinched. There was no point in lying to Becca when she was the one who'd pushed me to get on the wait list in the first place. "I did." Deftly I stripped out of my clothes and changed into my costume for the night. I kept my upside-down gold heart necklace and oversized gold hoop earrings on, though; those were part of *me.* I never changed them, and never planned to. It was reassuring to have one constant in my life that at least absolved me from making any jewellery decisions on a day-to-day basis.

"And?" Becca pressed, when I refused to elaborate.

"And I missed it."

"*Courtney!*"

"I was at work!"

"But you still have to make time for it!" Becca bit back, standing up to face me as if sitting down wasn't sufficient to demonstrate how important her words were. "They only call you three times before they put you back to the bottom of the list."

I knew this. Of course I did. But it had been hard enough already going to my GP and asking for help getting an ADHD diagnosis. Since then I'd been waiting for a call regarding the matter for over three years. God bless the NHS and socialised healthcare and all that, but when it came to mental health and neurodivergence in the UK you'd be better off self-medicating and hoping for the best. Which even *I* knew, for all my fondness of self-medicating, was not a good solution.

But at the end of the day, the thought of answering the phone and having that very call I'd been waiting three years for was fucking terrifying.

I sighed as if the entire weight of the world was on my shoulders. "Can we not talk about this tonight, please? I'd prefer to get drunk and have a great time."

Becca offered me the safest smile in the world, though I knew that behind that smile she had filed away a reminder to talk to me about this at a later date. "Of course. But we both know your problem will still exist tomorrow."

"Which means I can *handle* it tomorrow."

"Okay, okay, I get it. Whose turn is it to pay for a taxi?"

I groaned. "Mine." How much did I have in my bank account?

But Becca, because she was a saint, held up her phone and grinned. "Don't worry about it. It's on its way already."

I wrapped my arms around her in genuine, joyful affection. Becca responded by kissing the top of my head. "I love you.

Please never leave me."

"I'll have to one day."

"Just not one day soon."

Was it my imagination or did Becca falter on our way to the hallway to put on our shoes? But then she laughed, and we both downed another glass of prosecco, and then we were in the taxi and I forgot all about it.

Chapter Six

SIMON

Thomas Henderson shared many traits with his grandfather. One of those traits was being the perfect host, as demonstrated by the thirtieth birthday party I now found myself involved in at his townhouse. I'd spent many a drunken night over at his place during my undergrad years; being surrounded by tipsy strangers delighted at the venue for their friend's celebration was a fond trip down memory lane.

For of course Tom had hosted every party in our youth. He lived in a fancy house in Park Circus, *alone,* for god's sake. Well, he'd lived with his grandfather for the first year I'd known him, but then his grandfather passed away and it was just Tom and a house that was far too big and far too empty. I'd always wondered why he'd continued living in it. Sentimental reasons, probably. All I knew was that, even with Liz now living in it with him, the place was much too big for Tom.

But it was amazing for parties.

Tom had rolled out a red carpet from the front door all the way down the hallway and into the dining room to 'introduce' each of the film star guests. In the dining room was a professionally lit backdrop for everyone to take their red carpet photos; there was even a hired photographer for the night. In the living room was a DJ playing the greatest hits from all the best films over the years – right now it was *All Star* by Smash Mouth, because a man dressed as Shrek had just entered the house – as well as a huge table with a generous spread of canapés. Two serving staff for the night kept the food and complimentary prosecco on the table topped up with regular visits to the kitchen.

Along the wrought-iron bannister of the stairs were many hundreds of tiny, twinkling lights, with a large mirrored disco ball hanging from the ceiling way up on the second floor. Spotlights directed at the ball reflected dazzling flashes of light across the entire hallway. The rest of the rooms of the house which folk were allowed access to – all on the first floor, because the second floor was home to Liz and Tom's bedroom, bathroom and office – were decorated to emulate old cabaret bars and speakeasys.

Why was Tom a scientist when he clearly had an immense talent in event design? Even *I* was blown away by the entire affair, and I'd been to many a fancy event down in London. In any case he had well and truly outdone himself.

"Tequila, Simon?" Liz asked me, though she was dressed like Meg Ryan in *When Harry Met Sally* and was therefore almost unrecognisable beneath her wildly curly blonde wig. When Tom sidled up behind her, dressed in an impeccable cream sweater and with his hair fluffed to within an inch of his life, I realised he was supposed to be the Harry to her Sally.

I groaned. "A couple's costume? Really? The two of you are embarrassing as hell."

"I figured it was about time I finally got to do a couple's costume with him," Liz said, grinning at Tom with rosy cheeks and the kind of genuine love that stopped me from being able to hate how PDA the two of them were. "It's usually Daichi who gets to claim Tom as his costume partner."

"Ah, the illustrious Daichi Ito. Is he here tonight?" The

man had been Tom's other best friend slash work wife for years, but I hadn't seen him in almost a year. We'd joked before about the two of us having Japanese partners in crime, though aside from their nationality Daichi and Kei were like oil and water. I had no doubt that if they were ever in the same room together Kei would set Daichi on fire for being too optimistic about life.

Tom shook his head, then handed me a shot of tequila even though I never said I'd wanted one. "He has the baby tonight. Well, toddler. May's working a double shift at the hospital."

"Remind me to never have children."

"Or work in a hospital," Liz added on, "but definitely the kids part." The three of us laughed at our silly little in-joke; of everyone I knew in my life, Tom and Liz were the only ones happily together with no intention of getting married or having children. I was still on the fence about marriage – if it was the right person and they wanted it then I'd do it – but I'd recently come to the conclusion that kids weren't for me. I had too much I wanted to do, and what felt like entirely not enough time to do it.

Besides, there were plenty of other men out there to be fathers instead of me.

"Back on the subject of costumes," I said, as I surveyed Tom and Liz's ridiculous couple's costume, "why didn't you dye your hair, Tom? Or wear a wig? The blonde kind of ruins it."

Tom's gaze shifted from Liz, to me, then back to Liz. "Let's just say I have PTSD about hair dye and leave it at that. And wigs itch my head too much."

"I definitely don't want to know the backstory to this."

"You definitely don't. So why'd you go for the arsehole boss from *Office Space*? With that shirt you could have gone for *American Psycho*."

I plucked at the white collar of my blue shirt, then readjusted the stupid glasses I'd purchased last-minute on

Amazon. "I prefer the real-world evils of corporate late-stage capitalism to the fantasies of those responsible for it."

"You just wanted to wear the braces, didn't you?" Tom pinged them to prove his point.

"Guilty as charged. I – hold on. Why do they look familiar?" I peered over at a pair of men, one of them insanely tall, well-built and with a shaved head, the other smaller, lither, and with a full head of floppy black hair. They were definitely familiar, though I knew for certain I'd never met them in real life.

Liz watched where I was looking in interest. "Oh, that's Rob and Joe Cooke. They're friends of Chloë and Harry from their musical theatre days. I think they run a food blog...?"

"*Ah,* that'll be it. Excuse me, but I need to go and say hi." I necked back my tequila when it became evident Tom wouldn't let me go until I did so, then walked straight over to introduce myself to the Cookes. I'd been following their work for a while now, and indeed had already planned to reach out to them regarding the opening of my restaurant. To meet them like this felt serendipitous.

Perhaps this party wouldn't end up being a huge waste of my time.

I approached the two men – I wasn't sure which one was Rob and which one was Joe – and wasted no time in introducing myself when it became clear I was interrupting a conversation about myself.

"I swear he's the one who opened that bakery in Covent Garden," said the shorter guy. "The one with the fuck-off amazing pain au chocolats—"

"Why the fuck would he be at a house party in Glasgow, Joe?" the taller one – Rob – fired back. Then he glanced in my direction and was startled enough to take a step back when he saw I was standing about two feet away from him.

"I am indeed the one who opened that bakery in Covent Garden," I said, my mouth splitting into a grin at their baffled expressions, "and I am equally at a house party in Glasgow. Tom Henderson is my best friend. The name's Simon Saint." I held out my hand; Rob shook it first, then Joe.

Joe let loose a bark of nervous laughter. "*Saintly Pastries.* That was it. Sorry for talking about you behind you back."

"I don't mind when you're saying nice things."

"Then I guess we're all good." He pointed at his chest. "I'm Joe; this is my brother, Rob."

"Of *Two Many Cookes.* I follow your blog. And your YouTube channel. And your Instagram. You make for a scarily impressive team. Are you really brothers? You look nothing alike."

"We're twins, if you can believe that."

"I...cannot."

"Non-identical, obviously," Rob said. With a flourish he waved at his brother. "Joe takes after our mum; I'm a carbon copy of Dad."

"Minus his pretty blonde hair," Joe muttered.

"Hey, shaving my head was a choice."

"Yeah, a *choice* not to show off your receding hairline."

Rob scowled. "Shut up, you fucking emo."

I could do nothing but watch as the brothers fought like, well, brothers. When they reached the end of their spat they turned their attention back to me with foolish grins that, despite all of their dissimilarities, were identical.

"Sorry," Joe said, not looking sorry in the slightest. "What are you doing in Glasgow, Mr Saint?"

"Call me Simon." Joe and I took a glass of prosecco when a member of the serving staff offered us one, though Rob refused in favour of opening another beer. Then: "I'm opening a ramen restaurant."

"Aha!" Rob bit out, recognition lighting up his face. "I read about that somewhere. You poached Kei Nakamura from *Shoryu,* didn't you?"

I laughed a triumphant laugh; I was still very pleased with myself for wrangling that. "Guilty as charged. I was actually intending to reach out soon to see if the two of you would be interested in coming along to the launch party? We open in April."

"We would be fucking *delighted.*" I wasn't sure which one of them spoke – it might have been them both.

We clinked our glasses together. "Then I'll be in touch soon," I said, before saying my goodbyes in order to find Tom to tell him about the good news. But I left my conversation with the Cooke brothers so reinvigorated to jump back into work that I was tempted to leave the party – even though I was yet to say hello to the birthday girl in question.

It was then that I spotted someone dressed as what looked suspiciously like Jennifer Aniston in, of all things, *Office Space.* Well, that's what it looked like from the back, but I knew I could be wrong. Unable to suppress my curiosity I twisted my way through the crowded living room towards the double doors into the kitchen until I was standing beside the woman. "I don't think you have enough pieces of flair," I said, raising my voice to be heard over the eighties synth wave music playing that I knew had to have been Tom's choice.

"I have the requisite fifteen pieces of flair," the woman said, turning to face me. "I think you'll find that's quite a—*Simon*?!"

It was Courtney. Courtney-the-receptionist. Courtney Miller. Right here, in front of me. Dressed in a costume that could almost pass as the other half to mine (if Joanna had ended up with Bill, which would have never happened, but I digress).

I couldn't believe my luck. If I was smiling any wider my face would split in two. "Fancy running into you here," I said, crossing my arms in a perfect imitation of Bill. "Did you just arrive?"

Courtney beamed. "Yeah, literally a minute ago. God knows

where Becca ran off to; I don't know *anyone* in this room."

"If you don't know anyone then how do you know the birthday girl?"

"She's a friend of my flat mate's boyfriend. How do *you* know her?"

"She's a...friend of my best friend's girlfriend," I laughed. God, this was ridiculous. "Said best friend is hosting the party."

"Must be one loaded friend. His girlfriend chose well."

"Liz's taste in men is debatable, but Tom is indeed loaded."

Courtney cocked her head to the side, a look of confused recognition on her face that I hadn't expected to see. "As in... Tom Henderson? And Liz—"

"*Courtney?*" cried Liz as she entered the kitchen from the hallway door. She ran over and smothered Courtney in a hug. "No way! The hell are you doing here? Tom, Tom, come on over!"

A moment later Tom appeared with Chloë (Satine from *Moulin Rouge*), Harriet (Anna from *Van Helsing*), a friend I think was called Ray (Van Helsing from *Van Helsing*), as well as a masked Spiderman and Spider-Gwen close in tow. "No shit," Tom said, laughing as he high-fived a stunned Courtney. "When did you break into my house?"

"How do the two of you know Courtney?" I asked, unsure about who was the most confused in this situation but almost certain I ranked high on the leader board.

"She works at Ludo's dog day care centre," Liz explained, "and she sometimes takes him overnight as a favour to us. She's my friend."

"And she's my flat mate," the woman dressed as Spider-Gwen said. She took off her mask and smiled broadly at me before holding out her hand. "I'm Becca, Peter's girlfriend. I don't believe we've met. Are you Simon?"

"The one and only. Has Tom been bad-mouthing me

behind my back?"

"Oh, no, Peter was just telling me that he and Chloë could finally steal Liz away to go climbing because Tom's London boyfriend was up to stay."

"That was private," Peter-the-Spiderman muttered, though he didn't sound like he cared.

"So who are you dressed as, Simon?" Becca asked curiously. "I'm not really a 'movie' person; I still have no idea who Courtney is even though she's told me—"

"Like four times," Courtney cut in, speaking for the first time after having been bombarded by a litany of new faces. She scanned over them all, clearly decided she liked what she saw, and relaxed her previously tense posture. "He's actually dressed as someone from the same film as me."

Becca, Harriet, Chloë and Ray *all* clapped their hands together and cried, "No way!" They reminded me of Daichi.

Liz cackled, whilst Tom cast a calculative gaze my way. "So you already knew Courtney, Si?" he asked. "Did you know she was coming and planned your *couple's costume* together?"

It was Courtney who answered. "Mister Saint is a long-term guest of the Crowne Plaza. Rest assured neither of us had any idea we were both going to be here. The costume is pure coincidence."

"*Ahh,*" said Liz, catching on to what Courtney wasn't saying. "So Simon is the one who—"

"*Another time, Liz!*" Courtney gasped, mortified. I made a mental note to ask Courtney what this was all about...in private.

The conversation then devolved into everyone talking over everyone else the way things always ended up going in situations like this. I began to get a bit overwhelmed, especially when Chloë, Harriet and Ray began discussing their favourite costumes of the night at a furious pace I couldn't keep up with, so I excused myself to the bathroom and proceeded to head up to the furthest-away one on the second floor of the house. It was only once I instead walked straight into the spare bedroom and sat on the window seat, with its beautiful night-time view over Kelvingrove Park, that I realised Courtney had followed me.

She offered me a little wave. "Mind if I join you? That was a bit much, wasn't it? Which is saying something coming from me." She let out a shy little laugh which was, quite frankly, adorable.

"I would be incredibly unhappy if you left me here alone," I said, because it was the truth. I motioned for her to sit beside me. When Courtney did so a storm of nerves hit me. I felt like a school boy trying to handle his first crush, which was ridiculous. I was thirty-fucking-six years old.

I was beyond relieved when Courtney spoke first. "Do you want to play Twenty Questions?"

Considering who was asking me, I only had one answer.

"I'd love to."

Chapter Seven

COURTNEY

"Where did you grow up?"

"Seriously?" Simon blinked incredulously. "You're starting with such a pedestrian question?"

I swatted at his arm in protest, wondering if it was acceptable to *keep* my hand on his triceps – those dips at the gym were clearly no joke – before regrettably pulling my hand away. "Would you have rather I stalked your social media to make this conversation redundant?"

"...did you?"

"God no!" I bit out, faux-scandalised. "Everything I found out about you so far I found out when I was working. How unprofessional do you think I am?" Then, when Simon looked confused over how serious I was being, I added on, "I'll check you out online after tonight to cross-reference everything you're about to say, of course."

He laughed, and I saw some of the nervous tension that was keeping Simon sitting stiff as a board leave his body. I wondered if he was drunk: he'd been far more natural – far more comfortable – when we'd been flirting at the Plaza. Then

I realised that he'd come upstairs to get away from the party, so he was likely overwhelmed. It was up to me to set the mood.

I sidled closer on the beautiful window seat. The curtains were pulled open, so we had an unencumbered view over Kelvingrove Park. Outside the sky was dark and twinkling, the ornate streetlamps outside a hazy orange, painting the edges of the fancy Park Circus cobblestones with fire.

Jesus, Tom and Liz really were lucky. And loaded.

"Tell me where you grew up," I pressed again, letting my knee knock against Simon's. "And then ask *me*." He turned incrementally to face me. Was that a blush I spied across his cheeks? God, this guy was adorable, even dressed in the ridiculous glasses, shirt and braces combo that his costume demanded. I was kind of into it, if I was being honest.

Finally Simon relented. "I lived in Glasgow until I was ten, then I moved to London. You?"

"Glasgow my entire life. Maryhill. Although I lived in Australia for three years straight out of uni."

"What did you study?"

"Geography. I take it you went to uni, too?" It felt stupid to ask this; *of course* Simon Saint went to university.

Which was why I wasn't surprised when he said: "Economics."

I could only laugh. It was so predictable. "Of course. Where?"

"Glasgow, actually," he said, scratching his nose as he did so. Then he turned around properly, so we were facing each other. "It's how I met Tom."

Since I knew Tom had always lived in Glasgow this completely tracked. "We must have just missed each other. I'm only four years younger than you."

Simon frowned. "How did you—*ah*. My driver's license at the hotel."

I popped my tongue against my cheek. "Bingo. So why did you move to London when you ended up coming back to Glasgow for uni?"

"My mum died," Simon said, in that practised way that meant he'd become so used to telling people about it that it was simply another fact of his life, rather than a tragedy. But it was a tragedy nonetheless.

I squeezed his hand on impulse, and was gratified when I felt him squeeze it back. "I'm so sorry. That must have been tough with you being so young. What about your da—"

"He was never in the picture." Simon's answer was short and sure, but when he saw what must have been a bewildered expression on my face he added, "My grandparents raised me, hence moving to London. Moving *back* to London, really. Mum was raised there before she had me."

I bit my tongue, hating that I'd inadvertently careened what was supposed to be a flirty, fun way to get to know each other into upsetting territory. "Simon, I'm so s—wait." I swung my head from side to side, listening intently. "Can you hear that?"

"I can," he murmured, frowning, getting up to turn on the light both of us had ignored in favour of sitting in the glow of the streetlamps. "Oh. It's Liz's kitten."

"Jerry?!" I exclaimed, leaping up to locate the source of the tiny mewling noise I'd heard. Simon pointed to the left of the enormous bed – hidden from our point of view at the window – so I wasted no time in sliding over the covers to investigate. The bed was at least one hundred times comfier than my own bed. Damn rich people.

But thoughts of the bed quickly evaporated in the face of a tiny black kitten meowing pitifully for attention through the bars of a cage filled with blankets and toys. I opened the cage without hesitation, bundling the precious animal into my arms. When Simon came to sit beside me on the bed and began scratching Jerry's head and making a serious of incoherent baby noises at him my heart figuratively melted.

"You're a cat person," I observed in-between giving Jerry kisses that he eagerly returned.

Simon grinned, now completely and utterly relaxed. It was funny how tiny creatures could do that. "An animal person in general. Have you met Ludo? God, of course you've met him. You look after him."

"He's my favourite dog at the day care."

He tore his eyes from the kitten to look at me. "So you work two jobs? Isn't that tiring?"

"Homelessness would be more tiring, I imagine."

A self-deprecating chuckle. "Noted. Do you have any pets of your own?" Carefully he took Jerry from me, allowing the kitten to muss his hair and lick at his glasses. If ever there was a man I wanted to kiss senseless, it was Simon.

"I wish," I replied, a beat too late. But Simon had the grace not to ask me what had distracted me. "I can't afford it. You?"

"I travel for work too much for it to be fair on a pet." Simon sounded very much like he hated this aspect of his work.

"I suppose you have to travel a lot when you open restaurants all over the place," I said, but Simon shook his head.

"That's not what I do – not really. Call that a...side project."

"So what do you do usually?" I grabbed Jerry back and clutched him to my chest protectively. "You aren't an assassin-for-hire, are you?"

Simon sighed dramatically, holding a hand to his forehead as if he were a swooning maiden. "You've got me. No, I work for my grandparents' investment firm. Specifically I've been overseeing investments in catering for the last few years."

"I think I preferred assassin-for-hire."

"I think I do, too."

"So you don't enjoy it?"

Simon didn't have to say anything: I could tell from his face, the set of his shoulders, the sag of his spine, that he didn't. Carefully I put Jerry back in his cage, despite his vocal protests, then took Simon's hands in mine. "What's your dream? If everything that's clearly been holding you back was out of the picture, what would you do with your life?"

For a few seconds Simon did nothing. His breathing was accelerated, but so was mine. How often did he talk to anyone about what he really wanted? It didn't seem like the answer to that was *often.*

Instead of answering, however, Simon raised both of my hands to his lips and brushed a kiss over my knuckles. It was my turn to blush. Okay, more than blush. Simon was acting as chaste as damn Mr Darcy and he had me combusting like a building on fire.

"Can we move on from *Twenty Questions*?" he asked. His grey eyes were warm, almost molten. I never thought grey could be so expressive. But they were ultimately still hidden behind those ridiculous glasses which, at this point, was kind of ruining the vibe. When I gently extricated my hands from his Simon deflated, disappointed, but he immediately perked up when I removed his glasses and all but climbed onto his lap.

I knew what I wanted, right here, right now, and it was him. Whether my forward-thinking attitude was fuelled by booze was entirely irrelevant.

I wrapped my arms around Simon's neck. All my stupid pins and badges clicked and clanked and rustled as I squirmed against him. "I'd *love* to move on from *Twenty Questions*," I purred, well beyond horny. Going by Simon's erection currently swelling rapidly beneath me he was in the same boat.

To be honest I'm not sure who kissed who first. It didn't matter. I'd physically wanted Simon from the moment I saw him, regardless of the fact he'd stolen my sausage rolls and my taxi and hit me on the head with a door.

Simon tasted of tequila. I loved tequila. With a moan I

relaxed my mouth, parting my lips so his tongue could dip inside. He ran it along my teeth while his hands roamed up my back, finding purchase in my hair to tip my head back.

God, the guy could kiss. I couldn't remember the last time I'd had a first kiss *this* good.

I twanged Simon's braces against him, savouring the shudder that pulsed right through him, then slid them off his shoulders. With deft, sure fingers I began loosening his tie. Simon groaned into my mouth when he felt my hands on his neck, then pulled away just a fraction to gulp in some air. I felt dizzy; when I fluttered my eyes open I could see stars.

"I don't suppose," Simon began, voice low and gravelly and very, very unsteady, "you'd be interested in getting the fuck out of here and—"

"Did you leave the light on when you last checked on Jerry, Tom?" Liz's voice called out just before she threw open the door that I'd stupidly left ajar. When she caught sight of me and Simon her mouth formed a wordless *O*. Both Simon and I disentangled ourselves and all but fell off the bed in panic.

"Shit, Liz, I'm sorry," Simon bit out, grabbing his forgotten glasses from the bed before straightening his tie. "I swear I didn't come in here to—to—"

Liz cut him off with a peal of ugly, gleeful laughter. "Oh, Tom is gonna *love* this. *Tom!*" she cried down the stairs. But I was far too mortified for any of this. I'd completely and utterly forgotten where and when I was, my damn *space* and *place* colliding to include just me and Simon and the sinfully comfortable bed we were rutting on.

"I—I – bathroom," I muttered, fleeing the bedroom with a clumsy side-step of Liz.

But when I passed her she grabbed my wrist, looking both entirely drunk and very apologetic. "Sorry. That wasn't cool of me. I'll get out of your way."

When I laughed I sounded like a maniac. "No. It was good

you came in. This was *so* not the place for...well."

I heard Simon come up behind me. "She's right. Sorry, Liz. I didn't realise you'd put Jerry in here, either. We shouldn't have disturbed him."

"I'm sure he enjoyed the attention. He goes feral when he's ignored for longer than ten minutes."

When Tom came bounding up the stairs I knew that was my cue to escape. He raised a quizzical eyebrow at me as I ran past him, but I didn't hang around to hear what Liz and Simon would tell him.

I had no idea where the bathroom was but eventually I found one on the first floor. I spent ten minutes regretting all of the life choices that led me to this point, then got my shit together and headed back out to join the party. I couldn't see Simon, which was just as well. I didn't trust myself around him right now.

I'd practically jumped him back there. No, *literally* jumped him.

And he'd loved it.

That man was dangerous. Before I knew it we'd be sharing our deepest, darkest secrets and presumably spending every night giving each other multiple orgasms. But then he'd see me for the mess I really am, and he'd resent me for putting him in a position where he'd have to put up with and care for me.

This was why I didn't do relationships.

Eventually I found myself wandering over to a long table laden with all kinds of finger foods. Amusing myself with the fact that Tom literally had a house party *catered* for – and decorated more professionally than most any event I'd ever seen organised at the Plaza – I stuffed several mini pizzas into my mouth before helping myself to a glass of prosecco from one of the many bottles poised and waiting in ice buckets for people to help themselves to. It was just as well I found the free bar *after* my incident with Simon; lord fucking help me if I'd been wasted before it.

Liz wouldn't have found us merely kissing if that had been the case.

I didn't really feel much up to talking to anyone right now – the manic excitement I'd had for the party had pretty much been drained out of me the moment I fled to the bathroom – and I couldn't see Becca, so I contented myself with listening to a couple arguing by the food in lieu of finding someone to talk to.

"Don't embarrass me like this," the guy all but hissed at his girlfriend, who was staring at the empty plate in her hands instead of him. "We are *not* going to order food from fucking McDonald's again just because you're too scared to try a damn canapé."

The girlfriend shook her head miserably. "But I don't – I don't know what they'll taste like. I don't know what's in them. I don't—"

"Then *try it* and you'll fucking find out!"

"Excuse me," I said, interrupting them before I knew what I was doing. But my proverbial Spidey senses were tingling, and I was *not* about to listen to a drunk arsehole berate the girlfriend he obviously didn't deserve over what was clearly a serious mental issue she had. He glared blearily at me when I stood between him and his girlfriend. "She said she doesn't want to try it. Why is that a problem for you?"

He gave me the finger. "Who are you? Fuck off."

"I don't think so."

When he made to shove me out of the way a stranger grabbed his arm. No, not a stranger: Harriet, girlfriend of the birthday girl, dressed like than woman from *Van Helsing*. "Stop it with your shite, Ryan," she warned him. She looked over my shoulder. "Dani, are you okay?"

"Yeah," Dani mumbled behind me. "I'm sorry for causing a fuss." Then, when I turned to face her, she very quietly added on a, "Thank you."

I wanted to pull her away from Ryan – to spend my entire night protecting her and telling her she deserved better – but Harriet indicated for me to follow her, so reluctantly I did so. "I'm sorry about that," she said, when we were in the hallway and well out of earshot of the couple, "but thanks for stepping in. Ryan's my brother and I *swear* he isn't like this most of the time." Where had I heard that before? Oh yeah, basically every time one of my friends had the exact same, carbon copy, 'not usually a prick' boyfriend. Sensing my disbelief she added, "He's just too drunk. He dotes on Dani, I swear. They've been together five years already."

"They're always 'just too drunk'," I replied, not bothering to hide the venom in my voice. "That's the problem. There's always an excuse." I knew I could apply that exact line of thought to every time I'd made a mistake when drunk or high or whatever, but just because someone is a hypocrite doesn't mean they can't also be *right.*

Harriet nodded her head in rueful agreement. "I know. I'll talk to him again. He's just always struggled with Dani's... eccentricities."

"What, like having a clear food sensitivity issue? Because if he struggles with that then he should walk out the fucking door and leave her be. She deserves more than that." I had no idea where my resolve to defend this Dani girl came from, but it was here and it was strong and I didn't want to let up.

It looked like Harriet wanted to disagree with me – to defend her brother – but then she all but deflated. "You're right. I'll try to bring it up with him. Maybe if someone else points it out he'll see that he's the one in the wrong."

I wanted to tell her that it was unlikely, but I didn't want to upset Harriet. She seemed like a genuinely nice person. It wasn't her fault her brother was a dick. So I smiled, and lowered by proverbial hackles, and said, "Thank you. This is a wonderful party. Your girlfriend must be so happy."

At this Harriet beamed. "I'd been organising it with Tom and Liz and Ray and Peter for *ages*. But it has nothing on what I'm planning for...well." She tapped her nose. "That's a secret." Behind me someone called Harriet's name, so she gave me a hug and excused herself.

The moment I was alone I was struck by a sense of clarity. Dani and Ryan were a perfect, working example of why I didn't want a relationship. Dani had issues that weren't her fault. It was up to her to tackle them at a pace that she was comfortable with – if she was going to tackle them at all. And yet here was her long-term boyfriend, who was purported to love her, who was clearly 'at the end of his tether' with her. With her 'eccentricities', as Harriet put it.

I couldn't put myself through that. I just couldn't.

And I couldn't put Simon through it, either.

Feeling like a coward I grabbed my coat, telling Becca on the way that I wasn't feeling great so I was heading home, and ran for the door. My hand was literally on the door handle when I heard Simon cry out, "Courtney, wait!"

God, I wanted to just keep running. I was a coward like that. A self-aware coward, but a fucking coward nonetheless. But Simon deserved more than the text I'd been guiltily planning to send him once I slithered out of here.

It felt like it took me twenty years to turn around. There was no point in smiling or putting up a happy front for Simon; he could tell from one look at my face that something was wrong. He hadn't put his ridiculous glasses or his braces or his tie back on. That somehow made things more difficult, because he looked like himself rather than someone in a costume.

He bit his lip in concern. "Courtney, did I...did I do something wrong?"

"Jesus, no, this is all me," I said, practically tripping over the words with the speed with which I had to absolve him of all responsibility.

"So this is a 'it's not you, it's me' kind of situation?" Simon asked. He ran a hand through his hair. His nervous tic, back again with a vengeance. Because of me. "Courtney, I swear, if I said or did something then please just tell me."

I could only shake my head. "This is really, truly on me. I can't – I thought this could be fun. A fling. Whatever. But—"

"I can do a fling," Simon cut in. His entire fucking demeanour lit up, as if he had worked out the solution to my problem. "You'd be surprised how unserious I can be."

We both knew it was a lie. It had taken me all of two minutes to work out that Simon was long-term boyfriend material. *I* wanted him to be that. For me. But I knew I'd mess it up.

When Simon reached for my hand I narrowly avoided him. "I can't do that, Simon," I said, the words almost coming out as a whisper before I finally put some steel behind them. I forced myself to look him in the eye. Smile. Service face, service face. "You're a lovely guy. Really. But I can't do this. It was a mistake for me to make you think this could happen."

Then I thrust open the door and was off, off, off, across the orange-tinted cobblestones, beneath the pretty streetlights, until I was tearing through the dark and shadowy Kelvingrove Park to cut up along the river and back towards my flat.

God, I was a fucking coward. But that was better than having my heart broken, and breaking Simon's in the process.

Chapter Eight

SIMON

"Stop staring at your phone, Si," Tom sighed over a mug full to the brim with hangover coffee. "If she hasn't replied to your fourth text then she won't reply to your fifth."

"But if I—"

"No."

"But she—"

"*No,*" Tom repeated, with the stern resoluteness of a disappointed father. "I know you didn't want Courtney to cancel on you but hounding her with texts isn't the answer."

"That's rich coming from you, Mister 'I'm going to manipulate everything about Liz's life so she has no choice but to spend time with me'".

"That's 'Professor' Manipulator to you."

"Stop fighting, children," Liz complained, holding a bottle of ice-cold water to her forehead with a groan. The three of us were lying on the massive couch in Tom's living room, Jerry the kitten curled up on Liz's lap, Ludo's head resting on mine, and a riotous mess surrounding us.

But I was in a terrible mood, so I bit back, "It's true, though. Frankly it's ridiculous that you ever forgave Tom for all the shit he did to you."

"That was for me and Tom to sort out, and we did," Liz said, firm, before elaborating, "and I gave as good as I got. Don't take your anger out on us, Simon."

"But—"

"The fundamental issue Liz and I had back then was miscommunication," Tom chimed in, not unkindly, even though I was being a prick and I knew it. "Okay, yes, I was a monumentally immature bastard, and that definitely had something to do with it, but ultimately all we had to do was *talk* to each other, and make sure our feelings were genuine."

"...what's your point?" I grumbled, redirecting my misplaced anger into giving Ludo a vigorous head scratch. He wiggled in pleasure, so I kept doing it.

"His point is: do you know without a shadow of a doubt that Courtney meant what she said?" Liz asked. She forced herself into a cross-legged position, drank from her water bottle, then added, "Or is it possible that she ran off because of an issue you don't yet know about? Did you talk about *anything* last night that could give you a clue?"

It felt as if it was *Liz* giving me clues. She knew something, that much was for sure. Even through her hangover she had entered Helpful, Nosy Elizabeth mode.

Which meant there was something I needed to figure out, and fast.

I desperately tried to process everything Courtney had ever said to me, which was difficult considering the obscene volume of tequila I'd drunk the moment she rejected me and quite literally fled from my sight. "She told me on Friday night that she was trying to cut back on drinking because she was a manic drinker," I mused, after I realised that nothing she'd said during the party was of any help. I flung my hands up in resignation. "But that tells me nothing. She was probably put off by all my misery chat about my mum."

"Oh fuck off," Liz groaned. "Was that before or after I caught the two of you a hot second away from ripping each others' clothes off? I take that back, actually; she was *already* taking your clothes off."

"Fine, fine. Then it's the manic drinking thing. Why is she a manic drinker?"

"Why don't you ask Courtney and find out?"

"*That isn't helpful.* She made it clear that she didn't want to see me again."

"Did she?" Tom piped up. "Or did she tell you that going out with you was a mistake?"

"...the latter?"

"Then is it possible Courtney is scared, and talking to her about it might help you *both* work through it?"

"So what do you suggest I do," I said, frustrated by Tom and Liz's roundabout way of helping me, "go up to the reception desk at the Plaza and ask her to spill her deepest, darkest secrets to me?"

"Oh fuck no!" Liz all but screamed at me. She winced at the volume of her own voice. "If you go near her when she's *working,* Si, then I swear to god—"

"But where else am I supposed to see her? I only met her *because* she works at the Plaza. And as you can clearly see, she isn't replying to my texts. If I call her I doubt she'll answer that, either." I leaned forward until my head was resting on Ludo's, wishing that I, too, could have as simple a life as he did.

To my surprise both Tom and Liz looked right *at* Ludo, then at each other, then back to their dog. A conspiratorial grin spread across both of their faces.

"Care to let me in on what's going on in your twisted heads, guys?" I asked, unsure if I even wanted to know.

It was Tom who replied. "Courtney often takes Ludo for us

on Tuesday nights so we can go out for dinner. She'll be doing exactly that in two days."

"So, what, I rock up to her flat – wherever that is – and beg her to let me in?"

"Are you actively trying to get slapped across the head?" Liz said incredulously. "Get over your pity party and *listen*. She always, always takes Ludo out jogging to Dawsholm Park bang-on 6pm. They stay there for the better part of an hour, the fucking maniac that she is."

Tom nodded in approval. "Ludo deserves the exercise."

"Sounds like she's a woman after your own heart," I grumbled.

Tom gave me the finger, then kicked out a leg to nudge Liz's knee. "I have my very own cardio-hater right here. Can you imagine me being with a gym bunny? I'd forget all about my other hobbies. Heaven forbid I'm with someone who doesn't want to spend Friday nights watching *The Witch From Mercury* and—"

"Alright, you bloody nerd, I get the point. So what are you suggesting? I head up to Dawsholm Park for a 'jog' and 'just so happen' to run into Courtney?" Tom and Liz both nodded. "That's so stupid."

"It's better than cornering her at work, Si."

I cringed at Tom's words; he and Liz were right and we all knew it. But it still didn't feel right. Sure, only a fool could deny the immediate chemistry between me and Courtney. And the ease with which our *Twenty Questions* moved from flirtatious into serious territory meant I was desperate to explore something more than the fling I'd outright lied to Courtney that I'd be down for.

But she'd stopped all that. She'd said it was a mistake.

Sensing the souring of my already awful mood Tom sighed good-naturedly. "I wasn't going to tell you this, because I'd already said on Thursday that I didn't know anyone specifically that I wanted to set you up with. But that was a lie: Liz and I *both* wanted to get you and Courtney together. You're just neurotic enough to be right for her."

Liz nodded sagely. "Yup, an overthinker desperate for approval from the people he loves is perfect for her."

I didn't know which of the two of them to focus on. "I'm not sure if you're making fun of me or bigging me up. Or are you making fun of Courtney, too?"

"Oh, abso-fucking-lutely not," Liz said. "We're being serious. Try your hand at getting to know her on more than a surface-level and you'll see what I mean."

To be perfectly honest I still wasn't sure what the two of them were getting at, but I supposed that was the point. If I wanted to get to know Courtney then *I* had to put in the work. Through the right channels, without freaking her out, and without putting her on the spot at work.

Abruptly I got up, though Ludo whined when I did so.

"Where are you going?" Tom asked, curious.

"For a shower. Hell if I'm sitting around feeling sorry for myself with your hungover arses."

My best friend grinned. "That's the spirit. Never give up—"

"Never surrender. Shut up, Commander Taggart."

"It was Dr Lazarus who said that."

"I know." As if he didn't know *Galaxy Quest* was in my top five films. "But if you think you're even half as cool as Alan Rickman then you have another thing coming."

The task before me seemed difficult. The odds of succeeding were likely low. But I was nothing if not, as Liz so astutely put it, desperate for approval from the people I cared about. And I cared about Courtney Miller, even though my relationship with her thus far had been fleeting.

It was more than worth my time to give this a final shot.

Chapter Nine

COURTNEY

IF THERE WAS AN UPSIDE TO cancelling my date – and all future
potential dates – with Simon Saint, it was that I got to show up
at Rich's doorstep on Monday night and surprise the hell out of
him. Rich was delighted we could have our usual Monday night
together. Of course he was. So was I. It was what I needed:
routine, safety, reliability.

It absolved me from ever making a choice I'd inevitably
regret. A mistake, if you will.

"She's cycling through those guys like nobody's business,"
Rich said, halfway through our third episode of *The Button.*
"How many has she rejected in a row now? Seven? Ei—oh
damn. She just got rejected!" He whooped in triumph as Miss
Too Good For Everyone finally got her comeuppance. Or was
it that all of the men simply weren't good enough? As with most
speed dating shows, we'd probably never know.

And that was the beauty of them. They were flash-in-a-pan.
Contestants were one-dimensional characters. The first
impression you got of them was the only one that mattered, and
you never felt the need to change it.

"Courtney?" Rich pressed, when I didn't respond. His arm tightened around me; we were sharing the same recliner portion of his couch even though the couch could easily fit five people. His entire two-bedroom flat was pretty massive, to be honest. But I didn't begrudge Rich the fact his parents moved to the countryside to retire and left him his childhood home to live in. Because of that the place *felt* like a home, loaded with photos and candles and side tables and a million ornaments that Rich's mother and grandmother had picked out which he didn't have the heart to throw away.

Long story short: I loved it here. I hadn't felt this comfortable in a home since I was twelve. Before my *behaviour* started causing real issues and my mum stopped liking me as a person.

"Hmm?" I murmured, realising in that moment that I had neither heard what Rich said nor was aware of anything that had transpired over the last hour. When I went to bed that night I'd no doubt remember everything and obsess over it instead of sleeping, but that was a problem for future me. "Sorry. I wasn't listening."

"Clearly!" Rich huffed, sitting up with enough force to swing the recliner back into an upright position. He shifted over a few inches so he could turn and study my face, concerned. "What's up? Usually I have to tell you to shut up every five minutes so I can actually keep track of what's happening on TV."

It was a friendly jibe, but tonight it rubbed me the wrong way. "Sorry I keep pissing you off, then." I looked away, unable to maintain eye contact when I felt so raw and vulnerable. I tried not to talk over things and people, I really did, but it was difficult to always remember to do that. Especially when I was at Rich's, or in the flat with Becca, or back in the day when Ailish and I used to be close. Before she took mum's side and started criticising everything I did.

At the end of the day it was exhausting having to *remember* to do things all the time. When every little thing – such as not talking when a TV show was on – became a task I had to actively work on, my entire life became an endless chore.

One I frequently wanted out of.

Rich rapped the knuckles of his left hand on my head. "You know I didn't mean it like that. I don't judge you for the way you are."

"You just wish I was better than that."

"*Courtney!*"

"I know, I know," I muttered, shrinking into myself with every passing second. "That's not what you mean, either. I'm just in a bit of a low mood."

"And that's exactly what I'm here for. You know as well as I do that I've seen you at your worst. And guess what?" Rich pointed at himself. "I'm still here. So tell me what brought all this on, and maybe I can help you fix it."

I grimaced. "I highly doubt that."

"Is it because of that date you cancelled?" My stomach twisted horribly at the mere thought of Simon, and the look on his face when I told him agreeing to go out with him was a mistake. When I nodded Rich said, "If you cancelled it then you clearly knew it wasn't the right thing for you. That's a *good* thing, Courtney. Being able to say *no* to a situation instead of feeling obligated to go through with it is a huge step forward for you!"

Here's the thing: Rich was right. Through that lens I should be proud of myself. I was awful at saying no.

So why did I feel so guilty? And sad? And disappointed?

When I didn't respond Rich muted the TV. Gently he tucked an errant strand of hair behind my ear, even though I hadn't washed it since Saturday so it probably felt disgusting. "Look, Courtney," Rich began, in a tone of voice that felt like something important was coming. Which meant I kept my eyes on my hands fidgeting in my lap so I could actively listen, even though this usually pissed people off.

But not Rich. Never Rich.

"We've been best friends for years now, and I'd go to the ends of the earth for you. Quite literally."

I chuckled despite myself. "Australia is hardly the ends of the earth."

"I was being dramatic. Anyway, for the last few months I've been thinking about what I *really* want out of my life. You know I've been seriously considering expanding my business, but I've also been considering what I want from my personal life, too. And when you told me you were going on that date – fuck, it really threw me for a loop."

At this I looked up at Rich. Raised a quizzical eyebrow, wondering where he was going with all of this. "I've told you about a million dates I've gone on in the past," I said.

"Yeah, but this one felt different, because *I've* been feeling different. About you. Us. What I...what I'm hoping we might be able to be."

Oh.

"And I'm not looking for an answer from you, like, right now," Rich added anxiously, no doubt when he saw the blank look on my face. "But I just...I want you to consider me. To be more than just your friend, I mean. And let's be honest: we're practically dating already."

"I spend nights curled up with Becca on the couch watching trash TV and cuddling and sleeping in her bed; does that mean I'm dating *her*, too?"

"Do you sometimes spend your time with her kissing? Because I'm sure Peter would *love* to hear about that."

I knew Rich had a point, but if I had to answer him with anything but humour right now then I was going to implode. Because I didn't know. I didn't know what I wanted in the slightest. Hadn't I just turned down Simon Saint because I was scared of even *trying* to have a relationship? What kind of hypocrite would I be if I settled down with Rich immediately after that?

Except Rich was different from Simon. He was safe. He knew what I was like. He made daily life decisions for me all the time so I didn't have to stress myself out over menial things, and often big things, too.

Including changing our relationship?

Rich's face softened. His big Bambi eyes were warm with an understanding I far too often took for granted. "I was serious when I said you don't need to make a decision *right now*. But just...promise me that you'll at least think about it?"

I nodded, because I didn't know how else to respond. It wasn't as if I'd never viewed Richard Blake through a romantic or sexual lens before. Christ, I did that a dozen times a year. When we slept together the moment we both landed back in Glasgow, me heartbroken over my cheating ex and him dutifully returning to our home city to give me his full support, I remember it being pretty good. Not mind-blowing, but a solid base to work from.

Rich was probably much better in bed now, anyway. It wasn't as if he'd lived the life of a monk since we got back to Glasgow eight years ago. And we *did* already spend so much time together. Working together didn't ruin our personal relationship or vice versa. I loved him. He loved me. It made *sense* for us to be together.

So why did accepting Rich as my boyfriend somehow feel like a betrayal to Simon? To what I saw – fleetingly – on Saturday night? How *good* it could be to be with Simon, providing I wasn't...well, me?

"Let's reheat some of this pizza and watch a stupid eighties action film," Rich said, in an obvious attempt to lighten the mood. And because I would otherwise be paralysed by indecision, and I didn't want to ruin his night, I put on my best service face and said yes.

Chapter Ten

SIMON

I'D NEVER FELT SO CLEARLY LIKE an idiot as I did now. Dawsholm Park was near enough pitch black at 6pm, with a relentless bitter wind trying its best to cut through the multiple layers of athletic gear I'd piled on to prevent myself from succumbing to the cold. It was still January, after all, and this was Glasgow.

And I hated running. Ergo, this entire situation made me out to be an idiot.

I hoped Courtney would arrive soon so I could end this madness.

As I reluctantly jogged beneath the bare trees, narrowly avoiding slipping on some ice as I traversed my way down a narrow set of steps cut into the rock itself, I reasoned that even if this entire plan blew up in my face I could at least say I'd tried my best. It was more than I could say regarding talking to my grandparents – something which Kei had relentlessly needled me about all day. But, after tonight, perhaps I would finally be able to have that difficult conversation, no matter how long it took.

For better or worse tonight would mark the end of one part

of my life, and the beginning of the next.

So where was Courtney Miller?

A nervous-looking young woman came into my field of vision, the reflective patches on her jacket making her shine like an extra-terrestrial against my retinas. I gave her as wide a berth as the path would allow, though I also gave her a smile and a non-committal 'hello' as I passed. One time Liz sent me a video of a man showing he was non-threatening when jogged past women by making comments to them about Taylor Swift, *House of the Dragon* and some other equally silly topics, but I was not nearly so charismatic as to be able to pull that off in a dark and freezing park.

No, I stuck to Nirvana playing in my earbuds and a slow, plodding pace across wet leaves, and let my mind grow increasingly and erratically frantic that I'd made a terrible decision. It was always a bad idea to listen to Tom and Liz, to be fair. Despite me ripping into them about how they got together they truly were made for each other. Which made them a menace to everyone else.

Namely, me.

So when someone came up behind me and grabbed my shoulder and I shrieked like a five-year-old girl I blamed the two of them entirely. I swung around, eyes wide, tearing out my earbuds only to drop one of them right onto a beast of a dog. A beast of a dog who seemed oddly familiar.

"Ludo?" I said, voice shaking pathetically as I tore my gaze from his excited face to take in the person who had scared me out of at least twenty years of my life. Courtney Miller, bent over double as she cackled her arse off. Dimly I picked up my dropped earbud, shoved them both in my pocket and began scratching Ludo when he sniffed at my hands.

"How long were you following me?" I asked, a wary smile creeping across my face as I watched Courtney continue to revel in my predicament.

She wiped a tear out of her eye. "I don't know. How long

have *you* been out here trying to follow *me*?"

"I wasn't doing a very good job of it, it would seem. You aren't...mad at me?"

"What, because Tom and Liz told you my jogging routine so you could 'run into me', or because you thought it was a solid idea?"

"Courtney—"

"No, no, I'm not mad at you," she bit out the moment she saw the horrified expression on my face. She straightened up, shook out her shoulders a little, then readjusted the tiny sports bra she'd forced her boobs into before speaking again. "Not mad. Curious. Why the hell would you still want anything to do with me after I ran out on you like that? Are you a masochist?"

"Only when it suits." It was out of my mouth before I could stop it. But Courtney didn't give me time to regret it.

"Oh, I think I could work with that," she said, grinning wickedly.

I think I could work with that, too.

I knelt on the frozen ground to play with Ludo properly, though the muck beneath my knees soon started seeping through to my skin like some kind of cosmic horror searching for my soul.

A beat of silence passed. Two. Then—

"Look, Simon—" Courtney said, just as I called out her name. She shifted on the spot, fixing her ineffectual sports bra again before saying, "You first."

It was easier to pretend I was talking to Ludo, so that's exactly what I did. "I'm sorry I put you in a position where you felt like you had to apologise for cancelling on me," I began. "Your decisions are your own, and I never wanted to upset you."

Courtney tickled Ludo's head, her fingertips coming into my field of vision. A perfect French manicure, save for a chipped nail on her index finger. "I'm the one who should be apologising for running off like that," she said. "I panicked and overreacted and...Christ, this is why. So you wouldn't have to deal with me at my worst."

I looked up at her. Courtney had the most miserable, faraway expression on her face. It was worse because it looked familiar. Worn-in. Like she was old friends with this expression.

"I think you'd be surprised how bad you'd have to be for me to not want to 'deal' with you, Courtney," I said, easing back up so that I now stood taller than her, "but in order for me to do that you'll have to, you know, let me *actually* get to know you."

Courtney shivered; her entire chest was covered in goosebumps. Seeing where my lecherous gaze had wandered she held out a hand. "Jacket," she demanded. "Hand it over."

Of course I complied but not before asking, "Shouldn't you be dressed in more than leggings and a sports bra that – forgive me for pointing this out - is four sizes too small for your boobs? It's barely above freezing."

"With what money?" Courtney laughed airily. "When I started jogging back in – when was it? Late 2021? Anyway. I started jogging because my dad was getting a bit overweight, and he wanted to get fitter. So I joined him because otherwise there's *no way* he'd have stuck to it, and—"

"I'm sorry to interrupt," I said, chuckling into my hand, "but are you getting into the vicinity of a point or am I simply being blessed with a heartwarming story about you and your dad?"

Courtney gave me the finger, then huddled into my jacket. It was far too big for her but nonetheless looked as if it had been made for her. "I was trying to explain why my sports bra is too small."

"Ah, in which case please continue."

"So when I started jogging I was way smaller than I am now. Teeny. I never ate, really – it was such a hassle *remembering* to eat that—"

"Hold on, you *forgot* to eat?"

"Let me finish!" She stamped her foot impatiently. It was adorable. "*Anyway,* I was much smaller. My boobs were barely a B cup. Then I really, really got into jogging with my dad, and I suddenly realised I was starving. It got easier to remember to eat when I would literally drop into my bed, dead asleep by 6pm, if I didn't. But the problem is that now I'm more like an F cup and all my nice sports clothes – any of my clothes, really – don't fit anymore. And rent and food and energy bills are so expensive that I literally do not have money to replace stuff like bras. The end. Stop smiling like that."

"Like what?" I asked, a shit-eating grin plastered to my face. "Smiling like you're ridiculous, but that I *love* ridiculous? Nah, sorry, not going to stop." When Courtney made to punch my arm I grabbed her hand, instead, and she let me. "You're a bit manic, aren't you? I don't mean that in a bad way."

She made a face. "What other way is there?"

"Well, if you're manic, and I *like* you, then it must be a good manic."

"Infallible logic, Spock."

"Let me take you out. For real this time. Please." Courtney twisted her hand out of my grip, but then she seemed to think better of it and took my hand again. She traced cold, manicured fingertips across my palm in small circles.

"Manic isn't always good," she said, "and I can't guarantee I'll always be on my best behaviour even if I swear I will be."

"Nobody is always on their best behaviour, Courtney."

She searched my gaze then, her pale eyelashes fluttering over irises the colour of grass. I wanted to say more in my defence – I hadn't nearly made my point strongly enough – but before I could say another word Courtney said, "Okay. But can you wait a couple weeks? I have a Sunday off then."

I did the maths in my head. "...right before Valentine's Day?"

"God, don't give me that look," Courtney said, rolling her eyes. "I covered Sam for New Year so I got Valentine's. All I planned to do with it was go on a two-day bender."

"Healthy. How about going on an overnight trip, instead?" I didn't know who was more surprised by my idea: me or Courtney. But I stuck to it. "Separate rooms, of course. Just so we can...I don't know. Let loose a little. Relax away from our friends and our work."

Courtney side-stepped a neglected Ludo until she was right within the circle of my arms. She reached up and brushed my cheek with her lips. They were cold and chapped and I wanted nothing more than to kiss her properly, but I resisted.

"That sounds wonderful," Courtney said. She leaned against my chest, witness to my pounding heart and the lurching of my stomach. "I'll look forward to it."

I stroked her head, and it was the most natural thing in the world. "Me, too. I just have one question."

She jutted her chin up to look at me. "What?"

"Am I allowed to contact you in the interim? Like, text you or say hi to you at work or—"

"Oh my fucking god have you *ever* done this before, you fucking saint?"

"It's in the name. Literally."

Courtney whistled out a laugh. Then she gave me her best crooked smile. "Spam me with texts. Please. Especially during work. The more memes the better. And if you don't personally say hello to me during every shift then I'll personally see to it that a spider is hidden in your bed sheets."

"Consider me warned."

"Spiders are no joke, Simon," Courtney said gravely. "You should have seen the size of the one I cleaned out of my bathroom. Damn thing *bit* me. Though it has nothing on the spiders in Australia—"

"Tell you what," I cut in gently, taking Ludo's lead from Courtney's hand before linking her arm with my own, "how about you regale me with spider facts whilst we walk? I'm about to freeze to the pavement."

Courtney happily agreed and, indeed, spent the next fifteen minutes talking to me about spiders.

It was the best 'not a date' I'd ever had.

Chapter Eleven

COURTNEY

"So now you *are* going on a date with Simon?"

"Yes, and we can just shut up about it for now."

"Hell no!" Liz complained. "He hasn't told me *anything* about it. It's like your date is some big secret. So spill."

My chest warmed with the idea that Simon was planning something secret. It made me feel special. Important. My heart was fluttering, and were those butterflies in my stomach? God, I was actually excited. I'd never been so happy as I was when I spied Simon trying to surreptitiously 'run into me' in Dawsholm Park, though I wasn't about to admit that to Liz given that it had been her idea.

And then Becca brought me clanging back down to reality. "Wait, you have a date with the guy from the Plaza?" she asked around a strawful of chocolate milkshake. "I thought Rich *only just* asked you out!" When Becca had suggested meeting up with Liz, just the three of us, after the surprise at Chloë's birthday where everyone already, in fact, knew each other, both Liz and I had been delighted by the prospect.

Now I regretted it.

Liz peered down her nose at me. "Rich as in Richard Blake, from the dog day care?"

"My best friend, yes."

"He *asked you out*?"

"God, no, not exactly." I ran my hands through my hair, but then I stopped midway because it reminded me of Simon. "He asked me to consider him as a romantic prospect. That's all."

"That's all my arse," Becca protested. "The man's been in love with you since before I met you."

"That isn't fair. Don't make me think I've been *friendzoning* him for a decade. He's had serious girlfriends in that time. Besides, the friendzone is a misogynistic concept that men created to justify why girls didn't like them. It isn't real." Becca and Liz looked at me for a suspiciously long time. I buckled under the weight of their stares. "Fine. Obviously I've considered the fact he may or may not have been in love with me at various points throughout the years. But I'm not responsible for his feelings, and he only *just* made those feelings known to me."

"And your answer is to...go on a date with Simon?"

"My answer is to give myself the time and opportunity to *find* an answer."

"Yeah, and we all know that's worked out so well for you in the past," Becca retorted. If anyone else had said that I'd have fled the café in tears, but Rebecca Luton had every right to say that. She'd witnessed first-hand just how many times I'd given myself *time* and *opportunities* to work out what I wanted, but then I'd squandered both and ended up worse than when I'd started. But I wanted this to be different.

It *had* to be different.

Sensing my imminent dismal mood Liz threw a handful of chips onto my plate, having clearly observed that I'd been eyeing them up. I swallowed them down like the grateful seagull that I was.

"On the subject of finding answers," Liz said, when I'd swallowed down the last of her chips, "did I tell you Ray finally got his ADHD diagnosis?"

Becca clapped her hands in delight. "No way! He must be so happy!"

"Who's Ray?" I asked, though admittedly the name felt familiar.

"You met him briefly at Chloë's party. The one who likes plants." My blank stare spoke volumes.

It was Becca who said, "He was dressed as Van Helsing. Peter's flatmate."

"*Ah.* Yeah, I remember him. He has ADHD?"

"He went to the doctor about it years ago but they just gave him antidepressants," Liz explained. We all exchanged a look of understanding; doctors almost always went there first before considering any other answer. "But Peter didn't let up on him to *actually* find out what was wrong, because hell if Ray was depressed."

"...how long did it take him?" I asked, guiltily thinking about the fact that I'd missed my second call regarding the same manner because I'd been helping my dad get his stuff together to prove he was eligible for Universal Credit.

Liz smiled sadly. "His parents sent him the money to go private. I know that isn't feasible for everyone but I'm glad he had them to fall back on."

Liz and Becca exchanged some back-and-forth about Ray, Peter and some other stuff I was no longer able to pay attention to, because Liz's previous words were repeating in my head over and over and over.

Sometimes I couldn't bear living in my own head, either. Was I doomed, and that feeling would only get worse and worse until I found myself sobbing to my mother for help?

No. I had things covered. I'd never have to stoop so low.

Right?

"...so I thought I'd see if you could do it. Court? Courtney?" Liz said, waving a hand in front of my face. "Are you okay?"

"Sorry, I was just thinking about the fragility of my mental state," I replied, which was the truth, but the way I said it sounded like a joke and it landed as such.

Through a chuckle Liz said, "I just found out that Tom is taking me to *Japan* for two weeks at the beginning of April. For my thirtieth."

It took me a few moments to chew this over. "I thought Jerry was your thirtieth birthday present?"

"Apparently he was the decoy."

"I wish I had a boyfriend who got me a kitten as a *decoy* present," Becca sighed wistfully. Then she laughed. "But Peter's allergic, and unfortunately I care about him slightly too much to dump him in favour of a fur-friendly alternative."

Liz winked at me like the cringeworthy child that she was. "Do you know who could get *you* a kitten as a decoy present, Court?"

I could only scowl (although admittedly the idea that Simon would waltz into my living room and hand me an animal as a sign of his affection was just about the most amazing thing I could imagine). "Stop playing matchmaker. What do you need?"

"Can you house- and pet-sit for us while we're gone? We'll pay you, obviously. It would be good practice for you."

"You're going to *pay* me to live in your mansion with a dog and a cat? Fuck yeah I'm...wait." I blinked. "Practice?"

It was Becca who chimed in, her face pained. "I hadn't told her yet, Liz," she said awkwardly. Liz looked like she wanted to punch herself, but Becca continued talking before she could do or say anything to that effect. "Court, Peter asked me to move in with him. We're looking at flats to move into when our current lease ends."

"And that's - that's—"

"The end of April. I'm so sorry. I meant to tell you before the party but I—"

"Don't be fucking daft. This is great, Becca! I always knew you were destined for happy, monogamous life."

"Courtney—"

"I'm serious," I cut in, putting my service face to best use. Because of course I felt like Becca had just shredded my life into ribbons. Sure, I knew in my heart that she'd have to move on eventually, but it hadn't really *clicked* that her moving on could be...

Well, now.

"Where are you looking to move?" I asked, pulling out my phone and opening Google Maps. "Now all those months of looking at houses we could never afford makes so much sense!"

Becca looked at me as if she knew I was putting on a show for her, and that she didn't like that, but she appreciated it nonetheless. She rolled her eyes in a very exaggerated manner. "Yeah, you can exclude Park Circus and that townhouse in Hyndland that we saw. Not everyone's a millionaire like *Professor Thomas Henderson.*"

Liz looked scandalised. "Did you just sass my boyfriend?"

"I did indeed just sass your boyfriend. Does that mean I've been accepted into your trusted circle of friends?"

"Fuck yeah. Right, so where are you *seriously* looking? I always loved further up north, close to Summerston."

"By the canal?" I asked. I loved it up there; it was a scant ten minute walk from my current flat.

Old flat. Because I couldn't afford to stay in it on my own, and I couldn't handle living with someone new. I swallowed a lump in my throat as the conversation continued on about the best locations in Glasgow, but my heart wasn't in it.

Liz and Becca had their own lives. Their own career ambitions. Their own loves. I had none of those things. Well, none that really *mattered*, or were any more than childhood dreams. Was I doomed to fall further and further behind my friends? Was I going to be the one they pity-invited to everything but always invariably regretted doing so because I'd get too drunk and make a scene, until eventually even the pity invites dried up?

Was that really it for me?

I couldn't bear that being the truth.

By the time I got to work at the Plaza I was feeling well and truly wretched. I was almost tempted to call in sick. But then my phone pinged with a message from Rich.

> Becca told me about her moving out. Want me to come round later with ice cream?

I smiled. Of course Rich was ready and waiting to help me out of a low period the moment I dropped myself into it. I appreciated it more than he'd ever know. I drafted a reply, getting ready to send it off when—

"I thought you might appreciate this," a soft, masculine, familiar voice called out over the reception desk. The smell of savoury deliciousness wafted into my nostrils, and I jerked my head up. Simon, holding out a Greggs paper bag for me to take. He proffered it in my direction when I didn't immediately take it. "There's two in there. Consider my debt repaid."

I smothered a smile. "You still have to repay me for the stolen taxi *and* the bump to my head."

"I'm sure we can set a date where I can fix all my past transgressions." Simon gave me a disarmingly polite smile, inclined his head in a very businesslike half-nod, then added, "I'll let you get to work. And hello."

I frowned. "Hello?"

"Yes, *hello,* lest you put spiders in my bed."

I couldn't stop myself from laughing like a maniac, even

though that got me some major side-eye from the trainee receptionist, Eilidh, who by my measure wasn't going to last until Friday. "I swear on these sausage rolls that there are no arachnids in your bed, nor anywhere else in your room."

"That's what I like to hear."

"Thank you. Seriously. I needed this."

"What, high-calorie sustenance?" Simon's tone was jovial, but I could see the look of concern plain as day on his face. He was dressed in a large denim jacket and tan-coloured corded trousers, with his hair messy and unstyled – the most casual I'd seen him dress so far, and effortlessly fashionable. I wanted to ask him where he'd been to be dressed out of his usual suits. Who he was with, what he was doing, how his day had been.

But I was at work, and had a lot to think about.

"Let's pretend you believe me when I say yes," I said, sort-of answering his question. Simon spread his hands across the desk, ever-so-slightly leaning into my space. He was close enough that I could count the six freckles on his face.

Too, close, too close. My breathing hitched.

"And then...?" he asked, voice taking on a low, gravelly tone that sent my mind racing.

"And then I'll text you about the bad day I had once nobody is watching me?" It was the best – the only – compromise I could think of between ditching work and ignoring Simon, both things of which I either didn't want to do (ignore Simon) or couldn't afford to do (ditch work).

For a moment it looked as if Simon was going to completely reach over the desk to kiss me. God, I wanted him to kiss me. But at the last second he remembered where we were and refrained from any bodily contact. "That sounds great," he murmured, moving agonisingly away from my personal space. He smiled, and it was warm and comforting. "Take it easy, okay?"

"There's no other way to do it." That was a lie because I

took everything hard, hard, hard; with Simon around that was the opposite of a bad thing.

Once he was gone I told Rich that I needed to be alone tonight but thanked him for the offer. Then I settled into telling Simon via text all about my housing dilemma, whilst my brain imagined all the filthy things I wished I'd let him to do me on top of the damn desk instead of sending him on his way.

Chapter Twelve

SIMON

You'd think naming a restaurant would be the easiest part of opening one. The most enjoyable task. The fun job. But the other stuff was easy for me. Finances? I could do that in my sleep. Furniture and aesthetics? I'd been dreaming about this place for months and had about 3 GB of photos on my laptop serving as inspiration. But a name?

Jesus, I was stumped.

Kei wasn't helping. Or, rather, his suggestions ran more along the lines of what I *couldn't* name it rather than helping with what it was going to be. "I don't want 'ramen' in the name," he'd told me, and, "If there's any weeaboo shit on the shop front then I will personally fucking end you." Which was all well and good, but it still left me staring at a blank piece of paper with no better ideas than I'd had last year.

Which was to say, I had no ideas at all.

"Food of the Angels?" I muttered under my breath, writing it out then immediately scoring through it. Yes, my surname was Saint, but who in the general populace would know or even care about that? It sounded sanctimonious as shit. "Saint's

Ramen?" I tried, then promptly remembered the first of Kei's only two rules.

I gave up and took a sip of lager, instead. Hell if I could do this completely sober. Living in a hotel like the Crowne Plaza had its perks: namely, access to a nice bar from which to work. The tall, sweeping, floor-to-ceiling glass walls provided me with one of the best views of the Clyde you could get in the city (although the Radisson with its rooftop bar on the other side of the street would happily debate this). It filled me with a sense of peace that London had never given me, even though it was currently dark and windy and dreary as hell outside.

But I was safe and warm *inside,* which was of course the best way to enjoy dismal weather. All my best memories from my childhood were of huddling in an armchair with my mother in the nook of a tenement bay window, watching torrential Scottish rain lash at the window whilst she fed me chips and cheese and I read her my favourite books aloud. I'd been a huge Michael Morpurgo fan when I was a kid; later, when I read his books with adult eyes, I realised six had been much too young for books like *Kensuke's Kingdom.* But they'd made me who I am today, and they formed the core of the precious time I spent with my mother, so hell if the books I'd been reading were appropriate or not.

"Mister Saint?" a waiter inquired politely, standing at the edge of my table in such a manner that suggested he'd actually been there for quite a while and I simply hadn't noticed him. "A package arrived for you at the front desk. It needs signed for. Would you like me to bring it over or—"

"No, I'll get it," I said, brushing my failed brainstorming session into my bag before thanking the waiter and heading to reception. I almost did a double-take when I realised Courtney was working. Had I been sat in the bar for so long? Checking my watch I saw that it was just after 6pm, which was when she started work. I'd been sat in the bar for almost ninety minutes with nothing to show for it!

Courtney was busy talking to a curly-haired man around her

age when I came upon reception. Not wishing to interrupt her I sidled over to the end of the desk, where the courier and a temp receptionist (who I was pretty sure was two seconds away from being fired) stood waiting for me. Going by the austere packaging I knew the delivery could only be one thing: a contract from my grandparents regarding me becoming named partner in their investment firm.

Abruptly the lager I'd been drinking settled like lead in my stomach. I'd told them I didn't want to discuss this until I was back in London, but as usual they'd ignored what I said and what I wanted. Resisting the urge to simply rip up the contract and chuck it in the bin after signing for it I began storming away from reception, only for Courtney to call out, "Simon, hold on!"

It was as if my mood flipped entirely. Hearing Courtney call my name out, unbidden, had me walking on air. Sparing a glance at my reflection in the glass wall to fix my hair and straighten my tie – why I was dressed for business just to sit in a hotel bar I had no idea – I turned back towards Courtney with a mega-watt smile. "You called?"

She inclined her head towards the package in my hands, curiosity written in big letters across her face. "What is that? Seems important."

"I think it's from my grandparents. Legal stuff. Very boring."

"Sounds like you have an exciting night ahead of you." Courtney shifted her gaze to the man she'd been talking to, who was watching us with disconcerting scrutiny. "Simon, this is Richard Blake. I work with him at his dog day care when I'm not dealing with all of your unreasonable requests." I snickered. "Rich, this is Simon Saint. He's the one staying in the penthouse for three months that I was telling you about."

I held out my hand to shake Rich's when he proffered it to me. "It's wonderful to meet you."

"Likewise," Rich said, but his smile was tight.

Something told me he didn't want to just work with

Courtney.

"So you run a dog day care?" I asked, testing the waters by asking the safest question I could think of. "Having seen Courtney with Ludo I can imagine she's just as good at her job with you as she is here. Ah, Ludo is my friend—"

"He's Tom's dog," Rich finished for me. He crossed his arms. "I know. So you're opening a restaurant?" I nodded. "So what's next after that? Courtney said you have a bakery in London, so I can't imagine you plan to stay here long."

Ah. So he'd done his research. Or, at least, had written to memory everything Courtney had ever said about me. It felt nice – better than nice – that she'd been talking about me to other people. It was reassuring. But right now, going by Rich's demeanour, I felt anything but reassured.

I felt like I had to be on the offence.

"Courtney," I said, shifting not insignificantly back towards her. She was in a good mood, practically bobbing on the spot as she waited for me to say whatever I was going to say. "About Sunday—"

"I'm sorry, Simon, but I'm not working on Sunday," Courtney said without a trace of deceit. "You'll have to get Sam to take care of your request."

I wasn't stupid. Of course I wasn't. I heard what she was saying loud and clear: Rich didn't know about our impending date, and Courtney didn't want him to know. Which meant he *was* more than her work colleague, or her friend.

Luckily I didn't back down from a fight.

"I best deal with this," I said, indicating towards the contract my grandparents had sent me. "Have a good evening, Courtney." Then, to Rich, "It was wonderful to meet you."

Rich didn't reply, only nodded.

If I had competition – which I was increasingly certain I did – then I'd have to pull out all the stops to impress Courtney.

And I could start with our impending overnight trip. My eyes scanned the contract in my hands, grip tightening on the paper as if I meant to strangle it. But I knew the document gave me leverage – at least as far as being able to pull off impressive, if ultimately meaningless, stunts.

I emailed my grandfather and told him I'd discuss the contract with him in person, as per his wishes, if he did me a favour.

Chapter Thirteen

COURTNEY

"And what time did he say he was picking you up?" Becca asked, fidgeting impatiently as we both sat by the bay window in our living room to watch the empty street below us. Despite getting in from work at three in the morning she'd insisted on getting up early with me, determined to see me off 'just to be safe'. And by that she meant she was being nosy.

"I never said *Simon* was picking me up," I said, turning the selfie camera on my phone to check my make-up for the tenth time in five minutes. I hadn't wanted to go overboard so I'd gone for dewy skin, peach lip tint and blush, with no mascara. Along with my freshly-cut and styled curtain bangs (Becca's doing, because she'd spent two years training as a hairdresser before deciding it wasn't for her) and my signature oversized hoop earrings I figured I looked pretty seventies-boho-hippie.

If only my damn dress fit me properly, but alas none of my clothes really fit these days. At least it was February; I could hide the fact my boobs were practically spilling out of the sweetheart neckline of my otherwise very pretty leopard-print skater dress with a burnt orange crop-fit jumper.

It wasn't perfect, but it would have to do. I could hardly

wear a bodycon mini dress for an overnight trip, after all. Or could I? I had no idea what to expect from this trip. Was I making a mistake? Was Simon going to steal me away to a secondary location, have his wicked way with me and then calmly and carefully carve me into pieces like an expert serial killer? Hell, I didn't even know what the *primary* location was.

"*Courtney!*" Becca cried in familiar, fond exasperation. She pointed down at the street. "Get out of your head. There's a fancy car down there waiting for you, I think. So are you saying Simon isn't in it?"

I shook my head, my entire body trembling slightly with an equal mix of nerves and excitement. "He told me he was sending a car to pick me up because he needed to finalise our travel arrangements."

"How rich *is* this guy?"

"I think it's his family that's rich. His grandparents."

"Ah, a nepo baby. Makes sense why he's friends with Tom."

"Fuck off," I laughed, punching Becca's shoulder before swinging up to my feet, grabbing my tiny travel suitcase before rushing for the door. When I reached it I blew her a kiss. "Have a lovely night with Peter! And remember—"

"Not a word to Rich about this," Becca finished for me, sighing enormously. "I know. But you're gonna have to tell him sooner or later if you plan to actually date Simon. I know he said you could take all the time you need to think over your relationship with him but literally going out with someone else while you do that is a bit cruel."

"What a way to dampen the mood." I stuck out my tongue, keeping up an act of not caring even though of course I did. I just didn't know what to do. "Love you."

"You too. Now get going before Simon thinks you stood him up!"

I didn't need telling twice. I left our flat and practically tripped over my feet running down the uneven tenement building stairs until I slipped out onto the pavement. As soon as I locked eyes on the sleek black car with its tinted windows the front window came down. A man in a black flat cap nodded at me.

"Miss Miller?" he said. When I nodded the back door clicked, signalling it was unlocked, and the driver got out of the car to help me with my suitcase.

"Oh, that isn't necessary," I tried to say, but he pulled it from my grip and placed it in the boot of the car anyway. Then he held open the back door of the car to let me in. In all my thirty-two years on the planet I'd never been treated like I was anyone important. It was nice. In the back of the car there was a bottle of water and a little bottle of prosecco on ice waiting for me.

Definitely nice.

"Are you ready to leave?" the driver asked, glancing at me from his rear-view mirror. With a look out of the window to see if Becca was watching – she was – I signalled for the driver to start the car, then off we went.

No sooner had the engine revved up and we'd moved away from the pavement than my phone pinged with a message. I knew it was Simon without having to look at the name.

> Simon: All good?
>
> Me: If by 'all good' you mean I have permission to crack open that prosecco despite it being 8am then yes, we're all good.
>
> Simon: Well I didn't put it there as decoration. Have at it and I'll see you soon.

I realised I was beaming like a fool, though the driver didn't seem to care. God, I was really doing this. Going on a mysterious overnight trip with a wealthy man I barely knew. It was exciting. It was impulsive. It was unknown.

It was everything I loved about life and then some.

I was most of the way through the little bottle of prosecco –

alcohol had never tasted so good – when I realised where the car was going through the dreary, slow Sunday morning traffic.

"Excuse me," I said to the driver, frowning into the distance, "but are you taking me to the airport?"

"I am indeed, Miss Miller. Mister Saint is already there, awaiting your arrival."

A thrill ran through me at whatever it was Simon had in store for us. But then I gasped. "I didn't bring my passport! We need to—"

"That won't be necessary."

Ah. So wherever Simon was taking me was within the UK. I briefly checked my wallet to make sure I had my driver's license (provisional, since I'd never had the money nor the dedication required to spend more than an hour behind the wheel) for identification so I could get on the flight, breathing a sigh of relief when I found it exactly where it had sat in my wallet for the last fourteen years. Then I necked back the last of the prosecco just as we pulled up to the airport.

I let the driver get out first and open the door for me. It wasn't every day I was in a position to get spoiled like this; I planned to soak up every last second of it.

He took my suitcase out of the car, pulled out the rickety handle for me, then proffered it over with a gentle smile. "You'll find Mister Saint waiting for you inside Starbucks. Have a wonderful trip, Miss Miller."

"Thank you so much," I replied, before heading towards the entrance to the airport. I took a deep breath before walking through the revolving door, my head already spinning a little thanks thanks to my breakfast of two units of bubbly alcohol on an empty stomach.

Was I still nervous? Hell yes. Did I kind of feel like running away? Maybe a little. But the moment I saw Simon sitting in a little booth in Starbucks, eyes glued to his phone whilst he tapped his foot incessantly under the table, all such feelings melted away. The guy was an absolute 11/10, and *he* was nervous?

It was adorable.

"Fancy seeing you in anything but a suit," I whispered into his ear, having successfully crept up on him using the din of the airport to mask my approaching footsteps. Simon did a double-take, almost knocking over his coffee in the process, but when he realised who I was he laughed throatily and got to his feet.

"I figured you were bored of the suits by now," he said. He swept a hand down his outfit. "What do you think of casual Simon?"

What I thought was that I was going to have to hide him under a damn blanket so every other red-blooded woman wouldn't look at him. Simon had paired the most perfect black turtleneck sweater I'd ever seen with crisp, cream trousers, a pair of black pointy-toe leather boots and a black woollen trench coat. His hair – which he usually kept styled away from his face – was soft and slightly wavy across his forehead, the grey at his temples barely visible. It made him look younger. More innocent, almost.

And insanely fucking hot.

Simon watched me ogle him with increasing enjoyment. His face flushed in pleasure. "I take it you like what you see."

"I hate it," I immediately quipped, though I was smiling so Simon knew I was full of shit. But then I added, more seriously, "Now I'll look even more out-of-place next to you." I ran a finger under the neckline of my sweater self-consciously. It was so hot in the airport, but damn if I was going to have my almost-spilling-out boobs on full display next to Simon the fucking Adonis.

His expression softened. With a wordless hand on my back he careened me over to airport security. "Don't worry about your clothes, Courtney. And if they're bothering you that much then that's easily rectified."

I raised an eyebrow. "How so?"

"Because I may want to take you shopping so you can buy an entirely new wardrobe that actually fits you, sports bras and all."

We checked through security, and Simon directed me towards a private runway. A private fucking runway. "Where are we going, exactly?" I asked, no longer able to contain my curiosity.

As we passed through a set of double doors and out into the cold to board the tiny plane he offered me a boyish grin. "London, by way of my grandparents' plane that they very generously loaned out to me. And by 'loaned' I mean it was heading back in that direction with a load of important documents, anyway, and we're merely hopping a ride."

When he gave me a hand to help me onto the stairs leading up to the plane I paused, staring him down as if I could glean his true intentions straight through his beautifully grey eyes. "Are you doing all of this just to impress little old me, Simon? Or are you simply showing off?"

Those eyes twinkled. "The former. And I'm hoping that this disgusting display of wealth means you'll allow me to spend an inordinately large amount of money on you during this trip without feeling weird about it."

Well, who was I to argue with him? Simon earned so much more than I did; my idea of a large sum of money was likely pocket change to him. Pay equity and all that. And I *wanted* to be spoiled. To be treasured. To be the only one he was looking at.

I squeezed his hand, then walked up onto the plane. "Then spend away."

Chapter fourteen

SIMON

A BOTTLE OF CHAMPAGNE AND AN hour later, Courtney and I had landed in London. The entire flight I'd enjoyed watching Courtney look at the world go by through the tiny window, listening to her tell me all about her week and the terrible customers, human and canine alike, who'd pushed her to the limits of her patience. Patience which had – to my eyes when seeing her in the Crowne Plaza – seemed limitless, but now that Courtney was proverbially letting her hair down I discovered she actually had quite a short fuse when she wasn't in service mode.

I found that disparity incredibly intriguing, not to mention appealing. She spat out everything that bothered her in one manic, rambling complaint, safe from the ears of those who would punish her for it, and then she let it go forever. I could only aspire to be so mature.

"So where are we off to first, Simon?" Courtney asked, her face flushed both from alcohol and the stiff breeze whipping our cheeks. She huddled into her jacket and sweater, both of which were much too thin for what was turning out to be an Arctic eleventh of February. But she hadn't removed either layer on the plane, which had been warm and pleasant, which meant I could only conclude that Courtney was self-conscious about how her dress fit her.

Which was a shame, because Courtney Miller looked absolutely stunning.

She was pared-back, soft and *earthy* today, somehow. I couldn't put my finger on it. She was always so polished at work. Red lipstick. Mascara. Perfect, slicked-back ponytails, not a hair out of place. And then, at Chloë's party, Courtney had been dressed up as someone else entirely. To see this version of herself that she was *actively choosing* to present to me made me aware of how privileged I was that this fascinating, gorgeous, witty woman wanted to spend her precious free time with me.

I had to pull out all the stops. This date had to be perfect.

"We can go anywhere you want," I said, even as I veered Courtney towards Oxford Street. "I figured, since you need an entirely new wardrobe, that we should start with the basics first. But then..."

"But then?" Courtney wheeled around to face me, her eyes bright and alert and twinkling with mischief. She ran her hands up the front of my chest, gently grabbing at the lapels of my jacket. God, I wanted to kiss her so badly my heart ached. "What have you got up your sleeve, Simon?"

I slung an arm around her waist, a sly smile curling my lips when she gasped in surprise. "I may have cashed in a few favours so we could shop in private at a couple stores. More expensive ones."

"Are you Pretty Woman-ing me?"

I barked out a laugh. "Not unless you have a secret third job as a prostitute."

"It would certainly pay better than hotel reception," Courtney said, giggling, before picking up the pace until we were practically skipping along the busy street. "If that's the case I want to hit up Uniqlo first. Then Pull & Bear. Oh, and

Bershka, and I would be an idiot not to hit up Stradivarius while we're—"

"We can go quite literally anywhere you want to," I cut in, happiness spreading through me like fire at how excited Courtney was by the sheer prospect of simply *shopping* together. "Just so long as we're done and ready by seven."

Courtney spared a glance in my direction as we neared the tell-tale boxy red sign for Uniqlo. "What's at seven?"

"Dinner. Somewhere nice, of course."

"So what are we doing for lunch?" Courtney asked, pulling out her phone to check the time. I subtly pushed us out of the doorway to the shop when folk around us started grumbling and glaring in our direction at having stopped the flow of traffic. "It's not even eleven yet."

"I figured we could stop by my bakery and maybe Chinatown after that." When Courtney stared at me incredulously I laughed. "The best food isn't always the most expensive. Trust me, once you have a char siu bun from London Chinatown you'll never look back."

"I'll take your word for it. Ailish has been harping on about the place ever since she moved down here, so it'll be nice to see what all the fuss is about."

"Ailish?" I asked, as we finally entered the shop and I watched Courtney's pupils dilate as she processed everything on display.

"My sister," Courtney replied, but her attention was already elsewhere and I knew I'd glean no further back story to her life. Well, at least not right now.

Now was dedicated to getting Courtney Miller a wardrobe deserving of her quite frankly amazing body.

My experiences of women shopping were split into three categories. The first was my grandmother picking over things with slow, deliberate ease. Demanding the sales assistant go over every little detail of the product she was interested in to ensure there were no secret flaws only my grandmother could discern.

My second experience was rooted in my increasingly dim memories of my childhood: my mother fretting over whether she could afford that new pair of shoes she desperately needed. She always prioritised my every whim before she tended to herself. I'd never appreciated it as a kid but now, looking back, I realised she taught me a lesson about money and family and love that fundamentally defined me as an adult.

My final experience of women shopping was the worst one. There were occasions here or there throughout the years when I went clothes shopping with wealthy friends or casual girlfriends who treated money like air. They didn't care what they picked up – no matter the price, or how much wear they thought they'd get out of the garment, or if they had something like it in their wardrobe already. They simply bought it all.

But Courtney shopping was a wholly unique experience. As we went from shop to shop her energy did not once waver. Her excitement going from one rack of skirts to another rack, which were seemingly identical to me until Courtney insisted otherwise, was infectious. She viewed the purchase of a multi pack of socks with the same level of detail as she did a far more expensive merino wool cardigan, even when I reminded her that money was not an issue and she could buy whatever she wanted.

"Yeah, but it isn't about what I *want*," Courtney told me breathlessly after we left our fourth shop – Stradivarius – with our arms laden with shopping bags. But not nearly so many as I'd expected, and not even close to how much I thought it would cost.

I could only laugh. "The whole point of this shopping trip is to get you want you want."

"No, it's to get me what I really need, in fabrics that will actually last, but I'm picky enough over my clothes that the things I really need also just-so-happen to be what I want. It's an important distinction."

"That's an awfully mature approach to shopping."

"And yet still I find myself spending any money I actually have on shite I don't need," Courtney sighed, as we headed in the direction of my bakery. It was almost two in the afternoon, after all, and whilst our morning of champagne had been delightful the alcohol had now worn off and I was starving.

We stopped at a bustling corner, waiting for the pedestrian light to turn green. I gave Courtney a careful once-over. "Why do you think you do that?" It was one of the first questions I always asked people when they came to me for financial advice.

Courtney squirmed uncomfortably. "I tend to make most of my decisions impulsively, and usually always regret them. But I'm...I'm bad at forward planning. If it feels good in the moment I tend to do it." When she laughed it was sad. "Funnily enough, 'good in the moment' almost always leads to bad future consequences."

"Hey, you're aware of the problem," I said, anxious to help her feel better. "That's more than most people can say, and I know that for a fact."

As we crossed the road Courtney kept her eyes on me, her legs following my long strides without any effort at all. "You mean that, don't you?"

"Mean what?"

"Trying to make me feel better," she said. "Usually when people do that to me they lie or say I haven't been *that* bad, because they know that if I fall off the deep end...well." Courtney ran a hand through her hair to pull it away from her face. "But you aren't lying to me. You really do believe that knowing I have a problem means I'm on the right track towards fixing myself."

It was at this point that I knew for sure that Courtney was most definitely not only talking about her finances. We were almost at the bakery, so I took Courtney to sit on the closest bench I could find that wasn't wet or covered in bird shit. When we laid our shopping down I dared to take her hands in mine; they were freezing.

"Tell me what's going on with you," I said, trusting Courtney not to be offended. Trusting her to know why I was asking, because I wanted to know *her*.

Courtney considered my question for a few drawn-out seconds, but then she exhaled and said, "I have **ADHD**. Well, I haven't been diagnosed yet, but I know it's true. For my dad, too."

I frowned. "Your dad?"

"Yeah. We're so similar it's hilarious. Or tragic."

"So what's stopping you?"

"Stopping me what?"

"Getting a diagnosis."

Courtney waved a hand down her body. "Me. Obviously. Well, I've been on the wait list for years but they've called me *twice* already and I just haven't been able to bring myself to answer the phone. It's stupid, I know. I'm the one who wants the diagnosis and I can't even pick up the *damn phone—*"

"If you thought sorting this out was going to be easy then you wouldn't be in the position where you have to do it," I countered, trying to combat Courtney's disparaging view of herself with logic. "You managed to get on the wait list and then had to wait for so long? Why is that?"

"You might not have noticed in your ivory tower but the Tory government have been shelling out the NHS for years now." Her jibe at me wasn't cruel; it was simply proving a point. One that was so succinctly made that I didn't ask my next question: why not go private? Because of course I knew the answer to that.

It was too expensive.

There had to be something I could do for her that wasn't simply throwing money at the problem. A doctor I could recommend. A good therapist. Anything.

For now, though, it was clear Courtney wanted to continue having a good time together, and so did I.

I got to my feet. "Let's get some lunch. Not to brag but I'm pretty sure Nicola makes the best pain au chocolats in all of London."

"Wait, you're not...not going to tell me I'm overreacting?" Courtney asked, disbelief plain as day on her face. "You're not going to tell me that I'm probably just depressed, or lazy, or that if I had ADHD I'd have been diagnosed as a kid or—"

"Why would I do any of that? You told me what's going on. What you're dealing with. And I believe you."

"...why?"

"Because I trust you."

It was such a simple thing to say. Simple, but not a sentence to fling around lightly. Yet as I watched Courtney absorb my words I realised they were true, despite the fact I hardly knew this woman and the last time we'd been physical together she had literally told me to my face that it was a mistake.

But it was true nonetheless. I trusted Courtney Miller, and that made me happy.

"That's...I..." Courtney gulped, her eyes a little too bright. But then she smiled and she was once more golden and lovely against the dreary London afternoon. "I trust you, too. I don't know why. I shouldn't. But I do. So get me some of those pain au chocolats and we'll put that trust to the test."

Courtney's hand found mine, and we walked over to the bakery looking and feeling every inch a perfect couple. But it didn't take long to realise that the bakery was busy. *Too* busy.

"Here, follow me," I told Courtney, giving her the bags of shopping I was holding so I could use both of my arms to brute-force our way through the queue. I ignored the expletives and abuse thrown our way, and only stopped once I reached the till.

A harried young woman immediately said, "You can't skip

the queue, sir, so please...oh my god, it's Mr Saint!" Her flushed face went even redder when she realised her mistake.

"It's not a problem, Emma," I replied kindly, once I was sure I remembered her name. "What's going on? You seem awfully short-staffed today."

"Nick and Flavien have the flu," Emma informed me whilst she resumed bagging up orders for impatient customers. "It's just me on the till this afternoon."

"No it won't be." Without another word I headed behind the counter, threw off my jacket and put on an apron. Courtney caught my eye, and the approval that was written all over her face was like a bolt of lightning to the heart. "Courtney, I'll send you the details of the rest of the shops I had planned for the afternoon. A car will pick you up at the end to take your belongings to the hotel and you to dinner, so would you be able to—"

"Don't say another word," she said. "Let me steal one of those pastries and I'll be on my merry way." Emma gave her four, with a horrified but grateful apology at having interrupted our date. But Courtney was a service girl through and through. "If he abandoned you in your hour of need just to shop with me then this date would be over, anyway. And besides" – she gave me a wicked grin – "this way I can pick out a *very* nice outfit for dinner in private."

Oh.

I liked that. I liked that very much.

"I'll see you at seven!" I yelled out after Courtney as she left, before throwing myself into work.

It was funny the way things worked out. I should have been furious that my meticulously-planned date was falling apart. Instead I felt good, as if this date was the thousandth date we'd had together and it was only natural that sometimes one or both of us would get pulled away for work.

Courtney understood me. She trusted me.

Work flew by.

"You really are a saint," Nicola said when she appeared from the kitchen covered in flour. Going by the way she looked me up and down I gathered I wasn't much cleaner. My clothes smelled of butter and coffee and sugar, which was an amazing combination but not one I wanted to smell of for dinner. It was just as well I had a change of clothes ready and waiting for me, as well as a hot shower to wash off the sweat that was dripping off my skin beneath my turtleneck.

"Take this as a sign to add an extra couple of front-of-house staff to the roster," I said, smiling in satisfaction when Emma and I finished cleaning down the countertop. Then I turned to her, pulled out my wallet, and handed her whatever notes I had in it. "Please don't take that as a crude gesture," I added quickly, when Emma stared at the wad of cash in her hands. "You were wonderful today. You never lost your cool. Take that as a very late Christmas bonus and I'll discuss increasing your pay with Nicola."

I thought Emma would burst into tears. Instead she flung her arms around me and squealed in delight. "Go get your girl," she said, then: "Thank you. Thank you so much."

I didn't spend long at the hotel – I barely had a second to spare – and was grateful that traffic was quiet enough that I reached Clos Maggiore just in time to see Courtney step out of a car right before me.

"*Wow*," I mouthed, wasting no time in jumping out of the car to surprise her. She was bundled up in an oversized fawn trench coat, a hint of bare legs and black skyscraper heels all that was visible to the naked eye. She appeared to have absolutely no problem walking in them. It sent my mind racing.

Courtney's face flushed with pleasure when she caught sight of me. "Glad you didn't ditch me for the hot bakery girl," she teased, sliding her arm through mine. She waved towards the restaurant door. "Shall we?"

I matched her crooked smile. "We shall."

When we entered the restaurant, with its blossom bough-covered ceiling and its rustic wooden doors and gargantuan stone fireplaces, the front-of-house staff were quick to remove our jackets and direct us to our table. It was in this way that I saw how special Courtney looked, dressed up just for me.

An off-the-shoulder, crushed velvet dress cinched in at her waist and fell to her knees, the deep, rich, dark brown colour of the material complimenting the slight tan of Courtney's skin and her permanent gold hoop earrings and necklace. Courtney had put her hair up in a twist and kept her eye make-up natural, though she'd added a layer of mascara to her obscenely long lashes. Finishing off the look she'd painted her lips a dramatic dusky brown to match her dress.

"Wow," I said again, having apparently lost my entire vocabulary in the last sixty seconds. "You look...wow."

"You look wow too," Courtney said, a devilish look in her eye that told me she was very much telling the truth. But then she frowned into the distance, to my left, where a pair of woman were waving at...Courtney?

"Ailish?" she wondered, grip tightening on my arm as she spoke. "Mum?"

Oh Jesus fucking Christ.

Chapter Fifteen

COURTNEY

This wasn't happening. Simon had not flown us all the way down to London, spoiled me with the most expensive shopping trip of my life then taken me out to a beautiful French restaurant only for my mum and sister to destroy *everything*.

And yet here we were, the staff of Clos Maggiore far too graciously sitting the four of us together when it became clear we knew each other. Simon on my left, Ailish opposite him, Mum directly opposite me. She was yet to make eye contact for even a second.

Ailish, for her part, was beyond excited to see me. As if I'd *planned* to surprise her with my presence. I wondered why the hell she was so delighted, but then I remembered: her thirtieth birthday was on Tuesday. To Ailish's eyes it probably looked like I'd organised all of this on purpose. That I'd bit my tongue and reached out to Mum despite the fact I wasn't talking to her, all to surprise my sister.

I hated that this wasn't true. I hated even more that I'd have never done it even though I knew how happy it would make my sister, because the thought of breaking the ice with Mum first made me want to die.

And now Simon was involved. Poor, confused Simon, who was once again the most gorgeous man I'd ever laid eyes on even as he folded awkwardly into his seat and tried his best to appraise the situation. A man who was supposed to be mine and mine alone this evening after sacrificing our afternoon to help out a desperate shop assistant. A saint in both name and nature – one I didn't deserve but who was excited to be with me, anyway.

I'd wanted tonight to be perfect, and now it was ruined.

Fuck, fuck, fuck.

I coughed to hide the strangled cry that left my throat. "Ailish...Mum. This is Simon Saint. Simon, this is my sister, Ailish, and my mum, Josie."

The beam of approval Mum fired Simon's way made her look like a stranger to me. She'd never looked at me like that. "It's so lovely to meet you, Simon!" she exclaimed, shaking hands with him. "Do you live around here?"

"I've spent most of my life in London," Simon replied, flashing his winning, pointy-canined smile in Mum's direction, "but I grew up in Glasgow as a kid. I also studied at Glasgow Uni."

"Ah, that explains the lovely twang to your posh accent, then." Mum fucking winked at him. I had to fight not to vomit. "I'm from the west end of Glasgow – Hyndland, the nice bit – but I moved down here when Ailish did and haven't looked back since. It's far more cosmopolitan down here. Much more my *vibe,* as the kids say these days. I—"

"Are you a clothes model or something?" Ailish cut in, for which I was grateful. When Mum went on a ramble she never stopped. "I've never seen a real-life man dress that well. Or did you dress him up, Courtney?"

Simon had the grace to laugh. "I dress myself, thanks. And I'm no model; I just like clothes." Now that I'd seen him in a few outfits I could see that this was true. I mean, yeah, Simon had money to spend on super-high-quality clothes that most of us lowly mortals could never hope to afford, but money couldn't buy style. Every single one of Simon's outfits thus far fit him like a glove, clearly expertly tailored and draped to match his frame.

And by fucking god did I appreciate a man who knew how to dress.

Take tonight, for example. Simon was wearing a fine wool suit in pale, warm grey, paired with a black polo shirt tucked into the high waistband of his trousers and unbuttoned to his clavicle. Not once in my life had I seen a man pair such a casual top with a suit, but here was Simon Saint pulling it off like he was born wearing the damn clothes.

And now my mum was slavering all over him.

"Forgive me for saying this," Simon said, after Mum ordered red wine for the table without asking anyone if they actually wanted any, "but Courtney doesn't seem to look much like either of you. Does she take after her dad?"

Simon couldn't have known this was dangerous territory. Beneath the table I squeezed his knee – digging my nails in a little too hard – until he glanced at me, saw from my face that he'd walked onto a landmine, and mouthed *sorry.*

Mum waved a flippant hand. "Both of my girls are blonde, like their dad, which is so tragic! Because it's not *blonde* blonde, more of a dirty straw colour if you get me? I always thought darker hair would suit their faces better, so when Ailish started dyeing hers I was so happy. See how it makes her blue eyes stand out so much more? Why, it's like looking at myself in the mirror twenty years ago!"

"Mum, we talked about this," Ailish said, surprising me by actually saying something instead of passively ignoring her insensitive comments. "That was really rude."

Mum seemed grossly taken back by Ailish's intervention. "Oh," she said, softly, "you know I didn't mean it like that. You're both so beautiful—"

"So why hate on what we were born with? What's wrong with the way Courtney looks? She's the most gorgeous woman in this restaurant, if you spared a second to look at her."

Oh fuck me. Who was this version of my sister? I didn't know her. She was defending me, to Mum, without me having to beg her to do it?

"Thanks, Ailish," I mumbled, making eye contact and offering her a careful, grateful smile. When she grinned at me it physically hurt. All my guilt at keeping her at a distance the last few years – especially over the last few months when she'd actually been reaching out to me more often – felt like lead in my stomach.

But what I expected even less than Ailish's support was Mum taking a pause, swallowing her pride, and saying, "I didn't mean it like that. But I'm sorry if it came out that way."

Only then did I let go of Simon's knee, and in the process realised that he was gritting his teeth against personally saying something in my defence. But I didn't want there to be fighting tonight: not from me, not from Mum, and most certainly not from Simon or my sister on my behalf. So I did something I almost never did.

I bucked up to be the bigger person.

"Thanks, Mum," I said, taking a large glug of wine when it arrived at the table. "I'm glad you reached out to me to surprise Ailish like this. So let's have a great night."

The look Mum gave me spoke volumes: *I never spoke to you. How did this all happen?* But she didn't say a word, and as a result our accidental meeting-turned-lie cause Ailish to flush with happiness.

She held out her glass. "Cheers to that!"

We clinked glasses, then we ordered food. Then Simon bent low to whisper in my ear, "We can leave if you want. I had no idea they were going to be here."

I gave him the most subtle side-eye I could manage. "How

could you have known they'd be here? *I* didn't know they'd be here." I made sure Mum and Ailish were happily discussing my sister's hectic work schedule before mumbling, "We'll have dinner with them then go for drinks somewhere else. I'm sure you know all the best places."

This time it was Simon who squeezed my knee. "I most certainly do. There's—"

"How about the love birds leave the pillow talk for a pillow?" Mum complained. I just about gagged, but both Ailish and Simon laughed at her outrageousness.

"You're right, Mrs Miller—"

"Macgregor, but call me Josie."

He gave her his famous angelic smile for the second time in a row. "Josie. I was being rude. I apologise. Forgive me for wanting your daughter all to myself."

Mum positively *tittered.* "What do you do for a living, Simon? The men Courtney goes for are usually...well. Not like you."

"*Mum,*" Ailish warned, once more jumping to my defence when in time gone by she'd have ignored her or, worse, sided with her.

I loved her.

Simon glossed over Mum's jibe and answered the question, anyway. "I work in finance, but I want to move into the restaurant business full-time."

"He has a bakery down here," I chimed in. "*Saintly Pastries.* Have you—"

"*Oh my god I love it there,*" Ailish cried, delighted. "Your pain au chocolats are to die for."

"Aren't they just?" I grinned at Simon, who had grown quietly bashful behind a long draught of red wine. God, he was adorable. I turned back to address Ailish. "I ate four of them this afternoon."

"That'll explain the weight gain—"

"*Mum!*" Ailish and I said in unison. So much for my truce with her; this was exhausting. And all too painfully familiar.

"I didn't mean it in a bad way," she huffed into her wine. "Ailish is right; you look really good, Court. Healthy. I was worried about you...well, before. But you seem to be doing well now. That's good."

No thanks to you, is what I wanted to say, but I held my tongue.

"How did the two of you meet?" Mum asked, directing the question at Simon when I didn't respond.

He looked at me, eyebrow raised, then said, "I'm staying at the Plaza for three months to open a ramen restaurant in Glasgow. The moment I walked into the hotel I saw Courtney, and that was that. I *had* to ask her out."

Mum and Ailish gushed over this embarrassingly romantic take on how Simon and I first met, but to be honest it was nice. Mortifying, but nice. Leaving out the part where he hit me on the head with a door was very much appreciated.

"I actually turned him down at first," I said, enjoying the scandalised gasps the comment elicited. "I have very high standards, as you well know."

"And I was only too happy to try again," Simon countered, bumping into my shoulder as he spoke. It was the tiniest amount of contact – far less than me grabbing his knee earlier – but it sent a bolt of electricity running through me. We were flirting, in public, with my sister and my mum present, and nothing felt wrong. Nothing was awkward.

Were we...actually having a good time?

"Are you wearing the necklace I got you for your thirtieth, Court?" Ailish asked, peering at the hollow of my throat after an absurdly pleasant hour of banter and conversation and Mum narrowly avoiding saying something unforgivable every five minutes. The food had been amazing so far, and though I'd ordered a dessert at the very beginning I had no idea how I was supposed to fit it in my stomach now – or my dress.

I twirled the heart-shaped pendant between my fingers. "I am, yeah. I never take it off."

"*Same*!" Ailish pulled out a delicate gold chain from her high-necked blue dress, revealing the sister pendant to mine: an upright heart, where mine was upside-down. She'd bought them as a pair for my thirtieth birthday – a sign that we were getting closer, I'd thought at the time. But then Mum pushed me over the deep end one time too many, and when Ailish moved to London alongside her we grew more distant than ever before.

I wondered if the new, better-dressed, goes-on-dates-to-French-restaurants Courtney Miller could bridge that gap.

Simon looked from Ailish, to me, then back again. "The two of you are so cute. Makes me wish I had a sibling growing up."

"They were like cats and dogs when they were children!" Mum chimed in. "Ailish wanted to be just like her mum. She even went for the same career path as me! Courtney was talented enough to go into biomedical sciences – and her English teacher always said how imaginative and hard-working she was with her writing – so I thought she'd follow the same path into medical writing, too. But she's very much the epitome of 'head empty, no thoughts', just like her dad."

"More like 'head full, *too* many thoughts', Mum," I replied tersely, though the red wine I still didn't like the taste of was going a long way towards dulling the knife edge to both of our comments.

"She always wanted to do so many things, Si," Ailish explained for Simon's benefit. "I can call you Si, right?"

"That's reserved for family and annoying best friends," Simon chuckled. He snuck a glance at me, his grey eyes molten. "But I think I can make an exception for Courtney's sister."

Ailish flushed. "Courtney didn't want to follow the usual careers that children all want to be," she said. "Vet, doctor, lawyer, astronaut, ballet dancer, whatever. No, she was really into Pokémon so she wanted to be a bug collector. Then she saw *Die Hard* and wanted to be the person who constructed the explosions on screen. But the best 'career path' she had, god, Court, do you remember?" I was of course mortified about where this was going, but I hadn't seen Ailish this happy to talk about me and my eccentricities in, well, forever. If she planned to embarrass me in front of Simon for the sake of a good story I could allow her the opportunity.

Just this once.

"Okay," Ailish continued, when I didn't tell her to shut the fuck up, "so when we were kids Courtney wanted to be – I shit you not – a farmer who also ran a café that served food from all the countries across the world that she planned to travel to when she grew up. That's mad, right? I said I wanted to work in the café! We were so set on this infallible plan until Mum told us being a farmer who ran a world-cuisine café wasn't a real thing."

Everyone was laughing at the story – it was funny, even I could see that through my abject humiliation – but what I wasn't expecting was that Simon was most definitely not laughing *at* me. There was a fondness to his expression that threw me off. A softness. As if, later, when we were in private, he'd tell me my stupid dream wasn't all that stupid at all.

And I would believe him.

"What did you want to do when you grew up, Si?" Mum asked, taking his familial nickname for herself. "I don't imagine a child dreams of being in finance."

It seemed that only I noticed Simon tense up – just a little. I suppose it wasn't a surprise; I was the only one at the table who already knew his tricky history with his career choices. "I wanted to open the kind of restaurant my mum would love," he said, his grey eyes going soft and sad.

"Oh, so does she like Japanese food?" Mum said, completely oblivious to Simon's tragic past. "I can't believe you've achieved your dream so young!"

"No, I...she passed away. When I was ten. I'm yet to deliver on my childhood dream."

I'd never seen my mum look so horrified and so, so sorry. A pang of sympathy ran through me; she'd asked the question to be nice. To be engaged in back-and-forth conversation. The mood at the table turned heavy. But Simon was quick to correct it. He offered Mum a gentle smile then, when my hand just barely brushed his where it lay on the table, he took it in his own and squeezed. "It was a long time ago. I'd like to think she's proud of me, regardless."

"I'm certain she is," Mum replied, voice small and full of tears. She'd always been quick to get emotional, even though she saw the same behaviour in me as a flaw. "You're quite an outstanding young man, Simon."

"Ahh, I'm not so young any—"

"Simon?"

Simon flinched at the sound of his name being called. It hadn't come from our table but instead from behind my head. A man's voice. Low, gravelly, authoritative.

"It *is* you, Simon!" came another voice – feminine this time. I turned my head and saw an absurdly well-dressed elderly couple, the man with a full head of fluffy white hair, the woman with jet black hair pulled elegantly back into a knot at her neck.

His...grandparents?

I watched Simon construct a perfect service face, one I knew well from my years in the industry. Then he regrettably let go of my hand, got up and turned to face them. "Fancy running into the two of you here!"

"I could say the same of you, Simon," his grandfather said. He gave the table a once-over and clearly didn't like what he saw. "When you told me you were coming down for two days I didn't realise it was a...social call."

Simon nodded his head in my direction. "This is Courtney Miller and her sister, Ailish, and mother, Josie Macgregor. We're celebrating Ailish's thirtieth birthday in style." God, the guy was smooth. Mum and Ailish beamed with approval at the introduction.

Simon's grandfather offered us the tightest smile I could possibly imagine; his wife gave us nothing at all. "Rupert Saint. This is my wife, Maria. Simon, you told me you were coming down to speak to us about the contract."

Just like that, we'd been dismissed. Me, my sister, my mum. Not worth noticing.

Simon's hands subtly curled into fists.

"I never said I was going to speak to you during this trip, Papa. I said I was going to speak to you about the contract *soon*."

Maria rolled her eyes. "Semantics, Simon. Come join us for drinks. We can discuss things like adults."

"Please excuse me," I mumbled, getting unsteadily to my feet in my stupid giant heels before fleeing for the bathroom. I hated conflict like this. I didn't want to see Simon arguing with his grandparents about the fact he wasn't going to do as they asked. Worse: I didn't want him to *agree* and cut our date short. Even with the unexpected addition of Ailish and my fucking Mum I'd still been having a lovely time.

Was it all going to be ruined in one fell swoop?

But the moment I left the bathroom a hand wrapped around my forearm, stopping me dead in my tracks. "I asked a waiter to get our coats and wait for us outside the door," Simon's low voice whispered into my ear. It sent chills down my spine. "What do you say to running away like cowards whilst nobody's looking? Don't worry; I covered the bill for your family already."

I'd never agreed to anything faster in my life.

Chapter Sixteen

SIMON

"So WHEN YOU SAID YOU WANTED to go for drinks somewhere nice, what you *really* wanted was to steal off to our hotel room to have your wicked way with me," I joked, when we walked through the hotel lobby and made a beeline for the lift.

"I would have taken grabbing a Coke from fucking Greggs to get out of that situation," Courtney replied, inspecting her reflection in the mirrored elevator to check for...I don't know. She didn't have a hair out of place. I was the one who felt ruffled. Unsettled.

Off-balance.

I couldn't believe I'd fled the restaurant with Courtney instead of dealing with my grandparents. I was craven through-and-through. A big, massive scaredy-cat.

Right now I couldn't find it in me to care.

"Will your grandparents be mad at you for fobbing them off?" Courtney asked as the elevator climbed up, up, up. It took me a moment to understand what the words out of her mouth meant.

Perhaps it was because of the wine, or perhaps it was because I trusted Courtney to understand that it wasn't her fault – nor mine, not really – that I said, "Yes. Extremely. But I'm always paying for something or other with them so it's all good." It wasn't, but the anxiety knotting up my stomach was nothing new.

Courtney laid a careful hand on my arm. "You can call them if you want. I don't want to get in the way of your relationship with them."

I barked out a laugh before I could stop myself, but it was good-humoured. Sort of. I was being awfully honest today. "The only thing that gets in the way of my relationship with my grandparents is my grandparents," I said, "but that's a trauma dump for another day." I gave Courtney's reflection a dubious smile. "If you're into that kind of thing."

Her grip tightened on my bicep, and her reflection bared her crooked teeth. "As it transpires, I'm absurdly into that kind of thing. But it's most definitely for another day." The elevator pinged open, and we waltzed as if controlled by an external force into the suite I'd ordered. With two bedrooms – as promised – though by the anticipatory glances Courtney kept throwing my way and the fact she didn't seem to want to let go of my arm I imagined we might not need bedroom number two.

Or perhaps that was my tipsy, hopeful brain speaking, and Courtney was clinging to me so she wouldn't trip in her skyscraper heels.

Courtney let out a low, appreciative whistle. "You know, I barely had enough time after I went shopping to appreciate this place, but damn."

But damn indeed. For years I'd grown blind to the splendour of luxury hotel rooms; with Courtney beside me I found it easier to look at the place through her eyes. And it was a lovely suite, decorated in an art deco style with superb views over Soho. A long, deep couch overlooked the tall windows, with two large monstera plants bookending the windows. On our left was the bathroom, with a brass clawfoot bath and walk-in shower large enough to rival Tom's one back in the townhouse.

On our right were two bedrooms, both of them generously proportioned – for London – but with the master bedroom considerably larger overall. To my eyes the bed in there looked to be double the size of the one in the second bedroom. Far too large for anyone's needs, to be honest, but damn if it didn't send my mind racing with dirty possibilities.

There was a sizeable pile of shopping inside the second bedroom. The second, because Courtney had taken the smaller of the rooms as her own. Even on a trip I'd booked to spoil *her* she'd endeavoured to ensure I was taken care of first.

Would this woman ever let me look after her?

"Seems you managed to get everything you wanted," I mused when I walked into the room without thinking. I picked up the woven handle of a wicker shopping bag: the true sign of an expensive shop. I wondered what was inside. "Care to give me a fashion show?" I asked Courtney, flashing her a foolish, tipsy grin when she followed me into the room. I'd meant it in jest – why would Courtney ever entertain the idea of showing me all her shopping? – but in a moment she kicked off her heels and pushed me out of the room. "What—"

"Get out," she breathed, pupils dilated wide as saucers. "Order some champagne or whatever. I'll show you *everything*."

The way she emphasised the word left me helpless to obey.

I didn't need to order champagne – I'd already arranged to have two bottles chilled on ice ready for our return from dinner – so I poured us both a glass, took off my jacket and shoes and folded myself into the luxurious sofa that overlooked the view of Soho. Dimly I wondered what it would feel like to do this back in my hotel room in Glasgow, with a view that felt like home, but then the door to the second bedroom creaked open and all such thoughts as location were swept from my mind.

It wasn't that Courtney was dressed sexily – no corsets, no backless dresses, no thigh-highs – but that she was dressed the opposite of that. She'd come out with the sultry gaze of a high-end escort, but she was dressed in...a cream cable-knit jumper and straight-cut jeans in an acid wash. The jumper was sumptuously oversized, the jeans perfectly grazing her ankles.

They fit her like they were made for her.

"What do you think?" Courtney asked, visibly nervous for all of a moment. She did a little twirl. "The jumper's from one of those expensive shops you sent me to this afternoon but the jeans were only forty quid from Monki! Can you believe it?"

"You look amazing," I said, meaning it. And then, "Show me more. Show me everything my money bought."

So Courtney did.

She dressed in turtlenecks and camisoles and shirts, which for once actually buttoned over her boobs without gapping. She dressed in pencil skirts and skater dresses and shorts that fit like Laura Dern's in *Jurassic Park*. She showed me blindingly white Skechers and pretty sandals made for sandy beaches, and then a pair of thigh-high boots which I'd give the devil half my life for just to see Courtney wearing them and absolutely nothing else.

Courtney followed the shoes up with a couple of evening dresses – one floor-length and one that fell to her knees – and then some workout gear. Sports bras that actually fit her. Leggings that clung to her calves and thighs and hips like a second skin. I downed my second glass of champagne – my third? Courtney had been necking hers back between outfits – and swallowed in anticipation.

I could see Courtney appreciated the attention.

She'd grown bolder and, dare I say it, filthier in the way she presented the clothes. By the time she reached sports outfit number two Courtney was practically spilling onto my lap as she ran her hands through her hair and shook her arse for me to appreciate the fit of her leggings.

"You are figuratively killing me, Courtney," I bit out, when she came close enough for me to grab her only to wheedle out of reach at the last second. I'd had an erection for the last fifteen minutes but Courtney didn't seem to care. Or, rather, she very much did, but found pleasure in letting it stand like a monolith between us.

She drank deep from her glass of champagne, flipped her hair over her shoulder – she'd let it fall wild and loose at some point – and smiled at me as if the whole world was mine, but that *she* was the whole world. "Would you like to see the lingerie you bought me, Mr Saint? Although..." – she bit her lip – "I may have bought a lot. I wouldn't want to spoil it all for... future encounters."

"Damn straight you shouldn't spoil it." My voice was too rough, my throat too dry. "How about you show me the best set, and leave the rest for – for later?"

Courtney's smile turned wicked. If it would have been acceptable to come in my pants then and there I would have. But there was a lady present, and she was putting on one hell of a show for me.

I owed it to Courtney to restrain myself.

"I think I can do a highlight," Courtney purred, sauntering off to get changed one final time.

It felt like she was gone an eternity. My phoned pinged once, twice, three times, but I ignored it. The world could be ending and I'd have ignored it. Then music began rolling through the room from some tinny speaker – Courtney's phone, I could only assume – and the woman herself reappeared.

She was wearing her jacket again. The one from dinner, long and the colour of fawn, along with those skyscraper heels. With her hair pinned back up once more it looked for all the world like we were going out somewhere classy. Somewhere with other people. Then the beat dropped into something sultry and suggestive, and Courtney slipped the jacket down her shoulders.

Just a little.

"I really did feel like Julia Roberts today," Courtney said, her voice a husky whisper over the music, "picking out lingerie I thought might get you going."

I could hardly speak. When Courtney dropped the jacket again I spied thin straps in pale pink lace. She made a show of dropping the jacket further, toying with me, until finally tossing it carelessly to the floor.

"You're not a – not a prostitute, as I recall," I bit out, unable to form coherent thought as I took in the full sight of Courtney Miller in the barest pink corset, with fluttery lace straps and a waist pulled in so tight I had to wonder how she'd managed to get into it on her own. The matching thong may as well have been non-existent, it served its purpose so poorly. Sheer hold-up stockings with a matching pink trim completed the look. Through my short-circuiting brain I joked, "Unless this has all been an incredibly manufactured plot from your pimp."

I thought Courtney would laugh. Instead she walked purposefully towards me, spread my knees out wide, and dropped to her own between them.

Oh, fuck.

"This is all consensual and one hundred percent *not* based on the fact you made me feel important and wanted tonight in front of my family." Courtney swallowed, lowered her gaze, then brought her fiery green eyes back up to mine. "Okay, it's a little bit because of the latter, but I think that's okay."

"I'll always make you feel like that, Courtney. You...it's the least you deserve."

That beautiful crooked smile. "So I think the least you deserve is a good fucking blow job."

Well. I was hardly going to argue with that.

Courtney had her hands on my belt before I could utter a single word, unbuckling it then sliding down the zipper of my trousers whilst my breath hitched in my chest and my dick got harder and harder. She looked at the bulge in my boxers with some appreciation – damn it, I was so strained now that I was in physical pain – before pulling them down to free me from my cloth prison.

She quirked an eyebrow up at me. "I could smash a rock on this," Courtney said, grazing her fingers against the length of my cock as if we'd always been this comfortable with each other's naked body parts. I shivered when her other hand swept up my stomach, tracing the fine line of (still black, not grey, thank you very much) hair that trailed to my navel beneath my shirt. Why was I still dressed? *Why on earth* did we still have clothes on?

"You – you could," I coughed, bucking alarmingly when Courtney tightened her grip on my cock, "but I think it would kind of ruin the blow job."

A single snort of laughter. Courtney tucked an errant strand of hair behind her ear. Then her perfect mouth engulfed the tip of my penis, and any such words I could form were entirely of the monosyllabic variety.

"Ah, *god*, yes – like – like that," I gasped, when Courtney wasted no time in swirling her tongue around me as she made her way down the shaft. My hands were already shaking, desperate to hold onto something; I dragged them both through Courtney's hair, pulling it loose so I could grab on properly.

"*Mhmm*," Courtney purred when I pulled at her hair, the sound vibrating against my cock to ecstatic effect. Fuck, she was good at this.

Really good.

I could feel the ebb and flow of an orgasm building up inside me, rushing down, down, down as Courtney licked and sucked and tugged at me. There was absolutely no chance of me lasting longer than a minute with the way things were going. But when I slid a hand from her hair to her face, meaning to tilt her chin up and tell her to take a break, Courtney shook her head and continued on.

"Courtney, *stop*, I'm going to—"

She kept going.

Even when my grip on her hair became painful – her eyes were watering, smearing mascara across the apple of her cheeks – Courtney didn't stop. I moved a hand to the couch to grip onto it, instead, my hips bucking desperately as I chased my inevitable release. My eyes fluttered closed but something told me to open them again, so I did.

Courtney was staring straight up at me, a challenge plain as day on her face. *Keep looking. Don't break eye contact.*

When Courtney coordinated one final suck with the deft slide of her hand my orgasm came upon me with no warning. Stars blinded my sight, my breath coming in starts and stops, my brain swimming in a daze of chemicals whose sole purpose was to make me feel pleasure.

It was the best – and god damn it, the fastest – blow job I'd ever received.

I was barely cognizant of the fact Courtney swallowed everything I'd spilled into her mouth until she reached for the bottle of champagne on her left and poured it directly down her throat. When she licked her lower lip I found myself, dazed and satisfied, taking the bottle from her when she proffered it over and finishing the last of it.

Then I bent down, scooped Courtney in my arms, and carried her over to the main bedroom.

"I wouldn't have thought you'd be ready and raring to go so soon after you came," Courtney giggled into my ear. I could feel her heart beating wildly in her chest against mine. It was like music.

My responding laugh was barely a rasp. "Unfortunately I'm not nineteen anymore," I said, dropping Courtney atop the luxurious quilted duvet on the bed. My hands spanned the width of her thighs and squeezed. When Courtney gasped I slid them lower, easing her knees apart the way she'd done to me.

It was my turn to lick my lips. "But I don't need to use my

dick to get you off."

Chapter Seventeen

COURTNEY

I GOT GOOD AT GIVING GUYS head because it made them happy. I wanted them to like me, and I equated them enjoying sexual favours with them enjoying, well, *me*.

But with Simon...with Simon Saint I gave him a fucking blow job because I wanted him to see how much *I* liked *him*.

And now, with him sliding low over my body to dip his fingers below the waistband of my ridiculous, barely-there thong, I could say with absolute certainty that this man really fucking liked me back.

I'd never seen a guy look at me the way Simon was looking at me. The searing heat of his gaze threatened to boil me up from the inside-out. And damn if I wasn't already stupidly turned on. I mean, Simon had reacted to me sucking him off as if he'd never had a blow job before in his life. Maybe he'd simply never had a good one. Maybe—

"Courtney?" Simon murmured, a frown shadowing that heat in his grey eyes. "You all right in there?"

I let out a breathless laugh. "Yeah. Yeah, I am."

"Then stay in the moment."

Simon spoke it like an order. *Simon Says Stay in the Moment.*

So I did.

With long fingers Simon stroked my thighs, lowering his mouth over the silk of my underwear until I could feel his breath warming the material, dampening it against my skin. Not that I was anywhere near the vicinity of dry down there. When Simon darted out an exploratory tongue he realised just how wet I was, too.

"I don't think you need this," he said, rolling the thong down my legs and blessedly chucking it to the floor. He thumbed at the stockings covering my legs up to my thighs with a look on his face that suggested he might eat them.

"And these?" I pressed, when Simon made no motion to remove them. "Do you think I need the stockings?"

A minute shake of his head. "I don't think you need them, but damn if they don't make you look like the filthiest woman I've ever had beneath me. They can stay."

I still had the corset on, too, which was a little bit uncomfortable on my stomach considering how much we'd eaten and drank that night, but what was a little discomfort in the face of Simon Saint looking at me like that?

I could be naked next time. No, we could *both* be naked next time. Sexy as it was to watch Simon writhe beneath my touch, his cock standing strong and still even while the rest of him was fully dressed, it was pointless to lie to myself about the fact I was dying to see the man buck naked.

But it could wait.

Funny, I'd always found it difficult to wait for anything before.

I reached a hand down to run my fingers through Simon's hair, gentler than he'd been with me but with the promise that I could be much, much firmer if he wanted me to. "Touch me," I said, my voice husky even to my own ears. "Touch me and keep me out of my head."

Simon grinned, his magnificent pointy canines on full display, and then his face was lost between my thighs.

When his tongue first touched my clit my grip tightened on his hair. His tongue was big and wet and oh-so-sure of itself; my thighs wrapped around Simon's shoulders before I was really aware of what I was doing.

Simon made a muffled noise of approval when I did so, one of his hands gripping at my right thigh whilst the other began gently, then less gently, seeking purchase inside of me. I felt the ridge of his knuckles when he easily slid from one to two fingers inside me, moving with the rhythm of his tongue.

"Jesus," I bit out, when Simon added a third finger and he hitched me further up on my back to get a better angle. And fuck me did he find a better angle, his tongue doing the lord's work as I slowly but surely came undone.

Now I was the one writhing beneath Simon, gasping and grabbing at him for dear life. "M-more," I choked, on the edge of release. One final push and I'd become unspooled entirely. "I need more."

Simon paused for a fraction of a second, or a fraction of a fraction of a second, but it felt like an eternity. His eyes caught mine, and the expression on his face was *feral*. He almost snarled, canines on show, dark hair sweeping across his forehead to cast his gaze in shadow. Then Simon pushed a fourth finger inside of me, and his tongue lapped at me with pinpoint accuracy, and I shuddered out an orgasm so long and low I felt like a kettle coming up to boil.

The entire time Simon didn't stop kissing and licking until I was quite literally a whimpering mess. His grip on my thigh loosened – Christ, he'd been clinging on so hard I was certain I'd find fingertip-shaped bruises on my skin tomorrow – and he slowly sat up, kneeling between my legs. With another guy I might have felt too exposed like this, legs spread wide with all of me on show, but not with Simon.

In any case he wasn't looking anywhere but my face. With a trembling hand he wiped at his gleaming lips. "I hope that was to your satisfaction," Simon said, a note of uncertainty colouring what he otherwise must surely have intended to be a joke.

With some effort I propped myself up on my elbows and marginally closed my legs. "You *are* kidding, right?" I said, quirking an eyebrow. "I thought I was good at oral, but you...did they teach pretty boys how to please women back in your fancy economics class?"

Simon choked on a laugh. "Most of the guys back on my course wouldn't know how to please a woman if she gave him step-by-step instructions. Do you want a drink?" Simon indicated back towards the hotel suite proper with a thumb. "There's another bottle of champagne."

"Could we...find a film to watch?" I asked, a hazy sleepiness coming over me in the wake of my monumentally excellent orgasm. "We could cuddle and drink until we fall asleep."

If Simon was disappointed by the prospect of *not* having sex tonight he didn't show it. On the contrary he seemed rather excited by the idea of a film and cuddles. The smile he offered me was soft as he said, "Get yourself out of that corset and into one of those massive jumpers you bought. I can't imagine you're comfortable right now."

"Do I keep the stockings on?" I wiggled my toes suggestively until Simon laughed.

"Keep them on. I can't imagine anything sexier than a jumper and thigh-high stocking combo. Actually, I tell a lie. Those boots you got are killer."

He left before I could fire back a retort of my own so I rolled off the bed, picked up my discarded thong, and practically skipped over to the second bedroom to change. "I'm going to rinse off super quick if that's okay," I called through the open door, when the stickiness between my thighs began growing uncomfortably tacky.

"I'll order some chips, then," Simon hollered back. God, I could have professed my undying love then and there. Instead I made quick work of getting cleaned up, going through the motions of my skincare routine until I was make-up-free and glowy. Simon showered after I threw myself down on the massive bed in the main bedroom and flicked through the channels to find a promising film.

By the time he joined me the chips had arrived, we each had a glass of champagne in hand, and we were nestled together against a giant pile of pillows as if we'd been together our entire lives.

I picked at the edge of the sinfully soft T-shirt Simon was wearing. "Even your loungewear is gorgeous," I said. "Are you protecting your modesty for date number two?"

"Ah, so the party and our rendezvous in Dawsholm Park don't count?" Simon clicked his fingers in mock disappointment. "Damn it."

"Yes, because stalking me through the dark and winding winter streets is *so* romantic."

Simon ruffled my hair. "Point taken. So what are we watching: *Speed, Johnny Mneumonic* or *The Lake House*?"

"Is it Keanu Reeves day or something?"

"Clearly."

"Let's go for *Speed* and see where we go from there," I decided, throwing a chip in my mouth before all but shoving three into Simon's. He responded by biting my fingers.

Ten minutes into the film his hand found mine, and our fingers remained interlaced for the rest of the evening. "I'm not protecting my modesty, by the way," Simon said two hours later, the two of us practically horizontal as our eyelids drifted closed. "I just figured you wouldn't be able to control yourself if I was naked." We both sniggered, then Simon let out a giant yawn.

His grey eyes found mine beneath heavy lids. "Hell if I could control myself around *you* if you were lying naked beside me, Courtney."

"Well I guess it's good we've both remained clothed," I murmured, snuggling deeper into the crook of Simon's arm, "because when we bang I don't intend to get any sleep that night. Or morning. Or afternoon. I'm easy."

Simon kissed the top of my head. "Afternoon sex. I like that. Sounds sleazy. Like Carrie and Mr Big."

"Hopefully you don't turn out to be as huge an arsehole as Big, though."

"Fingers crossed you aren't a mega-narcissist like Carrie, then."

"I make no such promises."

I was impatient to have sex with Simon. To have him fuck my brains out so I could return the favour. But – perhaps for the first time in my life – I was willing to wait. Slowly falling asleep beside Simon as we drunkenly fired stupid film banter at each other was what I wanted. That, and the promise of more. More, more, more.

But not tonight.

Chapter Eighteen

SIMON

I̶ᴛ ꜰᴇʟᴛ ʟɪᴋᴇ I ᴍᴜsᴛ sᴛɪʟʟ be dreaming when I woke to find Courtney sprawled out on the bed beside me. At some point in the night she'd shed off her jumper, leaving her in a pale pink camisole and matching shorts. To my eyes the set looked to be the less obviously sexy cousin to the underwear Courtney had pranced about in last night. Although, given who was wearing them, they looked plenty bloody sexy to me.

Courtney must have sensed me watching her, for she roused from her sleep to peer at me beneath sleep-heavy lashes. "You're up."

"Not for long." I stroked her arm with my forefinger. "We'll need to be up and out soon, though; I'm afraid my grandparents will find a way to track me down if we stay in London much longer." It was annoying, because I'd planned to take Courtney out for brunch before heading back to London, but it was no joke the lengths they'd go to. Especially my grandmother.

She most likely knew where I was staying, and had someone downstairs waiting to corral me back to headquarters.

Courtney wrinkled her nose, yawned, then sat up. If she was disappointed she didn't show it. "Family are the best *and* worst of us and all that," she murmured, almost more to herself than to me. "I could do with some extra time today, anyway. I need to look for a flat."

As we got ready Courtney explained her living situation. I was grateful for the distraction: in the light of day the weight of everything I needed to say to my grandparents sat heavier and heavier on my shoulders.

Then, when we reached the lobby, a smartly-dressed woman in her fifties made a beeline straight for us.

"Holy shit, you weren't kidding," Courtney exclaimed, disbelief plain as day on her face. She glanced at me out of the corner of her eye. "Are you secretly in the Mafia or something? Whose grandparents go to such lengths to pin their grandson down?"

"Mine," I said, before grabbing Courtney's elbow and deftly leading her out of the lobby via the staff stairwell. Courtney followed along without question, a small smile on her face that I hadn't expected. "Is something funny?" I asked.

She shook her head. "I feel like we're in a spy movie. Or a Keanu Reeves vehicle. Is there a food trolley in the hotel that must maintain a speed of five miles an hour, lest it explode?"

I snorted. "Maybe one of the guests is an assassin with secret codes locked in his brain, and one of the cleaning staff has been hired to extract it."

"I'd go see that. Maybe you should stay in investments but move over to Hollywood," Courtney joked. "Or maybe you could open a restaurant that specialises in screening the best mindless action films."

"You know," I said, letting Courtney out onto the street when I found a fire exit before following suit, "that isn't a terrible idea, either. I wonder what rights you'd need to legally run such a venue."

The two of us exchanged easy back-and-forth banter all the way through London, to the airport, and even in the plane back home. It was as if Courtney knew I needed the steady flow of conversation to keep myself from thinking about my grandparents.

Or maybe she was literally just that easy to talk to.

When I dropped her off outside her flat – one of the classic Glasgow tenement buildings that I adored but knew from experience were cold, draughty and inordinately expensive to heat up – I was beyond disappointed that our date had come to an end.

"Can we get date number two in the calendar?" I asked, taking Courtney's suitcase from her to carry it up to the top floor on her behalf. Thank god walking steps was part of my exercise routine, otherwise the ascent would have killed me.

Courtney gave me a wry smile. "I thought it was date number four?"

"I thought you said me stalking you in the park didn't count? Although having you grind against my lap while we snogged like teenagers certainly feels like it qualified as date material."

A giggle, then Courtney reached up on her toes to kiss me. "Lets call it date number three, then. Do you want to go for coffee before my shift on Saturday?"

"I'd love to." And I really meant it. I wanted nothing more than to steal an hour or two out of Courtney's day before she had to work. It wasn't about getting her for the night or an entire day or anything inbetween – I'd take what I could get, and be grateful for it.

Sex could wait. I was horny as shit for this woman but it could wait. After all, if last night were anything to go by, Courtney was just as horny for me as I was for her.

We could afford to take things slow.

Chapter Nineteen

COURTNEY

YOU KNOW HOW IN ALL THE best romance films there's that moment when the heroine is simply going about her usual business but something has fundamentally changed for her, all because of the hero? The grey and cloudy sky is not quite so miserable, and the fifteen-minute wait for coffee becomes an opportunity to people-watch and prepare for the day ahead. You notice flowers in the windows of pubs and cats playing hide-and-seek with you as you wind down the street, and even when one of seven pugs tries to pee on your shoes after you say yes to helping out at work on your one full day off you can't help but smile instead of scold them.

Well, that was me all of Tuesday morning. Annoyingly positive. Bursting at the seams with sunshine. I was swooning over Simon Saint within the safety of my own mind but I wasn't doing much of a good job trying to hide my feelings externally, either.

"Care to not be *quite* so happy about going to London with that guy from the Plaza right in front of me?" Rich grumbled, bending down to mop up the puddle of pee I'd been left to stand in. Though Rich hadn't known beforehand that I'd gone on an overnight date with Simon I'd been forced to spill the proverbial beans after he'd asked Becca where I was and she very suspiciously told Rich she couldn't tell him. "In case you've forgotten I basically confessed to you."

"And in case you've forgotten, you asked me to *consider* you." I stuck out my tongue for good measure. Very mature, I know, but if I didn't react like this to something serious then I wouldn't be Courtney Miller. "The best way for me to do that is to explore the options I currently have open so I can make sure I make the right choice."

Rich gave me the finger. "You know I'm just concerned. This is Nate all over again."

"I thought we both agreed that we would never speak his name again?"

"Yeah but this is relevant." Rich put the mop away, washed his hands and then ran them through his mess of curly hair. It wasn't a nervous tic like it was with Simon: I knew this meant Rich was exasperated. He gave me some major side-eye. "You always told me you wasted those three years on him. That if you could go back and do things over you'd never have given him a chance. But he swept you up in how spontaneous he was, and you ignored all the warning signs that he wasn't good for you, and just like that three years went by. And for what – for him to cheat on you? Can't you see that you're doing the same thing again?"

I knew there was a kernel of truth to what Rich was saying. Which was why I let him get away with saying it, even though I knew part of the reason he *was* saying it was borne out of jealousy. I wasn't blind, for fuck's sake: Rich wanted to go out with me. That meant he was currently romantically invested in me and my decisions, even if he purported that I could take all the time I needed to work things out.

"I'm being careful," I reassured him, even though I didn't think that was true. "I'm just having fun with Simon." Also not quite true. Something had changed after London. Not just the nature of my relationship with Simon but with me, too. I could feel it. After dinner with my sister and my mum, after being treated like royalty all because Simon believed I deserved it, after opening up to him about ADHD and the way I was and him so completely accepting it all, *I* was different.

It should have terrified me. Instead I was excited about what came next for me, and for Simon.

For us.

Looking at Rich looking glumly at me, like he could tell where my thoughts had strayed, brought me back to reality. It wasn't fair to rub this in his face when he'd given me the grace to sort things out without too much pressure from him.

"What were you working on in the office all morning?" I asked, keen to change the topic of conversation. And I was curious; Rich was *so* not a tied-to-a-desk kind of person.

Rich brightened immediately. With a wave of his hand he directed me into the office, where the desk was scattered with floor plans.

"What's all this?" I had no idea what I was looking at. "Are you thinking of moving to another location?"

"Not moving *this* location," he replied, spreading out the papers as he did so, "but opening another. This place in the south side seems perfect." He stabbed a finger down onto the central floor plan on the table.

"Wait, does this mean your business development loan got approved?!"

He grinned. "Yesterday."

"You son of a bitch!" Flinging my arms around Rich's neck he wasted no time in spinning me around within the confines of the tiny office. We knocked into the desk and it wobbled dangerously, but neither of us cared. "I can't believe things are moving along so fast."

"It hasn't felt fast for me," Rich joked. I knew he was

speaking the truth. He'd planned to open at least two or three locations from the very first day he opened the current one three years ago. "In any case, Court, I'm going to need staff I trust if I want to make this expansion successful."

"Which means?" I asked, too happy for him to process what he meant.

"Which means I want you running this place full-time in my stead, and I want you to help me hire a part-timer for you and a part-timer for me."

Gently I pulled away from him to put a respectable few inches between us. "Rich—"

"I can offer you a better hourly pay than the Plaza does now I have the loan," Rich cut in, doe eyes earnest, "as well as actual job benefits. Imagine that!" A soft laugh, then he grew serious. "You're so good with the dogs and their owners, Court. I know you love it here. It would mean the world to me to have you on my side while I do this."

There was no pretty way to ask what needed asked, so I went for a direct hit. "Does this in any way, shape or form have something to do with you wanting to go out with me? Will my decision to work with you be subject to change based on what I choose to do regarding...us?"

"This is entirely separate," Rich said, and I believed him. "I swear it."

"We *do* make a pretty good team." It was definitely something to consider. "And quitting the Plaza would be amazing." Better pay would help me out with finding a new flat. It was truly a win-win-win.

And yet...

"Let me think on it," I said. Rich deflated, but only just a little.

"Of course. But don't take too much time. I want to open the new location by June, if possible."

As I left for home I realised I felt a whole lot heavier than I had that morning. More manic, and not in a good way. I needed to let off some steam lest the weight of all the decisions I had to make but didn't want to touch with a bargepole caused me to drown. I knew exactly what I needed.

I called the girls to get Tuesday-night-wasted.

Chapter Twenty

SIMON

"I STILL CAN'T BELIEVE YOUR TRIP went well considering everything that went wrong," Tom said as we made our way through Park Circus towards his house. He held out his left hand and lowered a finger for each set-back I'd faced: "You had to ditch Courtney to work for half the date, then her sister and – one must assume estranged – mother get in the way of your lovely dinner, then when you think you're out of the woods your snob grandparents show up for the grand finale." Tom chuckled good-naturedly, shaking his head in disbelief as he did so. "That Courtney still wants to have anything to do with you after all that is the surest proof I've ever seen that there's someone out there for everyone."

Tom's rude but succinct summary of my trip to London with Courtney might have worried the old me. A month ago I might have over-thought the series of unfortunate events that befell me to absolute death, then let them get in the way of whatever relationship I was building. But with Courtney it was different. With Courtney I felt understood and, more importantly, I knew that I understood her.

So what else was there to do but laugh along with Tom at

the way things had transpired?

"I thought my grandparents were a piece of work," I told my best friend between childish fits of giggles – fuelled by the whisky we'd been drinking during a spontaneous visit to the Glasgow University Union after Tom finished work – "but by god, Tom, Courtney's *mother.*"

Tom grimaced sympathetically. "That bad, huh?"

"No wonder Courtney has issues." I paused, considering Josie Macgregor for a moment, then added, "It seemed like her mum's been trying to better herself, though, going by how Courtney's sister kept reminding her of everything she's 'talked' to her about, so I suppose that counts for something."

"That counts for a lot, actually," Tom said, taking the lead up his driveway in order to unlock the front door to the townhouse. But when he slid the key into the lock he frowned, then held his ear to the door. "Sounds like Liz has company."

"Is it unusual for your thirty-year-old girlfriend to have people round on a Tuesday night?"

Tom gave me the finger. "No, but she usually tells me about it first so I can decide whether to make myself scarce or not." A pause. "That definitely sounds like more than one friend over."

"I can head back to the Plaza, then," I said, making to leave. "I don't want to interfere with her having a girls' ni—"

"This house has fourteen rooms in it; if she wants us out of sight we'll see ourselves off to the first floor lounge." The way Tom said it reminded me of just how privileged the two of us were, with our inherited wealth, fancy houses and rich people problems. It had been sitting heavily on my heart since Courtney told me about her problems with her mental health and finances – that my biggest issue in life was having the balls to tell my grandparents I didn't want to inherit their booming investment business. I'd never so hated being thrown into the world of millionaires after the simple but joyful upbringing I'd experienced at the hands of my mother as I did now.

Well, now was not the time to wallow. Now was the time to continue having a nice evening with Tom, so I followed him inside.

And was immediately met by the cacophonous explosion of noise only a gaggle of close-knit women were capable of making.

"We'll just pop in and say hi," Tom murmured, taking off his coat, scarf and shoes as I did the same. Vain man that he is, he paused in front of a mirror to re-tousle his hair and fix the collar of his shirt.

"It's cute that you still want to look your best for Liz even inside the comfort of your own home," I said, intending for it to be a jibe.

But Tom had taken it as a compliment. He beamed at me, rosy-cheeked from whisky, the cold night air and a healthy dose of lovesickness. "Have you *seen* who I'm with? The grey is going to come soon, I can feel it. I have to look after myself so Liz still finds me attractive when I'm sixty."

"*I'll* find you attractive when you're sixty, you fucking Adonis," I spat out, appalled that even Thomas Henderson could be worried about not looking good. "And everyone on both sides of your family didn't go grey until well into their seventies, unlike me and my poor temples."

"You suit the grey, though. It makes you look distinguished."

"Ahh, what every man wishes to hear in his thirties."

Tom thumped me on the back, then led me over to the living room. "I'll still find you handsome at sixty, too, so it's all – *Courtney*, hello!"

A hush fell over the living room as Tom and I made our entrance. Liz, Chloë, Harriet, Becca and Courtney were all piled onto the huge corner sofa, with Ludo collapsed over Courtney's lap whilst Jerry the kitten amused himself by hunting the charm hanging off Harriet's phone. The fire was roaring, the TV was blaring out *Chicago* to its inattentive audience, and there were at least seven empty bottles of wine strewn across the table (with two more currently open).

A standard girls' night if ever I'd seen one.

All eyes turned to me as I openly stared at Courtney. I knew a giddy grin was plastered to my face at getting to see her so unexpectedly. "Hey," I finally offered, giving the room at large a sheepish wave. Then, to Courtney: "Fancy seeing you here."

She saluted me back. "And you. Does *Simon Say* he wants a drink?" Everyone groaned, then the silence was broken as the girls welcomed me and Tom into the fold in that wholesome, accepting way that only drunk girls could do. I found myself sitting on the edge of the right arm of the couch beside Courtney (by design, I was sure) whilst Tom chose to sit on the floor by Liz's feet to steal Jerry away from an outraged Harriet.

"What are we celebrating?" Tom asked, before thanking Liz when she poured him a glass of red wine. He handed it over to me by way of everyone else on the couch before taking one for himself.

"We're commiserating, actually," Becca said. Then she frowned. "Or are we? Simon, maybe you should be the one commiserating."

Courtney threw a cushion at her flat mate. "Shut the fuck up, Bex."

But Becca eagerly ignored her. She leaned forwards so she could stare directly at me, eyes wide as saucers as she said, "Rich offered Courtney a full-time, better-paid job to run the current dog day care so he could expand into the south side."

That didn't sound like a bad thing to me. I glanced at Courtney. "Isn't that...good news?"

"He also basically offered her his hand in marriage."

I don't know who spat out his wine faster – me or Tom.

In contrast, Courtney proceeded to down her own glass of wine – which had recently been topped up – and grabbed one of the open bottles to fill it back up again. I could see in her eyes and her general demeanour that she was well past drunk, in that hazy, far away way when you know someone should probably think about switching to water and sobering up to go home.

Except Courtney didn't seem to want to do that in the slightest. She put her hand over her eyes, groaned dramatically, and said, "He didn't ask for my hand in marriage. He just asked me to consider him as boyfriend material, that's all."

"Oh yes, because that's what everyone's totally *not* completely in love with them best friend says on a daily basis," Chloë chimed in, her perfectly sculpted eyebrow arched in a critical manner. She directed her next question at Becca. "How long did you say the two of them had been best friends?"

"We've known each other since we were twenty," Courtney answered on her own behalf. "We were both working in the Hilton back then."

"And how long did it take for you to sleep together?"

This time it wasn't just me and Tom who spat out our wine. Courtney did, too, but she was quick to clean up after herself and refill her glass. She drank even more wine at a dangerous pace. "It was one time when we came back from Australia," she said, addressing the room at large. Then, glancing at me surreptitiously, "It's no big deal."

"So you..." I began, frowning. I wanted to understand the relationship Courtney had with Richard Blake as best I could without looking like a jealous, possessive idiot. "You travelled together?"

Courtney nodded. "Sleeping together was a one-time thing, though. I was pissed at my cheating ex. No harm, no foul. There's been nothing romantic between us since then."

"Until now," Harriet said.

Becca scoffed, flipping her perfect hair back in the process. "It would take a fool not to notice the way he looks at you,

Court. I've been telling you this for months now!"

I didn't know how to process this piece of information. First of all: I wasn't supposed to have heard it. This was girls' night, and I'd jumped into that knowing the risks. Namely that people say things, and admit to things, and spill secrets that aren't theirs, when their blood alcohol level is way too high.

Second of all: Courtney herself was saying it was no big deal. I knew she liked me, and I liked her, and at the end of the day we never said we were going to be exclusive whilst dating, either. She hadn't done anything wrong. If her best friend was in love with her, well...that wasn't exactly Courtney's fault.

So I ignored Rich being in love with Courtney, and professing his love for her, even though in truth an ugly snake of jealousy was rearing its head inside me. Forcing the topic back onto positive things I turned to Courtney and said, "This job, though. Is it not a good opportunity for you?"

"It *is* a good oppor-opportunity," Courtney said, hiccoughing. "I'd definitely like it better than my-my current situation."

"It's basically your dream job!" Becca protested.

But Courtney shook her head. "Only dream adjacent."

"I don't imagine you can be a farmer who runs a café," I said, remembering what Ailish had told me back in London.

Courtney stared at me, open-mouthed, horrified that I had somehow reached into her mind to take her secret, but then she seemed to remember how and when and why I'd learned that piece of information and grew scarlet all over. "So let's cut the farmer bit," she muttered, maintaining eye contact but looking mortally embarrassed. "It's hardly as if I've got the attention span to go to school to learn all about agriculture."

"So...a café with animals?"

Everyone in the room chuckled. "That would be the cutest thing ever," Liz said, scratching Ludo's head until he barked in agreement. "Have you never thought about seriously pursuing it?"

Instead of answering Courtney handed me her wine glass. "Here," she slurred, before staggering dangerously to her feet. Immediately I stood up to put a hand on her elbow, steadying her, but Courtney pulled out of my grasp. "I'm fine," she insisted, though she sounded anything but.

Only once Courtney left the room did I sit back down, a strong feeling that I'd said or done something wrong souring my mood. But Becca gave me a sympathetic smile. "She gets like this sometimes," she explained, not just to me but to everyone else in the room. "Whenever she has too much to think about she tends to go on a downward spiral. Don't take it personally."

My eyes strayed to the door. "Shouldn't we help her? She seems quite..."

"I'll go home soon with her, don't worry," Becca replied. "I've already told Rich that Courtney won't be coming into work tomorrow, so it's nothing that a lot of water, codeine and some trash TV in the morning won't fix."

I wanted to do something more for Courtney. She was clearly entering a manic phase, and not in a good way. I'd been reading up on ADHD almost non-stop since she told me about what was going on, in the hopes that it would help me better understand the patterns of her mood. But the do-gooder in me wanted to help. I wanted to look after Courtney, and take her home, and put her to bed, and it frustrated me that I couldn't.

Tom slapped his knees then got up to his feet. "Come on, Simon, let's leave the girls to it," he said, a not-at-all subtle signal that we should head upstairs and give the girls – Courtney – their privacy. The rest of the night was not for us to see.

I could only hope that, in the future, Courtney felt comfortable enough to talk to me about her problems instead of drinking them away.

Chapter Twenty-One

COURTNEY

Fuck me, my head was *throbbing*. My only solace was that misery loves company – especially equally hungover company – and Dad was only too happy to oblige.

"God, dove, there's nothing better than chips and cheese the morning after a big one," Dad sighed happily after a generous mouthful of chips. We were sitting outside our favourite café, wrapped up against the cold but needing the fresh air more than the comfort of central heating to clear our heads. Dad took a long draught of his black coffee before adding, "I'm glad I kept a fiver back last night just for this."

He was sickly pale, as he always was the day after drinking, but aside from that he was looking good. For most of his life he'd been on the other side of pudgy, but two years ago he'd announced that he seriously wanted to get in shape. So that he'd actually stick to it I acted as his body double, jogging absolutely everywhere with him and working out to YouTube aerobics and yoga classes. As a result I started eating more, gaining weight and got much physically healthier, and Dad lost weight, gained muscle and got just as physically healthy as I was. We were both proud of the progress we've made: the fact that we'd finally managed to maintain a routine – however menial it was in the grand scheme of things – and the fact that we did it together.

Now that my dad was in the best shape of his life the similarities between us were easy to see. We had the exact same straw-coloured hair, though Dad's was getting whiter with age, and though his eyes were blue and mine were green they were the same shape, and we had the same nose, and he wasn't all that much taller than me. You could certainly tell that we were father and daughter, unlike when I stood beside my mum.

"Has your universal credit started coming through?" I asked him, through the pounding of a horrible headache. Bless Becca's heart that she'd already told Rich that I wasn't going to come into work this morning. One whiff of dog shite would have sent me straight to the toilet for hours.

Dad nodded, then winced at the action. "It has, aye. Thanks again for coming to the interview with me. God willing, I won't be on it long!"

"You'll be on it at least until your back's healed, Dad, however long that is. Don't push yourself."

He grumbled in that way only dads could. "I like being independent. I hate not working."

This was what always struck a nerve with me growing up with my mum and dad arguing. Mum called Dad lazy, because he was unable to keep a job in the same position for longer than a year at time. But my dad was one of the hardest working, dedicated people I'd ever met. It was just difficult to keep his attention. The moment a job got boring, repetitive and predictable it was like pulling teeth for him to continue working it. That's why I was happy when they got divorced. It sucked, but I was. It was the best thing for Dad's wellbeing – and Mum's, too, if I was letting myself be honest for a change.

The last few years he'd managed to maintain a modest but respectable man-and-van business. The physical work, plus our exercise routine, had not only moulded Dad into fighting shape but it also showed him that physical labour was a whole lot easier for him to maintain. He could listen to audiobooks or podcasts or music or whatever he wanted whilst his body moved through the motions of satisfyingly tiring work. But that was until his back gave out, and now he was back to square one.

I shuddered to think what would happen if his back never healed.

"You're doing that thing we both do when you get lost in your head, dove," Dad said kindly. Kindly, because he knew how hard it had been for me, growing up, having Mum and Ailish shout at me the moment I did that exact thing. He had only ever been gentle with me. It was why I loved him so much.

"I just have a lot to think about," I said, which was the truth. But I didn't want to tell him that I'd been thinking about his work situation, so I settled on telling him the reason I'd ended up so shit-faced last night. "Rich give me a...a really good job offer last night."

"Aye, he told me about it over the phone the other day. It seems like a great fit for you, doesn't it?" It wasn't surprising that Rich and my dad had spoken on the phone – Rich was like a son to Dad. They even went for coffee together on Sundays.

"It's a great job offer," I relented. "But..."

"This wouldn't have something to do with that fancyman of yours that your mum and sister met down in London?"

Fuck sake, Ailish. Nothing was sacred anymore. Nothing was secret. I made a mental note to text her demanding that she stop gossiping about me to our father. Well, actually, I probably wouldn't, because then I'd be too scared to read her response and I'd avoid contacting her for months and months afterwards.

But there was no point in lying to Dad now that he knew. "Maybe." I circled the rim of the tall glass my vanilla milkshake was held in. Dad's hangover cure was chips and cheese; mine was pure, unadulterated dairy. "Rich told me he had feelings for me. He wants me to consider him in – in a romantic sense."

"And you don't want to?"

"I don't know! I'm just – I'm not in – I'm not in the right headspace right now to make this kind of decision." Simon was no small part of that, of course. God, Simon. I had no idea what I said or did last night in front of him. Why had he been there again? I couldn't remember. All I knew was that he hadn't sent me a text or a funny GIF or a link to an interesting article or whatever since before he saw me in my black-out state. I mean, okay, that meant I hadn't heard from him for a scant sixteen hours, but still.

"Do you want to be able to make this decision?" Dad asked, very kindly ignoring the fact I'd spaced out again. "Or is it that you aren't ready for a serious relationship?"

I barked out a laugh. "Good question. Would be great if I knew."

"Ah, speak of the devil," Dad said, waving at someone crossing the road. I turned my head to see who he was talking about, only to see Rich walking five dogs at once in our direction. "Morning!"

Rich waved merrily back. "Morning," he said when he reached us, chipper as ever. He gave me a sympathetic smile. "Glad to see Courtney's hangover routine is the same as always."

I groaned. "Don't talk to me about hangovers. Even the word makes me want to vom."

The way Rich looked at me told me he was far too close to being able to read my mind than I was currently comfortable with. "You've clearly been thinking too much. Just let me do what's right by you, Court."

I kind of tuned out whilst Dad and Rich exchanged pleasantries, then we watched the dogs so Rich could go inside to order coffee for himself. I petted Mrs Campbell's spoiled labradoodle and ruined his stupid diet by giving him a cheesy chip off Dad's plate before Rich came back, but he gave me a knowing look before heading back to the day care centre, anyway.

The moment he left Dad said, "Do you really want other people making all of your decisions for you?"

"Rich is right, though," I relented. He really was; he'd never steered me wrong so far. He was still here now, supporting and loving me, even when most other people were long gone. "He always has my best interests at heart. More than pretty much anyone else."

A pause. "You know if you just give your mum a cha—"

"Let's not talk about Mum right now, Dad." My pounding head couldn't handle it.

"Then let's talk about what's really bothering you."

To say I was conflicted didn't even cover it. Everything Rich was offering me was everything I could have honestly hoped for. Realistically it was the best offer I was going to get. Back when I was studying geography at uni I had some naïve thoughts of being a weather-girl – something my mum could proudly brag about to her friends – but it really wasn't for me. I thought travelling would satisfy my love of the subject, instead, but all it gave me was a frustration about how aimless I was...and heartbreak at the hands of my stupid guitar-playing cheating boyfriend.

When my phone pinged I half jumped out of my skin, along with my dad. But then he nodded and I let myself seek my phone from the depths of my bag to see who had contacted me.

It was Simon.

I'd been full of hangxiety all morning about what I said or did the night before, but the moment I saw that all Simon was asking was if I was alive and in need of caffeine before my shift at the Plaza all that anxiety washed away.

There was no judgement from him. Nothing but concern, and affection.

I didn't realise I was smiling. But I had to be because Dad was grinning like a Cheshire cat right back at me. "Clearly you *do* know what you want."

"Fuck off, Dad."

He laughed, and I laughed, because at least for the rest of that morning my life was easy and uncomplicated once more. All because of a silly text from Simon Saint.

Chapter Twenty-Two

SIMON

Fᴜᴄᴋ ᴍᴇ, ᴍʏ ʜᴇᴀᴅ ᴡᴀs *ᴛʜʀᴏʙʙɪɴɢ*. And not from a two-day hangover, though when I hit thirty-four I experienced one of them for the first time in my life and had suffered from them near-constantly ever since. Screw getting older, damn it. Courtney had been regaling me all day yesterday with how awful her hangover had been after her impromptu drinking session with the girls, though she'd made no mention of what may or may not have been said in my presence. I was relieved by this, sort of, though part of me really did want to sit down with her and talk about her coping mechanisms.

But not right now. Right now I could barely think straight.

I had no idea why I felt so out-of-sorts today. I rarely if ever had migraines – which was a blessing, because I remember Mum suffering from them scarily often. Barely a week went by when she wasn't dealing with one. She'd always told me it was because of stress, from working so much, and that she'd feel better after a little break.

She never took a little break.

"If you're done thinking about anything *but* the name of the shop, Simon..." Kei grumbled, crumpling a sheet of note paper in his hand and lobbing it at my face. We'd decided that today – right here, right now – was when we'd finalise the name. Sure, we had no suggestions to pick from, but regardless we were determined. If only my damn head didn't hurt so much. My vision was so blurry I could barely see.

"Can't we just go for our names?" I sighed. My hand brushed against a stack of papers that had nothing to do with naming the restaurant and everything to do with my grandparents' looming demands. Between that and the aching head I was absolutely not in the right mind for work. But this needed done, and at least if it was achieved today we'd never have to think about it again.

Kei considered this around a sip of beer. "Simon and Kei doesn't sound right."

"Kei and Simon, then."

"No, it isn't the order, it's..." My business partner said nothing for a while, doodling on a piece of paper before beginning to write out some kanji I recognised.

"Isn't that *my* name in kanji?" I asked, peering to focus on the characters with incredible difficulty.

"Sort of. Your surname, Saint."

"I thought we agreed that using the word Saint was a no-go, since my bakery is already called *Saintly Pastries*?"

"In Japanese, Saint is Seijin." Kei tapped his pen on the kanji several times, a contemplative look on his face. "Seijin and Kei, where the *and* is an ampersand?" He wrote it out, then turned the page to face me.

Seijin & Kei.

It was so perfect I felt stupid that we hadn't come up with it earlier. "Having both names in Japanese will definitely bring in the Japanophile audience more than *Simon*," I said, pleased. "Let's go with this."

Kei nodded, satisfied with our decision, then startled when my phone began buzzing incessantly on the table. When I made no move to answer it – I felt bad enough without taking a call from my grandmother, thank you very much – he asked, "What are you going to do about them?"

"About who?" I couldn't think straight. My head was swimming.

"Your grandparents," Kei said, uncharacteristically patient. "Their job offer. You could still have a hand in the shop and the bakery if you took over the firm, even if it means you won't be as involved as you are now. But say goodbye to opening any other restaurants."

I made to stand up to get a glass of water and staggered dangerously, narrowly avoiding toppling to the floor when Kei jumped up, alarmed, and grabbed my arm.

"Holy shit," he said, pressing the back of his hand to my forehead, "you're like a furnace. Why didn't you say anything?"

"It's nothing," I complained, even though it obviously was.

Kei forced me back into my seat and pulled out his phone. "I'm ordering you a taxi back to the Plaza. Get some sleep, Si."

Given the state I was in I had no capacity to argue. In all honesty I had no clue how I got in the car, reached the Plaza and stumbled through the revolving doors, but I did. If I'd had two healthy brain cells available to rub together I'd have pegged that it was after eight in the evening, so Courtney would be working. I always said hello to her every shift, without fail. Be it at six or nine or eleven, I *always* made time to say hi.

I didn't today.

Getting the elevator up to my suite was just as bleary in my mind as the taxi ride. I'd always thought the Plaza lift was a smooth ride but today I felt every jostle, every jerk, every stop. My stomach lurched the entire time, and I had to actively fight not to vomit all over myself.

But, somehow, I made it up. When I reached my darkened

suite I careened into the bedroom without taking off my coat or shoes or even turning on a light. I collapsed onto the duvet, useless as a small child, and fell deep into feverish oblivion.

Chapter Twenty-Three

COURTNEY

S IMON ALWAYS SAID HELLO TO ME when I was on shift. Even if it meant coming down from his suite specifically to do so, he said hello. But today, Thursday, when he basically staggered through the revolving glass doors into the hotel, he didn't even look at me. I was confused; weren't we going for coffee on Saturday before my shift? Had I somehow done something wrong since our last flirtatious text exchange the night before? Had I upset him? Offended him?

I had no idea. But now it was all I could think about.

I'd run to the Chinese bakery up on Garscube Road straight after my shift ended at the day care to grab some char siu buns for Simon to enjoy. I hadn't stopped eating them ever since we never actually *got* to head into Chinatown in London. Now I felt awkward about going up to give them to him.

But I was worried about him. Simon hadn't looked himself, not at all.

By the time my shift finished I was itching and impatient to go up and check on him. I mean yeah, it was almost midnight, but Simon was a night owl. I'd learned that very quickly over the last few weeks of getting to know him. Sometimes he'd come into the Plaza at seven or eight in the evening and literally say, "Good afternoon, Courtney!" with no hint of irony in his voice. So I had it on good faith that he'd be awake. And since I'd never been one to back down from a challenge, I figured it was worth tamping down my nerves to head up to the penthouse and check on him.

If Simon didn't answer the door then I would walk away gracefully. Maybe he just had a migraine, after all. Maybe he'd had an argument with his grandparents and hadn't been in the mood to speak to anyone. Of course, all of this mystery would be resolved by waiting until tomorrow to see if Simon's mood had improved, but I was impatient.

And like I said, I liked a challenge.

My heart was pounding in my chest as I ascended in the lift, feeling like a schoolgirl with her very first crush instead of a world-weary woman in her thirties. When I reached the door I paused for a moment before knocking. I closed my eyes, took a deep breath, then rapped sharply on the door three times.

"Simon?" I asked quietly. Then, louder, "Simon? It's Courtney. Can I come in?"

For a few seconds I heard absolutely nothing, and became convinced Simon must actually be asleep and that it had been rude of me to come up here just to satisfy my curiosity. But then I heard the tell-tale sounds of someone shifting through the room, and a moment later the door creaked open.

Holy fuck, Simon looked terrible. His skin was grey and pallid and gaunt; a sickly sheen of sweat covered his face. His hair was drenched in sweat, too, and his eyes were unfocused. Upon further inspection I saw that he was shivering through the suit he had been wearing earlier, that he clearly hadn't managed to change out of.

"You aren't well," I said, stating the obvious. Another woman might have taken this as a hint to leave Simon be, but I was impulsive. I pushed the door open wider and let myself in without waiting for permission. "Let me help you out."

"Cour—" Simon rasped, voice dry and thick with the cold. He coughed and then tried again. "Courtney, you don't need to —"

"I don't need to, but I want to. Have you eaten?" I held up the bag of char siu buns in my hand and shook them. "I come bearing gifts. Although..." I surveyed his pitiful appearance critically. "You might want something in more of a liquid form. Hang on."

I paraded Simon back to bed – the crumpled covers confirming that he had indeed probably spent the last few hours knocked out on it – before pulling out my phone and ordering some chicken noodle soup from my favourite late-night Chinese restaurant. Then I gave Simon my full attention once more.

I tutted good-naturedly as I took in the shoes he hadn't even managed to remove. "Get those off," I ordered, waving up and down his frame. "All of it."

Simon grimaced. "I thought you said I should get back into bed?"

"I changed my mind. Strip off, go stand or lean or sit in the shower, and give me ten minutes."

Mutely Simon obliged, too ill to fight back or protest. I imagined he wouldn't be able to stand up for much longer than ten minutes without passing out, but I knew the steam and the hot water would do him good. Once Simon was in the shower I moved like a whirlwind around his suite, straightening out the sheets and fluffing the pillows on the bed, opening one of the windows an inch to let in some fresh air, setting the air con to a pleasant temperature, and sorting out his discarded clothes. Then I called down to room service and had them bring up a bucket of ice and a jug of water and set this beside his bed. I finished things off by putting on some mindless gameshow on TV.

In the end I had to retrieve Simon; fifteen minutes had

been and gone with no sign of him. When I entered the bathroom I saw he had all but fallen asleep against the tiled shower wall, the water running down his gorgeous body in a way that made me wish I *was* the water. Forcing my head out of the gutter I grabbed a towel off the radiator and gently slid the shower door open.

"Simon, wake up," I said, keeping my tone soothing. Regardless the sound of my voice startled him awake, and Simon backed himself against the tiles.

"How—" Simon began, the epitome of dazed and confused. "Why are you – Courtney?" He looked at me blearily, as if he'd forgotten I'd ever shown up.

"God, why are all men so pathetic when they're sick?" I wondered aloud, rolling my eyes as I handed him a towel and directed Simon back into the bedroom. I had taken the liberty of going through his stuff to find a comfortable pair of sweatpants and a T-shirt for him to wear; he didn't question my choices as he put the clothes on and obediently slid into bed.

Simon drank from the glass of water I'd poured him that was waiting by his bedside. He was shivering all over; I watched with some concern as the water and the glass shook alongside him. "Here, let me—" but Simon waved my hand away.

"I can do it," he muttered, not looking at me. "I'm not *that* pathetic."

"That remains to be seen. How long have you been feeling like this?"

"My head's been throbbing all day." Simon laid down the glass, closed his eyes, and rested his head against the pile of pillows I'd arranged for him. He let out a heavy sigh. "I'm not used to getting sick. I'm sorry if I worried you."

"I wouldn't be a very nice person if I wasn't worried after seeing the way you staggered into the hotel earlier." I traced circles on the top of the duvet for a few seconds, before ultimately deciding to sit down on the bed beside Simon against all of the pillows. I glanced up at him from beneath my eyelashes, suddenly self-conscious. "You never said hello."

"If I'd had to speak a single word I would have thrown up all over your shirt. I didn't imagine you would want that."

I could only laugh. But before I could respond properly the phone rang; I picked it up long before Simon's reflexes realised what he was supposed to do. "Mister Saint's room," I said, easily turning on my service voice.

"There's a delivery of Chinese food down here," the late night concierge informed me. I could almost hear the frown in his voice. "Is that you, Courtney?"

"Yes. Just checking in on the sick and infirm. Send it up, Brian."

 Simon coughed again. He sounded surprised – if a cough could sound surprised. "What did you order?"

"Chicken noodle soup," I said, moving from the bedroom to answer the door. When I came back I set up a tray on the bed, then opened the steaming bowl of soup (my mouth started salivating at the savoury, slightly spicy smell of it) and took out the buns I'd bought earlier. "When was the last time you ate?"

"Courtney," Simon began, shaking his damp hair in the process, "this is too—"

"Don't you *dare* say it's too much. Haven't you had anyone take care of you when you were sick before?" He squirmed uncomfortably, and I immediately knew I'd stepped on a landmine. "Never mind," I said quickly. "You don't have to—"

"Mum did," Simon murmured, staring at his hands until I put the bowl of soup in them. The warmth of the liquid seemed to calm the shaking in his hands, for which I was relieved. "But once my grandparents took me in I was kind of... I don't know. Afraid to show them that I was sick. They wanted me to be independent. Hard-working. There was one..."

"Yes?" I pressed, when Simon didn't continue. "Drink your soup, Simon."

He gave me an unfocused frown. "What do you want? For me to tell you the story or drink the soup?"

"Both. Get that delicious chicken goodness down your gullet then regale me with childhood stories."

So he did. Simon forced down a few spoonfuls of soup – I handed over several high-strength painkillers for him to swallow alongside it – then he said, "One time I *did* get sick, just after Mum died. I think it was tonsillitis, actually, but I can't really remember." Simon paused to drink more soup; when I ripped off part of a char siu bun and handed it to him he dipped it into his bowl, spent a few seconds chewing, then swallowed with a contented expression on his face. "God, I missed these. Where did you get them?"

"The Chinese bakery up on Garscube Road. I've been going almost every day since we got back from London." For some reason this made Simon blush, which made *me* blush. I looked away, embarrassed. Jesus Christ, I'd given this man a lap dance and a blow job and *this* was what embarrassed me? I needed to get my head checked out. "Tell me the rest of your story," I said, desperate to distract the two of us from how disgustingly cute we had accidentally ended up being.

Simon ran a hand through his hair to push it away from his face. The blush remained, but his face turned sad. "Apparently I screamed and cried for my mother so much that Nan ended up hiring someone to look after me while I was sick, because I didn't want to see my grandparents. I didn't *know* them. That probably has something to do with why they never wanted to be around me when I was sick, after that."

"Simon, that isn't your fault," I said, appalled and mortified in equal measure. Just what had Rupert and Maria Saint done to Simon? "You were a *child*. And you...you just lost your mum."

There was a question hanging between us that I desperately wanted to ask. Morbid curiosity and all that. But of course I would never ask it; it wasn't my place to pry. But Simon, astute even through the cloud of sickness, inclined his head slightly. "It's okay. You can ask."

I gulped. Shifted position so I was better facing Simon. "Then how did she...how did your mum die? How did you and her end up alone, without your dad?" Okay, that was two questions, but if I didn't ask them now I felt like I could never ask them again.

"There was a car crash. Ice on the road." A pause. Simon closed his eyes, as if the story could only be told without him looking at me. "She was working really late that night, which was why she was on the road at all. She always worked late – that's why I'm such a night owl." Simon laughed, and it was sad. He opened his eyes and caught my gaze; his vision was too bright. "She was working extra shifts in the run-up to Christmas because I was dying for a Playstation. I know it isn't my fault, but still..." Simon paused for longer this time, wiping at his eyes without bothering to hide the fact he was crying.

Gently I took away the tray of half-eaten food, and took Simon's hands in my own. He squeezed my hands too tightly, but I didn't wince. He could snap my fingers in two if it gave him some comfort to do so. "Mum was only seventeen when she had me," Simon continued, after several seconds of silence. "She went to a gig and fell for a guy who was working behind the bar at the venue. I never knew his name; it didn't matter. Long story short, he got her pregnant. My grandparents are super conservative, so they were against Mum having an abortion, but they also wanted to control each and every aspect of her pregnancy. They forbade her from seeing her boyfriend." A short laugh. "Unsurprisingly, Mum did not like this. So she ran away up to Glasgow with her boyfriend. He was from Bridgeton or something – I don't really remember what she told me. I guess it doesn't matter. But then I was born, and the postpartum depression set in, and because my grandparents had cut Mum off there was no money to be had. Her boyfriend, realising what he was in for, just up and left her. Left my mum with me, penniless and alone."

I was crying – you couldn't go near me with an emotional story without a ninety percent chance that I would cry – but Simon was crying too and didn't seem to mind. "I'm so sorry," I whispered, squeezing his fingers as tightly as he was squeezing mine. "I am so, so sorry."

"It's fine. Well it's not, but it's done. What use is there in dwelling on the past?" Simon had recounted his mother's miserable life as impersonally as if it was a story on the news, or in a soap opera. But his tears, and the way he grabbed onto me, told me exactly how he really felt.

He was angry. He was distraught. He lost his mum, and he wasn't over it. In all likelihood he never would be.

"I'll wrap up the rest of the food for later," I said softly, taking the remains of Simon's meal and carrying the tray over to the living room portion of his suite. When I returned Simon looked halfway towards sleep; brushing my fingers over his forehead I discovered he was just as feverish as I expected him to be. "Those painkillers will kick in soon," I reassured him, "then you should be out like a light. There's water here for when you get thirsty, but hopefully you'll sleep through the night and feel better in the morning. Okay?"

"Okay dokey," Simon said, in a singsong voice that made me laugh. I realised I was still sweeping my fingertips across his forehead, clearing his hair away from his face each and every time. Simon didn't complain, so I kept doing it. It was soothing.

My heart twinged; these were definitely very real feelings I had for Simon Saint. Not infatuation, not lust – though there was a fuck-load of that, even for the pathetically sick version of Simon currently before me – and most definitely not trivial.

"Courtney..." Simon almost whispered, after a minute or two of comfortable silence. "Will you speak to your mother?"

It hadn't been the question I was expecting. Though, given what we had just been talking about, I suppose the connection was obvious. "I could," I relented, "but whether I *will*..."

"Funny. Very funny. You don't know how much time you have someone. And I know…I can see why your relationship is complicated. But it seemed like she was trying at dinner, didn't it?"

It did, but I didn't want to admit to that. If I didn't get to hold onto my anger towards my mother – if I didn't let it dictate my life and my decisions – then what was I left with? There would be a whole space my heart where before there had been rage and sorrow and bitter disappointment. What would fill that? There wasn't nearly enough love in my life to replace those feelings.

But to disappoint Simon, just for that? It hurt to even consider it.

"You're overthinking…" Simon mumbled, far more on the side of sleep than wakefulness. He rolled onto his side, slid his hand up to mine, still on his forehead, and tapped my knuckles. "Not everything is that hard. Sometimes you have to let go."

I swallowed. "Words to live by, but hard to follow."

"Amen, sister."

I laughed at the silly comment, but it was cut short when Simon began gently snoring. Waiting a few more minutes to make sure he was definitely out for the count, I covered his food and left a note telling him to ask the front desk to have it heated up for him when he woke up.

Then I left, closing the door as silently as I could, and asked Brian to wake Simon up at nine in the morning for a hot breakfast.

Hopefully, when I saw him tomorrow, Simon would be feeling a lot better.

Chapter Twenty-four

SIMON

"OPEN YOUR MOUTH FOR THE AIRPLANE!"

"I'm not a child, thank you very much," I replied sulkily. But I opened my mouth anyway and let Courtney spoon-feed me carrot and coriander soup, Courtney sniggering the entire time at how ridiculous we were being. After two more rounds of this I grabbed the spoon and bowl from her hands. "I think I've had enough of that. You're too slow."

"Not a problem you've ever been able to relate to, I'm sure."

"How fast you went from infantalising to sexually degrading me!" I cried, mock-outraged. I got rid of the spoon after a moment of consideration to drink directly from the bowl, sipping on the delicious contents in as offended a manner as possible. Was it possible to drink soup in an offended manner? "And I'll have you know that using only one data point to infer that conclusion is poor science, Courtney."

Courtney rolled her eyes. "Shut up, you sell-out economist. How are you feeling this evening, anyway?"

"Given that you've dedicated the last three nights to looking after me once your shifts end...a whole lot better." I put down the bowl and offered Courtney what I could only hope was my most charming smile. Given how awful I'd looked the last few days, it was probably more of a grimace. "Honestly, you didn't have to do all this for me. You must be exhausted."

Courtney took my hands in hers. It was so easy. So effortless. Ever since I'd feverishly told her about my mum we'd found ourselves holding hands a lot. "It was my pleasure," she said, gaze holding firmly on mine. "I mean it. It was even worth missing our coffee date for."

Something caught in my throat. I wanted to kiss her, or hug her, or...I don't know. Nothing felt like *enough*. How had we fallen so deeply, so fast? In the grand scheme of things Courtney and I had barely scratched the surface of each other, and yet there was nobody else I'd rather be with right now that her.

But then Courtney broke eye contact, let go of my hands, and the moment to do something was over.

"Um," I said, feeling suddenly awkward and fishing for a topic of conversation, "speaking of infants, do you know if you want children?"

"What the actual fuck?"

What the actual fuck, indeed. Courtney looked as shocked as I felt; I wished the ground would swallow me up. *That* was the topic of conversation I came up with? "Ignore me," I mumbled, sheepish as hell. "I got nervous suddenly. I don't know why I asked that."

To my immense relief, however, Courtney got over her bafflement with a soft snigger. "I don't want them. Never have. And...you?"

"I don't want them, either."

"Did you ever?"

"Maybe." I pondered the question for a few seconds then decided that, since I was the one who'd asked the question first,

I'd give Courtney a full and proper answer. "When I was a kid –
back when Mum was still around," I said. Courtney, sensing my
answer was going to be long, resettled beside me on the bed to
snuggle against my side. My thoughts strayed to entirely filthy
places. I tamped them down. For the love of god I tamped
them down.

"I thought it might be nice to have a 'little me' be my best
friend," I continued with difficulty, "but as I grew up I realised
that wasn't really a reason to have a *child*. And it all stemmed
from me being lonely and wishing I could have as strong a
relationship with someone else the way I had with my mum, so
at the end of the day it was nothing to do with wanting kids at
all. What?" I asked, running an awkward hand through my hair
when I noticed the way Courtney was looking at me. "What did
I say?"

"Oh it's – it's nothing, really. It's just...that's so mature of
you. So – so – what's the word? Astute? No, that isn't it."
Courtney's brow furrowed in concentration. "I mean that you're
very emotionally intelligent, I guess. To be able to pinpoint
your feelings and the reason for those feelings existing so well."

"I think most folk would call that 'overthinking' and tell me
to chill."

"And I think people who say that should fuck off." Courtney
traced a finger over the fabric of my T-shirt, drawing circles that
got wider and wider as the silence stretched between us.

"What is it?" I asked, desperate to know what was going on
inside her head.

"Well, um, I don't mean to pry, but..."

"By all means pry away. What else would I rather be doing
on a Sunday at" – I checked the time on my watch, on the
bedside table – "five to midnight than giving you an opportunity
to pry? Nothing, that's what."

Courtney nudged me, not-so-gently. It sent a shocking jolt of
electricity through my elbow, up my arm, then all the way down
my spine; clearly my body had recuperated more than enough

to feel things that felt grossly inappropriate given the fact Courtney was helping me get over the flu. "I can think of a few things that might be more fun that, ahem, *prying,*" she murmured, her mind apparently in the exact same filthy place mine was.

Oh yes. I could definitely feel things.

Unfortunately, my body chose that time to make me yawn, and the sexual tension was gone in a moment. Courtney's flirtatious expression softened, and she stopped tracing circles on my chest to turn on her side. When I did the same I caught a whiff of the scent on her skin. Courtney smelled of oil and salt and spice and herbs – the hotel restaurant had been understaffed, so Courtney offered to switch up jobs for the evening. Her hair was a flat, dull mess from all the sweat that had accrued in it from working. Her lipstick was smeared into oblivion and her mascara had smudged below her eyes.

I thought Courtney Miller was the most beautiful woman in the world. Exhausted or sick, it didn't matter. A blind man could see how sensational she was.

"Ask me anything," I said. "Please."

Courtney hesitated for a second, but then she asked, "Why haven't you spoken to your grandparents about the way you feel? About what you really want to do with your life, and...and the influence they have over you?"

It would have been easy to lie. Instead I told the truth. "Because I owe them everything, and they're all the family I have. I know they're from a different generation – if I tell them the pressure they're putting on me, the damage...they won't understand. They'll cut me out before they concede to change."

"You can't know that for sure. I'd wager you could persuade them, if you found the right words."

I gave Courtney my most disbelieving smile. "You *do* remember meeting them, right?" Another damnable yawn. "In any case, I know I have to speak to them, and soon. Maybe you're right and I simply need to fi—"

"Jesus, could you yawn any louder?" Courtney laughed, sticking a finger in my mouth to ruin said third yawn right in the middle of it. "You're making me exhausted just looking at you. And I still have to spend an hour *getting* to bed."

"Stay here."

I said it before really thinking through the ramifications. But when Courtney, wide-eyed, asked, "Can I?"

All I wanted to say, so all I *did* say, was, "Please."

"Sleeping only, right?" Courtney asked, a quirk to the set of her lips that made me wish I had even one iota of energy left. Fuck, being ill really took all the wind out of your sails.

"Perhaps some cuddling, if you're amenable," I said, putting on my best investor voice.

Courtney snaked her arms around me, a wicked grin on her face. A wicked grin for *cuddling*. "I like that. I like the sound of that a lot."

I don't know how I managed it but, for the second time in as many weeks, I'd found myself sharing a bed with a woman I had grown crazy for, and for the second time I found myself falling asleep willingly before anything X-rated could occur.

But then Courtney squeezed her laughably weak arms around me a little tighter, and I realised this wasn't me missing a prime opportunity.

This was happiness. I hoped to have ten thousand more nights like this.

Chapter Twenty-five

COURTNEY

WITH HIS HAIR DOWN, EMPTY OF product and messy as hell, Simon looked so much younger than he usually did as he slept peacefully beside me. Thank god the colour had returned to his cheeks; I'd been worried I'd have to pull out the dreaded covid test. I'd never much enjoyed looking after sick people but, strangely, I'd liked looking after Simon.

But he wasn't sick anymore. Not really. Which was just as well, because the thoughts racing through my head as I watched him sleep were absolutely *not* suitable for the ill and infirm. I suppose they weren't suitable thoughts to have about a sleeping man, either, but who was I to tell my brain to shut up?

I was horny as fuck, and could do nothing about it.

My problem was two-fold. First: the object of my desires was, as aforementioned, sleeping. Simon had barely been able to keep his eyes open after I came up to check on him after my shift. This wasn't surprising, given how sick he'd been, but it still threw a spanner in the works for horny me.

Second: I looked and smelled like an absolute state.

Grease and sweat and food and wine and all manner of other

things clung to my clothes and skin and hair after a manic shift working in the restaurant, helping out the wait staff with a stupidly busy Sunday evening dinner rush. Simon, being the gentleman that he was, hadn't commented on how bad I smelled, even though the horrible intermingled scent was so strong I found it clogging my senses and rendering me unable to sleep.

I tossed in the bed, away from Simon, crossing and uncrossing my thighs as I did so. So I was horny, and that feeling wasn't going away, and I had to accept that.

I'd resisted the urge to go on my phone so I didn't rouse a very heavily sleeping Simon, but now I was desperate to know what the time was so I knew how long this seemingly unending torment would last. I turned on the screen and stole a quick glance.

Three in the morning.

God, that was still *way* too much time to lie here, unable to sleep. I could do nothing about the rampant horniness – how did Simon look so *good* all gaunt and wrung-out from the flu? – but I could, at least, sneak off for a shower to wipe the grime of the day off.

I was very quiet as I stole out of bed and tiptoed to the bathroom, a skill well-honed after many a one-night-stand where the last thing I wanted to do was stay over at some random guy's place in his uncomfortable bed with a shitty mattress and flat pillows and torn duvet cover. At least – this time – the bed was nice, the man in it even nicer, and I actually planned to return.

And holy fuck did a shower feel good. The showers in the Crowne Plaza were a million times better than my own tiny cubicle back in my (soon to be old) flat. Once I was safely within the confines of the massive shower unit, the steam curling up my nose whilst the pressure sloughed off the sweat from my skin and hair, I felt my entire body relax. I'd always been one for a late-night shower after coming in from a long shift or drinks with the girls or sneaking off from aforementioned one night stands, but the ground I was treading now was entirely new.

The shower was cleaning me off, yes, but it was doing absolutely nothing to help ease me into sleepiness. Instead I felt wired and most *definitely* still horny.

I stole a glance at the bathroom door. I'd left it ajar just in case the click of it shutting woke Simon up. There was no sign of him...and I could be quiet. Real quiet.

After finishing washing my hair I slipped my hand between my thighs, practically gasping in relief when my fingertips found my clit and began to ease the enormous pressure building inside me. Something in the back of my brain told me I really shouldn't be doing this here: this was my place of work, after all, and I wasn't even a paying guest. And Simon was asleep one room over. I needed to stop. I needed to, but I couldn't.

When was the last time I'd had sex? Simon and I had been all over each other in London but we hadn't gone all the way. Two months, maybe? Three? More? I'd never felt so time blind as I did now.

But damn if it didn't feel good to relieve some of the tension in my body. I leaned against the glass door, panting with exertion, as I chased a release I was desperate to experience. My wet hair stuck to my face, getting in my eyelashes and dropping water down my face like tears, and the steam was kind of going to my head, but I didn't care.

Getting myself off in here, in secret, was such a major turn-on. Simon was dead asleep but was, unknowingly, the demon inside my head urging me to touch myself faster to the mere thought of him, with his beautiful grey eyes and defined shoulders and sexy expensive suits and silky hair and—

"Courtney."

I froze, gaze momentarily unfocused when my eyes flew open to look through the steamed-up glass. Simon Saint was standing right there. *Right there*, naked, in front of me. Just how long had he been there? Just how—

Simon opened the shower door then picked me up and slammed me against the tiled wall. His mouth was on mine before I could utter a single word. All I managed was a gasp when Simon slid his tongue into my mouth and propped me up with a tense, thick thigh between my legs. His dick was hard as a fucking rock already.

Just how long had he been watching me?

Simon's mouth left mine to trail kisses down my neck as I desperately rutted against him. Okay, this was infinitely hotter than masturbating all on my own. The feeling of Simon – all of him – sliding against me already had me teetering on the edge.

"How long – how long were you watching?" I bit out, panting heavily. Simon's hands were somehow everywhere: my neck, my boobs, my waist, my hips. "Why did – *ah* – didn't you say anything?" Fuck, it was hard to talk. It was hard to see.

Simon pulled away just far enough that we could make eye contact. Those usually cool, clear eyes were as hazy and unfocused as the steam softly wafting all around us. "Long enough," he growled. "Why didn't you wake me?"

"You were fast asleep."

"I wasn't. I was pretending."

"You...what?"

"Courtney Miller, be serious," Simon said, capturing my mouth with his once more. He bit into my lower lip until I groaned. "You think I could sleep with you right there, beside me?"

"So why didn't you *say* anything?"

"Why didn't you?"

Simon grazed his erection against my clit, and I decided I didn't care about the finer details. I dragged a hand through his hair, demanding Simon kiss me deeper, more insistently, like I was air and he was drowning. And Simon played the part of a drowning man to perfection; it was as if he couldn't possibly grab hold of enough of me.

"Watching you touch yourself in here was so hot," he murmured, eyes molten when we took a precious moment to catch our breath. Simon's hands shook where they touched my skin. "Were you thinking of me?"

"Guiltily thinking of the recovering sick man in his bed, yes," I admitted, laughing despite myself. "I have no shame."

"I like you shameless. I like it a lot. Only..." Simon teetered on the spot, knocking into me against the wall. "The steam is making me dizzy. Can we—"

"Fuck yes let's move this to the bed; my legs are cramping like hell in this position." It was Simon who laughed this time, deep and throaty as he carried me out of the shower and back into the bedroom. Neither of us cared that we were dripping wet, or that the sheets were going to have to soak all that water up – though I threw the duvet to the floor to protect it from the inevitable mess.

"In service mode, even now," Simon said, dropping onto the bed and pulling me on top. When I moved against his dick he let out a grunt of pleasure.

"I'm thinking I might be in a different kind of *service mode* at present."

"Another prostitute joke. Is this becoming our thing?"

"The bedroom is probably the only appropriate place to *make* a prostitute joke," I said, trailing my hand down Simon's abs – yoga and crunches clearly got the job done, Jesus Christ – until I found his cock. When I stroked it Simon squirmed. He was just about to make another joke when I kissed him, wet and eager and impatient; he got the hint to keep the talking for later.

His hands crawled down my spine to my waist, before one of them wandered around to touch my clit. The noise that emitted from the back of my throat when he did so was like nothing I'd ever heard.

"Fuck, Courtney, I can't wait," Simon whined, as we

touched each other and our breathing got faster and our skin slid across skin. "I *need* to be inside you."

I paused for a moment, my hand still but strong on his dick, and looked around. "Do you...?"

"Jesus, a condom!" If Simon had an available hand it looked like he would have slapped himself. Then he broke eye contact, suddenly self-conscious. "They're in my laptop bag. By the – um – by the door. I bought some for London and—"

"Have been carrying them around with you ever since?" Without another word I swung off of Simon, prancing off naked towards the bag in question despite his protests that he'd get it, instead. When I returned with a box of condoms I grinned like the Cheshire Cat. "I like a man who's prepared."

"Then it's a good thing I'm *always* prepared. Come here," Simon ordered, "and put one of those on me."

"You didn't say 'Simon Says'."

For a moment it looked like he was going to tell me to fuck off, but then Simon's lips quirked into the ghost of a smile, and he grabbed me and bodily threw me beneath him whilst I yelped in surprise.

"*Simon says* he's going to fuck you," he breathed, ripping open the box of condoms with adrenaline-unsteady hands. "*Simon says* you're going to like it." He opened one of the foil wrappers, then placed the condom in my hands and directed them to his cock. I could feel it pulsing beneath my touch. "*Simon says* I'm going to make you do everything Simon says. Has the joke gotten old yet?"

I gulped, finding it near impossible to decide what to stare at: Simon's eyes or his dick. "I think the joke just got a whole lot sexier." It wasn't a difficult thing to achieve; Simon Saint was perhaps the sexiest man I'd ever encountered. His hair, dripping wet and plastered messily over his forehead, along with the water droplets clinging to every line and muscle of his taut body, made him look like he was in some kind of raunchy music video.

"Can we leave the jokes behind now?" Simon asked between ragged breaths. He loomed over me, tight and barely-restrained, until I looped my legs around his waist and urged him towards me. His resultant grip on my thighs was strong as steel.

"Yeah," I said. My voice was barely audible. I stroked the side of Simon's jaw, covered in days of stubble. He'd suit a beard. "Yeah, I think I'd like it if you screwed me senseless now."

Simon turned his head. He kissed my hand where it lay on his jaw, so gently. So tenderly. My heart hurt at the motion, my lungs constricting as if I couldn't get enough air. This thing between us...it wasn't trivial. It wasn't passing lust that would fade in the light of day.

"Simon," I said, quietly, "I like who I am with you."

His eyes went wide, before growing heavy-lidded with desire. His mouth curled into a dizzyingly boyish grin. "I like who I am with you, too."

And then, with the barest hint of direction from my hand, Simon was inside me. I let out a noise somewhere between a whimper and a moan; when I tensed around Simon's cock he bucked alarmingly.

"Jesus, Courtney, you're going to make me come embarrassingly early if you keep that up."

"Then you'll just have to make it up to me in round two."

"I like the sound of that."

It took us a few seconds to find the right rhythm, but the clumsiness wasn't awkward. Our hands and lips and tongues were everywhere, everything wet and wanton and sliding in all the right places.

Then Simon flipped me onto my hands and knees, and he slammed back into me, and his fingers crawled around to touch my clit. To say I saw stars was an understatement; the man knew his way around the female anatomy.

"Simon, I – I don't think you'll be the one c-coming first," I gasped, grasping onto the pillow beneath me for dear life.

When I heard a guttural, unhinged laugh behind me my entire body clenched. Simon's onslaught on my clit intensified, and his other hand slapped my ass. "I've wanted to do that ever since I first watched you walk away," I said, after the slap rang out satisfyingly. He pulled out of me the entire way, paused a moment, then thrust back inside with almost painful enthusiasm. God, I was going to come. I was going to come. I was—

Simon bent over me to bite my shoulder, driving me face-down into the bed, and rutted into me like a beast. His breathing came in rapid stops and starts, signalling he was about to unspool entirely.

I was still the one who came undone first.

My orgasm ripped out of me in one feverish motion, my cry of pleasure absorbed by the pillow. I was suddenly too sensitive; too aware of things. Simon's hand pulled away from my clit, sensing it was too much, and instead rested both his hands over my boobs and squeezed, hard.

"*Simon*," I gasped, turning my head to the side for precious air, but the sound was smothered by the truly animalistic growl Simon let out as he came. His entire body shuddered; for a few seconds he continued to rock into me even though he was spent, and I was spent, but neither of us had the energy to break away from our positions.

Then Simon rolled off me, but he brought me with him. Now I was lying on top of him with my back against his chest, and his lean arms squeezed me tight.

I laughed; what other reaction was there but to laugh. "What are you doing? Let me go!"

"Five minutes," Simon muttered into my wet, tangled mess of hair. "Five minutes, Courtney Miller, you goddess, you succubus, you—"

"Do you always wax poetic after getting laid?"

"Only when I get my money's worth."

"So we're back to the hooker thing now?"

"You started it, Julia Roberts."

And so I let Simon hold me against him for his precious five minutes, until eventually it grew too uncomfortable and he was forced to let me go so I could lie beside him. His chest was heaving still, and so was mine.

"That was potentially some of the best sex I've ever had," I admitted, because it was true and I wanted Simon Saint to know.

He flashed those tantalising canines of his. Licked his lips. "It takes two to tango, and you are a *superb* dance partner."

"I'll take it."

"Can we take another five minutes and then I'll go down on you? I've been dying to get my head between your legs for days."

"You are one horny sick man, Simon."

"Is that a no?"

I kissed his damnably sexy lips. "That is the opposite of no, Mr Saint."

When we were done, a long, long time later, once more covered in sweat but for entirely different reasons than working in the Plaza restaurant, I had no issue falling into an exhausted and contented sleep.

Chapter Twenty-Six

SIMON

When I woke up Courtney was gone. I panicked, immediately awake; checking my watch it was barely seven in the morning.

"Court" – I coughed to clear my parched throat – "Courtney?"

No answer. And then, a moment later, the door to my suite clicked open and closed, and Courtney appeared swaddled in one of the room's complimentary robes carrying several bottles of water. When she saw I was watching her she flinched. "Sorry," she whispered. "I didn't mean to wake you."

"You don't have to whisper. Is there someone else sleeping in the room we need to be mindful of?"

Courtney gave me the finger, handed me a bottle of water, then slid out of the robe and back into bed. The fact she was entirely un-self-conscious about doing so was such a huge turn-on that I not-so-subtly placed the bottle of water over my dick.

She laughed. "It's pretty gratifying seeing how quickly you react to the mere presence of my nakedness."

"Can you blame me? Have you looked in a mirror

recently?"

"Not whilst thinking to myself, 'Am I sexually attractive enough to give Simon Saint an erection the moment I walk into a room?', no."

"Unforgivable. I think that about you at least three times a day when I look in the mirror."

"About whether you can give me an erection?" Courtney grinned, her hand sliding between the water bottle and my dick, then squeezed it for good measure. I groaned when she began moving her hand up and down, slowly, inexorably.

"Fuck me, Courtney, don't do that unless you're about to... well. Fuck me, I guess." Her eyes shone in the glim light of pre-dawn, intent and mischievous on mine as she decidedly continued to stroke my cock. I let the water bottle drop from my hand, off the side of the bed, then grabbed Courtney to place her firmly on my lap. She yelped in surprise. "I can think of better places to put my dick than your hand," I breathed into her ear, trailing slow kisses down her neck, her collarbone, her shoulder, until Courtney became soft and pliant beneath me. And then...

"I *can't*," she bit out. The worst phrase I'd ever heard. My grip on her tightened, and Courtney rutted against my erection despite herself. Fuck, she was still so wet.

"I don't think you *can't* do it." I kept her moving against me, heart hammering in my chest as Courtney's breathing hitched. She slung her arms around my shoulders, pulling herself closer, until her lips were on mine.

We kissed and rubbed and grabbed at each other for a very long five minutes, but still it was over too soon. Courtney sucked on my lip, moved away an inch, and whispered, "I have to be at the day care for nine, and I need to get back to my flat before that. I really need to go."

I wanted her to call in sick, or at least be late. How could I let Courtney go *now?* I wanted more of this; so much more.

I wanted all of her.

But work was work, and even though that work involved her spending time with a man who had professed his love to her, I knew it made me a controlling arsehole if I petitioned for her to remain with me.

Sensing my disappointment Courtney kissed me once more. "I fully expect a million eager messages from you throughout the day. GIFs of goats jumping on sheep. A link to an article detailing the fall of late-stage capitalism. Sexual positions you'd like to try next time."

"I take issue with your notion of 'eager' in relation to capitalism, but I'm only too happy to oblige." Of course I was; already I missed her, and wanted to talk to her, and be *in* her, and Courtney wasn't even out the door yet.

She bopped my nose and jumped out of bed, tossing on her filthy work clothes and heading for the door before I had the wits to stop her. "Stay in bed and catch up on your beauty sleep. I'll text you when I get home."

"You better!" I called out after her, but Courtney was gone. Like a sprite or a faerie or a figment of my perverted imagination, she spirited away to leave me alone.

But not for long. I had permission to bombard her with texts, and the promise of future sex to test out all those new positions she seemed very interested in me researching. The fall of late-stage capitalism could wait for another day.

For the first time in a long time, I fell back asleep fully content with the way my life was turning out.

Chapter Twenty-Seven

COURTNEY

I KNOW THAT, FOR SOME PEOPLE, sleeping with someone who they feel a connection with causes some vital change to their brain chemistry, or their routine, or something else fundamental to their life. I was too old – too wise, laughably – to feel that way after sleeping with Simon, but still...I found myself jogging in a different park this morning.

Nothing ground-breaking, but it was different for *me*.

So here I was, running through the pretty streets of Kelvingrove Park and thoroughly enjoying myself. It was almost March now, and the weather had taken a far milder turn. It was wholly welcome; though the sun was obscured by a familiar bank of thick, grey Glasgow clouds, it was warm enough that several park-goers had already shed their outer layer of clothing, citing global warming or whatever for the reason they had to take their jackets off in February .

One such man, dressed in a T-shirt and shorts – *shorts!* – and keeping perfect time with the lumbering gait of a very large dog approached me just as I headed up the hill towards Park Circus. A familiar man, and a very familiar dog.

"Fancy seeing you here," Tom said, waving merrily as he fell into step beside me. "What caused the change in routine?"

I shrugged. Hell if I was giving him any opening with which to question the reason for me being here, even if that reason was for all intents and purposes a good one. "Dawsholm Park is full of rotten leaves that haven't been swept up yet," I said, which wasn't technically a lie, at least. "I don't want to break my ankle."

Unfortunately Tom wasn't convinced. He gave me a smarmy, knowing grin that I imagine made Liz want to punch him in the face on a daily basis. "I heard Simon had his own personal nurse during his time of need."

"I'm a woman of many skills," I fired back without missing a beat. Tom laughed, and Ludo whined until I gave his head a scratch mid-stride.

"I'm glad." And he sounded it. Not that his best friend getting it on with me was something for Tom to be glad about, but guys were often weirdos like that.

"No, seriously," Tom insisted when I didn't say anything. Together we jogged to the bottom of the hill and carried on to the little duck pond by the play park. Most of the benches were full, or were covered in water from last night's heavy rainfall, so Tom and I made do with standing to watch an old woman scatter bread to feed the ducks. Well, one duck. It was mostly pigeons trying to eat the bread. Tom took a long swig of water from the bottle he was holding before elaborating, "I really am happy the two of you hit it off so well. I couldn't have hoped for it to turn out better than this."

Something about that rankled me. Now don't get me the wrong way: I already knew that Tom had aspired to set me and Simon up before we ended up meeting on our own terms. This wasn't new information. So why did it bother me? Maybe it was because it felt like my entire sort-of relationship with Simon had been decided for me without me actually being part of the decision-making process.

But I knew this wasn't true; of course it wasn't. Tom was my friend, in any case. He was only trying to help.

I didn't like it.

Sensing my discomfort – Tom and Liz were *both* far too observant for their own good, damn it – Tom laid a gentle hand on my shoulder, encouraging me to face him. "Okay, spill," he said, in a very big-brotherly kind of voice. "What's up? What did I say?"

I didn't want to divulge all of my deeply stupid insecurities to Tom – not least because they were ridiculous – but luckily, in this instance, I had another excuse primed and ready to go. One which was the truth, even if it wasn't exactly what I was thinking about right now.

"I'm worried about finding a place to live," I explained. My hands felt fidgety. I wished the old woman would give me some of her bread to chuck it at the birds even though I knew bread was bad for them. "Everywhere is so much more expensive than it was ten years ago."

Tom stretched his arms above his head until his shoulders popped. It was satisfying to hear, and to watch. "That's not a situation I can empathise with," he said, a shit-eating grin on his face, "what with me being filthy rich and all."

"You're a Grade A Arsehole, do know that?"

"I've heard that once or twice, yes." He laughed in a way that made me think he simply didn't care. I *really* wanted to hate him for it, but unfortunately Tom was one iota too likeable for me to tell him to fuck off. "Where have you been looking?"

I told him the truth. "I want to stay where I am right now. It's where I was born and raised. I shouldn't have to move out of north Glasgow just because it's gotten too expensive."

"Absolutely. So what are you going to do?"

"Well, I can afford an unfurnished place on my own." I grimaced, then added, "Just about. The thought of having to thrift furniture from a million different charity shops, though, and finding friends with cars who can help me transfer it all...I don't even know where to start. Honestly, it's my worst nightmare."

For a moment Tom considered things. He began stretching his left leg, then his right; behind us a group of three girls who were maybe in their early twenties openly ogled him. "Can you ask your parents for help?" he asked, either not noticing the girls or not caring. "I thought your dad had a removals van or something?"

"He's hurt his back though. If he gets even a hint that I need help he will literally injure himself trying to do so."

A pause. "And your mum? Can she help you?" If looks could kill, the glare I sent Tom's way would have eviscerated him. "Then focus on finding that one, perfect, unfurnished flat," he said, when I maintained a stony silence. "And take the next step when you get to it. There's no need to get overwhelmed by the bigger picture when you can achieve that picture in smaller steps. Besides, you have people around you who want to help you."

It was ridiculously sound advice. So ridiculous, in fact, that I couldn't believe that Tom was the one who gave it. He clucked his tongue defensively. "I'm a forty-year-old man, Courtney," he said, bending down to ruffle Ludo's ears and letting the dog lick his face in the process. "I might have picked up a trick or two when it comes to easy living during those forty years. Honestly, don't stress about it. Focus on what you *can* do, not what you can't. Ah, shit."

For the heavens had quite literally burst above us: the kind of sudden torrential downpour that only Scotland was capable of. Tom indicated back up the hill with a nod of his head. "Do you want to come back to mine and Liz's until it lets up a bit? This shouldn't last long, and she's working from home on a manuscript. She'd love an excuse to procrastinate over coffee."

But I shook my head, blinking heavily against the falling rain as I did so. "If I don't want to get overwhelmed about finding a flat then I should really, you know, find one," I said, offering Tom a thankful smile nonetheless. "But say hi to Liz for me."

"Only if you tell her I absolutely did not bring up the topic of Simon," Tom said, flashing me that stupidly perfect smile I knew had won Liz over; to my eyes it lacked pointy canines and therefore wasn't perfect. "She made me swear not to badger you about things when I saw you next."

"And you failed miserably."

"What's a secret between friends?" Tom waved just as merrily as he had done when we'd said hello, then with a goodbye bark from Ludo was on his way through the pounding rain.

I was in quite a conflicted mood as I battled the torrent to run the half an hour back home. Tom had given me a lot to think about, and not all of it good. It wasn't his fault – he was probably one of the most (annoyingly, but genuinely) helpful men I knew. But he'd shed a light on part of me that I was well past frustrated with.

Why did it bother me that it seemed as if Simon and I had been set up without my consent, but regarding my flat situation all I wanted was for someone to make every decision for me to absolve me of the risk of potentially messing things up? I was a hypocrite, and I knew it.

I liked Simon. I really, genuinely liked him. I didn't play nurse for just anyone. Or anyone, frankly. But now...now things were serious. Now things were scary, because I couldn't wait to see him again. Usually this heralded the end of my fledgling relationships; I knew that if I followed my usual habits then I was right on track to messing something up.

I didn't want to mess this up.

I wasn't working today, since I'd helped Rich last week on Tuesday so he gave me today off in exchange. Normally I revelled in having an unexpected day off. And yet two hours later, after washing away the rain in a hot shower, scarfing down no fewer than three cheese toasties in a row and watching someone on YouTube tell me all about how to make a vivarium (Liz was obsessed with them and I wanted to know why), I kind of wished I *was* at work. Behind the desk in the Plaza, waiting for Simon to come downstairs to chat to me or subtly make fun of the ridiculous complaints guests often fielded my way.

So when he messaged me at three in the afternoon my heart leapt into my mouth.

> Good morning! Would you like to have dinner with me tomorrow night?

I could only laugh.

> Me: Morning? You've slept in, even for you.
>
> Simon: I had something I very much needed to recover from ;)
>
> Me: Like telling Tom about me 'playing nurse'?
>
> Simon: I told him you brought me chicken noodle soup, damn it. He made his own conclusions.
>
> Me: Naturally. Do you feel better?
>
> Simon: Good as new. So, dinner?

I was tempted to ask Simon if he wanted to do tonight, instead. But I didn't want to rush things. I didn't want to pull a classic Courtney Miller and ruin everything before it had even begun.

> Me: Tomorrow sounds great. At seven? Though that's barely lunch time for you.
>
> Simon: Seven works for me. What's the lunch/dinner equivalent of brunch?
>
> Me: Hell if I know. See you tomorrow x

Simon followed up with a GIF of a goat riding a sheep.

Fuck me, I liked him. Maybe too much. So, even though it physically hurt me to do so, I turned off my phone, pulled out my laptop, and resolved to book in a few flat viewings before the day was up.

Chapter Twenty-Eight

SIMON

"Stop worrying," Kei complained, midway through me doing exactly that. Taking Courtney out for dinner was one thing, but inviting her to my *own* not-quite-open restaurant to try out the menu?

I was a fool. This was too much pressure.

"Why on god's green earth did I think her coming here was a good idea?" I complained, fretting over my reflection before checking the table settings for the fifth time. "We don't even have a bar top yet!"

"You don't believe in god," Kei replied, cool and calm and collected where I was a mess. He handed me a beer. "And you aren't the one cooking; I am. So what if there isn't a bar top yet? Unless you needed it for reasons that I really shouldn't be here fo—"

"Point taken!"

Ultimately I knew why I'd invited Courtney – who was due any minute now – to eat at my restaurant. It wasn't because Kei needed a guinea pig for his new miso chicken broth, and it wasn't because I didn't think there was anywhere else in

Glasgow good enough to spoil her at.

It was because I wanted Courtney to understand a little more about *me*. After she'd spent days looking after me, and after...well, what came after, I was desperate to connect even more with the amazing, bubbly, intelligent, caring woman who had somehow waltzed her way into my life by way of a stolen sausage roll.

That included showing her my hopes and dreams, even if I still wasn't sure how I was meant to go about truly following them.

Aside from the bar top the restaurant *was* looking good. Bamboo screens had been installed between the tables, converting each and every one of the tables lining the walls into comfortable booths with plush leather seating. Real bamboo grew in wooden troughs in front of the window and around the mirrored wall behind the bar, and the floor was a deep, lacquered mahogany to match the tables. I had the best selection of whisky known to man available for purchase, as well as a good mix of wines, beers and other spirits that I knew paired well with our menu.

The seventies funk guitar of Masayoshi Takanaka played quietly away in the background. Kei and I were still working out a decent rotational playlist to use week-to-week, but right now Takanaka was our mutual favourite.

I was happy with the place. It was deceptively expensively furnished, because in order to get my grandparents to approve of me building the place it *had* to be high-end, but it was simple and it was pretty and I was proud of all that Kei and I had achieved so far.

"Is that her?" Kei asked, when a taxi pulled up outside. He let out a low, appreciative whistle. "You never told me how hot she is. Does she have a sister?"

"Yes, but don't even go there," I warned, smoothing my hair back one final time before opening the door to let Courtney – wrapped in her new fawn coat that I would love forever – inside the warm and hopefully inviting atmosphere of *Seijin & Kei*.

Courtney let out a matching whistle to Kei's as she slid out of her jacket and surveyed her new surroundings. "I like it," she said. Simple and effective, but I believed every word. Courtney turned her megawatt crooked smile in my business partner's direction; it was satisfying to watch Kei practically take a step back from how dazzling she was. "You must be Kei," Courtney said, holding out her hand to shake his own and then laughing when Kei pulled her in for a hug, instead.

"Nice to finally fucking meet you," Kei said. "Simon hasn't stopped going on about you since he arrived in Glasgow." Courtney flushed, and I gave Kei the finger, which he responded with in kind. Then he headed into the kitchen before anything else could be said.

"He's charming," Courtney said, accepting a Peroni with lime – I'd learned she liked them over the course of our late-night texting sessions – when I offered her one. "How long have you known each other?"

"Long enough." I paused to consider it. "Four years, or thereabouts. We met just after I opened the bakery."

"I'd have thought you'd been friends since you were kids, to be honest."

"I don't have any real friends from pre-university." I hadn't meant to say it, because it was a fast track towards negative conversation territory, but Courtney had the grace not to look like she pitied me enormously. I indicated towards a window booth table: my favourite in the restaurant. During daylight hours it would be ideal for people-watching over a pile of steamed gyoza and perhaps even a sneaky Chu Hi. "Kei shouldn't be too long with the food," I said, once we'd settled into our seats. "He's been excited to try everything out on you all day."

"I do love exchanging the potential health of my stomach in exchange for free food."

"And good company, I hope?"

Courtney wrinkled her nose. "And good company."

I'd been worried that things would be weird between us. This was the first time we'd seen each other in person since we slept together, and I knew how awkward things could get after sex was added into the mix. Especially when that sex had been hours long and fucking mind-blowing. Especially with a woman I really, really liked.

Especially with Courtney.

"So this is the kind of place you *really* want to open?" Courtney pressed, when we were onto our second beers and the tantalising smell of spicy fried chicken filled the air. She relaxed against the booth to survey her surroundings in greater detail. "It's got a lovely vibe to it. And whatever Kei is cooking up in there smells *divine.*"

I ran a hand through my hair. "Sort of. Even this place is a little too...high-end. I want to open the kind of place that serves good, affordable, home-cooked food. Somewhere—"

"Somewhere young mums can take their only son to, and leave feeling happy and full?" Courtney guessed. I must have been smiling, because her face lit up as if I'd verbally answered *yes.* "It's a good dream, Simon. And attainable. I really wish you'd tell your grandparents where to stick it and then just...go for it."

"It's not as easy as all that, Courtney."

"I'm not saying it's easy. I'm saying *you* could do it."

"And you?" It came out defensive, so I coughed and tried again. "What about your hopes and dreams? You'll have to give Rich an answer soon about his – his job offer. What do you want to do about it?"

"I...hold that thought," Courtney said, quite obviously relieved when Kei sauntered over with a tray laden with food. "Kei, this looks amazing!"

And it did. "Karaage with spiced garlic honey, pickled radish and cucumber, and treacle teriyaki beef skewers," Kei announced, gently placing everything onto the table as he spoke. "After this you'll be trying a variation on my miso chicken and pork ramen. Enjoy."

Kei had used his service voice to inform us about the menu, something which Courtney clearly appreciated. It warmed my heart to think the two of them would easily become fast friends: I could see the two of them nursing a hangover after complaining about their worst customers over a bottle of expensive whisky already.

It was easy to forget how deftly Courtney avoided my question as we ate and drank and talked about menial things, such as the flats Courtney looked up in a price range she could never afford just so she could laugh at their poor taste in decoration, or the decision I had to make between sage green and jade green when I was getting the walls painted for the restaurant.

There was no mention of the fact we'd had sex, or if we were going to find ourselves in bed together again tonight, but then Courtney grazed her foot against my leg, and I bumped it with my own, and I practically felt the crackle of electricity between us.

"So I ran into Tom yesterday," Courtney said, when we were finished eating. "Quite literally *ran* into him. That's how I knew *he* seemed to know an awful lot about what we got up to at the weekend."

"Is...that a problem?" I asked, sick to my stomach for the second time in as many days that I'd confided in Tom about it at all. Was I not supposed to? Was this a secret? Was this—

"It's fine, Simon," Courtney laughed, eyes crinkling as she did so. "Your face is so transparent, did you know that? How have you gotten this far in the world of finance with such a bad poker face?"

"The key is to not care even one iota about what you're doing, then your face on the job all day, every day is a poker face."

"Sounds like a wonderful way to live your life."

I felt the needling there, again, like earlier. Courtney was being gentle about it but I could see the steel in her eyes. I *knew* what I wanted, after all, and she knew that I knew that. I had the money, I had the power, and I had the know-how to see it through.

But whether I had the guts was another thing entirely.

"It's complicated with my grandparents," I said, addressing the elephant in the room. "I told you that much already. I don't want to disappoint them, but I know that I'm currently trapped by them. It's just..."

"Complicated." Courtney reached out for my hand, brushing her fingertips over my knuckles, and all such difficult talk evaporated. "Do you...want to come back to my place tonight? Becca's at Peter's and—"

"Yes. Absolutely. Let's go." I rushed to my feet and pulled Courtney up with me, her bemusement transforming into joy as I grabbed her coat and bundled her into it. "We're off, Kei! Thanks for the food!"

"And what about the dishes?!" he cried, popping his head around the kitchen door.

I waved him off. "Tomorrow. I'll do it tomorrow."

For I could indeed do the dishes tomorrow, and ask Courtney about her dreams another day.

Tonight was not for talking.

Chapter Twenty-Nine

COURTNEY

A WEEK HAD PASSED SINCE SIMON and I first slept together. One week, and other than the immediate night afterwards we had spent every night since then with him either sleeping over at mine or me crashing out in his hotel room after work. It was so easy to get swept up in the joy of me and him, him and me, that all else in my life seemed very much to have fallen to the wayside.

I was making mistakes at work. Guests were annoying me more than usual. I was snappier with the owners of misbehaving dogs, and less forgiving when said dogs peed all over my shoes. Because they were expensive, quality shoes that Simon had bought me, and were therefore precious.

But then I realised I was making my entire life be about a man, and it all came crashing down. *This* was how I ruined things. This was how I got bored. So when Rich asked me if I was coming over that Monday night – having ignored our usual weekly ritual for almost a month now – I, perhaps too eagerly, said yes.

"You can't shout at Mrs Campbell like that, Court," Rich chastised, when we'd finished eating Indian takeaway and had resorted to watching silly dating shows on YouTube. Our favourite right now was *The Button*. "I know she's annoying as hell but come on. She's a good customer."

I groaned. "Can we not talk about work? I know I messed up. *Have been messing up*, present tense. I'm trying to sort it out, okay?"

My phone buzzed. It was almost definitely Simon. I ignored it. I could feel a bad, all-consuming mania rapidly creeping up on me so, even though I didn't like the idea of doing it, I ignored it.

Rich, however, noticed me ignoring it. "Is that – what's his name?" he asked, trying his best to sound like he didn't care even though we both knew he did. "Simon Saint?" He said his name like it was the name of a kids' TV presenter.

"Probably." I laser-focused on the TV.

"You aren't going to answer it?"

"Doing that when we're having fun together would be rude. You always tell me off for being on my phone when I'm with people."

"And yet you never listen." Rich laughed easily, and I felt myself relax a little. He knew exactly what to do when my mood was flipping. He never judged. He simply stayed there and let me be. But then he fidgeted with the bowl of popcorn he had in his lap. "So...how's it going with him?"

"We're just having some fun," I said, on reflex. "He's probably not going to be in Glasgow much longer." It wasn't a fair thing to say, but Simon had made it abundantly clear that he couldn't, or didn't want to, talk to his grandparents about what he really wanted. If I was good at anything I was good at identifying a pattern of bad behaviour in someone.

And Simon had a terrible pattern of letting his grandparents walk all over him.

I had been naïve to think that my mere presence in his life would change that. God, London felt like forever ago. How had everything been so easy back then? Or, rather, why had things suddenly become so hard?

I knew why. It was all in my head.

In my head, where I couldn't escape from it.

"Ah, yes," Rich said, putting down the popcorn as if what he was about to say demanded no snacks to be present. "The Courtney Miller version of fun! Where you experience an existential crisis and then refuse to speak to anyone for months afterwards because you don't want to face the fact you were wrong about someone!"

"What the fuck, Rich?!" I cried, turning to face him with a sick feeling in my stomach. "That's *so* uncalled for."

"You're the one wearing that same expression on your face that you always wear when you realise you got in too deep with someone, too fast." He held his hands up in a placating gesture. "I'm just trying to help you out with some tough love."

And he was. He really was. Rich didn't have a cruel bone in his body. Jealous and competitive on occasion, yes, but never cruel. All at once the tension left me, and I banged my head against the back of the couch several times. "He isn't...it isn't like that. Not really."

"And yet here you are, over-thinking something that should be simple. If you're with the right person."

"Is that always true, though? I've been thinking a lot about you, too. It's part of the reason this is all so hard." That last part I admitted so casually that I almost put a hand over my mouth in surprise; I'd been doing so well until now to not let on that Rich's confession had been bothering me, damn it.

To my shame, Rich seemed genuinely surprised by my statement. He looked away awkwardly. "I didn't really think...well. You seemed so wrapped up in this guy that I figured you were hoping I'd somehow forget I ever asked you to...ugh. You know."

I rolled my eyes harder than I'd ever rolled them up until

this point. An ultra-rare eye roll. "You should know me better than that by now. I over-think everything. I just don't always make that obvious to everyone else."

"Because heaven forbid they know what you're thinking!" Rich pretended to swoon, realistically enough that I began to laugh when it became clear he expected me to catch him before he fell off the couch.

I let him fall off the couch.

"*Rude*," he complained, landing with a thump on the floor. Rich pinched at my leggings until I kicked him in the chest. But then that pinching turned to gentle touches, sending a shock of pins and needles up my calf. "I don't like seeing you worry so much over something that isn't supposed to be serious," he murmured, looking at his hand touching my leg instead of at my face. "If Simon is supposed to be fun why does it feel like you're on the verge of a breakdown?"

Because it isn't just fun, it's serious, I wanted to say. *Because I can see myself actually being happy with him, and wanting to be better for him, and for me, and that's fucking terrifying.*

Instead I said, "You know I can't help what triggers a manic or low episode. For all we know it was the fact I finally walked in on Sam and the security guy getting it on in the supply cupboard that's setting me off."

"Liar. You loved that."

"You're right. I admit it. And now I have blackmail material against them."

"Definitely something a normal person relishes in." Rich got up to sit on the couch, closer to me this time. I didn't mind; rather, having Rich there was comforting. Usually when I was two seconds away from disappearing into my own world for a month the last thing I wanted was anyone touching me, but Rich was always an exception.

Then he stroked my face, and his gaze fluttered down to my lips beneath those damnable lashes of his, and he kissed me a microsecond before I knew he was going to kiss me.

We'd kissed before. Hell, Rich and I were kissing two weeks before I met Simon, when we got drunk off a box of cheap wine and watched all three *Lord of the Rings* extended edition films in one day.

But this was different. Wasn't it?

I kissed Rich back. On instinct, and because it felt nice, and because I knew him and trusted him and loved him, I kissed him back. His face was smooth and shaven, his lips soft and tasting of maple vanilla chapstick – his favourite. The way they always tasted. There was no fumbling, no working out what worked, because we both *knew* what worked. Rich wound his hand through my hair, urging me closer, and for a moment I eagerly reciprocated. But then—

Simon.

I remembered Simon, over and over again. Simon with his days of sickness-induced stubble. Simon who wasn't gentle. Simon who watched me get off to the thought of him and pushed me against the wall and fucked me senseless. Though we said we were keeping things casual, and Simon even knew about Rich's feelings for me, precisely none of what was going on between us *felt* casual. Even if the thought of being serious with someone – of being my genuine self with someone and having them accept me *and* challenge me – was the reason I was spiralling, it was something I knew I longed for.

I pushed Rich away. Gently, but firmly. The disappointment was plain as day on his face.

Heart throbbing I leapt to my feet. "I'm gonna—"

"Court—"

"No, it's fine," I bit out, because Rich hadn't done anything wrong. So why couldn't I look at him? I grabbed my coat – the lovely one Simon bought me that had become my most prized possession – and ran for the door.

Rich knew better than to run after me. Through the rain-soaked streets I jogged home, even though it was a good forty-minute journey back. But I was too buzzing in a sickening way to get a taxi, not to mention too poor to afford one. I knew with horrible certainty that I wasn't going to sleep well tonight, if at all.

I left Simon's earlier text ignored.

Chapter Thirty

SIMON

"It'll be fine, Simon. Don't be a coward."

"I'm not a coward," I muttered, nonetheless dithering in front of the door to the Blake Dog Day Care alongside Tom and Liz. "I just don't want to bother Courtney at work. Well, her other work."

Liz rolled her eyes in a long-suffering fashion. "We are picking Ludo up, and you are with us, and you are *not* standing out here like an idiot in the rain whilst we do so. What's wrong with popping in to say hi?"

"Nothing. Fine, let's go."

'Nothing' wasn't strictly true, but I couldn't pinpoint what was wrong, either. Technically nothing *was* wrong. I just had a feeling.

A bad feeling.

After the most amazing week where Courtney and I spent every night together, now I was on day four of her barely communicating with me and telling me she was too exhausted after work to hang out. I wasn't one to be resentful because she was busy – Courtney was looking for a flat, after all, and had her job situation to mull over (not to mention Rich's *other* offer) – but something didn't feel right. Even when she was working in the Plaza she kept our conversations deliberately short and sweet. Still lovely, still fun, and the way Courtney looked at me was reassurance that she still very much enjoyed my company, but it was clear her mind was elsewhere.

Courtney Miller was spiralling into a manic period, and I had no idea what precisely had set it off, nor if that 'something' was me. I wanted to help her, and badly.

But would she let me?

When we entered the day care I was overwhelmed by the smell of wet dog, bleach, and the faint scent of urine. That was to be expected in a place that looked after dozens of dogs – as was the cacophony of barking that greeted us when we made our way over to the hall where the dogs played for most of the day.

"Rich, hello!" Tom hollered over the canine crowd, Liz and I close in tow. Rich beamed at them but the smile quickly slid off his face when he spotted me.

"...hi," he said, guarded as a nervous pit bull.

"Is that Tom and Liz?!" Courtney yelled from a tiny office. She popped her head around the door frame and caught my eyes, which went wide with obvious surprise. "Simon? I wasn't expecting to see you here."

"We were driving him over to his restaurant so figured he could deal with us picking Ludo up first," Tom explained, allowing said dog to crush him in a bear hug.

When Courtney exited the office she was holding a black-and-tan puppy. She came over to Rich's side to pass over the tiny dog, who cooed at the creature and let it lick his nose.

"A bit early to get a dog, isn't it?" I joked, trying to fit myself into this space in which I clearly did not belong. "You don't even have a flat yet." Rich and Courtney looked like damn newlyweds with a puppy for a baby, huddled together to lavish it with all their love and attention.

To my relief, though, Courtney sniggered. "We're helping out a friend for a few days; their husky is recovering from getting the snip." She mimicked the motion of scissors cutting as she spoke.

"She is absolutely gorgeous," Liz said, coming over to join the puppy love-in. The dog yipped happily. "She's barely bigger than Jerry!"

"Oh, she'll get big." Rich held up one of the puppy's legs. "Rita here has *massive* paws. And look at her ears!"

"What breed is she?"

"A mutt. But she must have some big dogs in her family tree."

Courtney, Rich, Liz and even Tom spoke between the four of them regarding Rita the puppy for a minute, before moving on to discuss how Ludo had been. At least Ludo hadn't abandoned me, choosing to pad over to sit beneath my hand so I'd scratch his ears.

"Thanks, buddy," I whispered to him. But Courtney must have noticed, because a moment later she bounded over with the energy of a dog herself to say hello. Her hair was a flyaway mess, and her clothes were stained to shit, but I'd never seen her so happy.

"So you've found my second place of work," she said, offering me a luminous smile. "Glamorous, right?"

"The most glamorous of all. How do you have the energy to go from *this* to the Plaza all in a day?"

She shrugged. "Because I have to."

"Except you don't have to. Not anymore."

"True..." Courtney raised a careful eyebrow. "How are you? Spoken to your grandparents yet?"

I hated that our conversations kept circling back to this standstill we had about where our lives were going. It was like we were both waiting for the other one to make a move first. Instead we were paralysed exactly where we were.

Courtney could tell from my face what my answer was. "Forget I said anything," she mumbled, grazing my hand for the barest second. Then she turned her head to yell at Liz, "Did you get that invite to Cornstar Martini for a big group night out tomorrow?"

Liz popped up her head from Rita-the-puppy like an owl. "I did! Do you have any idea what it's all about?"

"Not a fucking clue."

"Even Daichi was invited," Tom added, "which he is positively buzzing about." Then, "Oh, Simon, you're invited too."

"Says who?" Rich asked, betraying his dismay before he could stop himself. "I thought he didn't know the friend group." Going by his indignation I inferred that he was also going on this night out.

Tom chose to ignore the tone of Rich's comment. "Harriet insisted. Clearly she took a liking to my top-tier best friend."

Liz elbowed him in the ribs. "I thought that's what you said when she invited Daichi?"

"That's because both of my best friends are top-tier."

"Did you manage to get the night off, Courtney?" Liz asked between scratches of Rita's ears.

"I did, yeah." Courtney caught my eye and offered me a secret, mischievous grin. "Had to phone in my blackmail chip against Sam and the security guy to get her to cover for me, but I'm sure it'll be worth it."

I'd been feeling horrendously left out of the group's conversation – like I was back in primary school after I'd moved in with my grandparents and couldn't make heads nor tails of what the other kids did for fun – but in that moment Courtney pulled me right into her circle once more. We'd been gossiping about Sam for weeks now.

I leaned down to whisper in her ear. "I wouldn't mind giving Sam an opportunity to gather appropriate blackmail against *you* for a similar sin."

"*Simon,*" she gasped, delighted and scandalised in equal measure. "That would be—"

I kissed her. High off our little joke, and fuelled by jealousy at how easily Rich and Courtney fit in with Liz and Tom and all their friends, like they were meant to be together, I kissed her. Courtney hesitated for the barest fraction of a second and I thought my heart would bottom into my stomach. But then she reciprocated, and everything was all right with the world once more.

Courtney's fingers gripped into the fabric of my coat sleeves when I wound my arms around her, pulling her closer to my chest, tilting her chin up and deepening the kiss. Her lips were chapped but neither of us cared, mashing ourselves together with reckless aplomb.

We had an audience, and this was inappropriate. But I couldn't stop myself; I wanted to kiss Courtney forever. I wanted to tell her to ditch work and whisk her away to London once more, where nobody could interfere with us.

Except they could. My grandparents were there, and Courtney's mother, and those problems wouldn't magically disappear if we went to London.

Australia, then. Except Courtney had an ex there.

Well, there was still the rest of the world.

When we pulled apart, both of us breathless and surprised, for one precious moment all Courtney focused on was me. Her lips quirked into a smile; her hands tightened on my sleeves. Kissing her had been the right move, audience be damned – I'd finally broken through Courtney's mania to remind her that I was here, and I wanted her, and she wanted me.

But then she remembered where we were, tore her gaze

away, and hopped out of reach with scarlet-stained cheeks. "I-I need to finish up here, otherwise I'll be late for work," she stammered, running off to the day care office in an obvious sign of dismissal. Several feet away stood Rich, glaring at me whilst he squeezed the living daylights out of a tattered football. Thank god he seemed to have put Rita down, else I feared the puppy would have been eviscerated. A pug whined at his feet until he threw the ball.

"Come on, Casanova," Liz urged, not-so-gently tugging on my elbow to direct me out of the hall. Once we were outside she slapped my chest in outrage. It actually hurt, she was so angry. "Not cool!"

I held up my hands. "What did I do?"

"You know exactly what you did, and why! Aren't you a grown man?"

"Cut him some slack," Tom said, allowing Ludo to pull him over to the car. "People are allowed to get jealous, Liz."

"Yeah, but you aren't supposed to *act* on it and put the person you like in an awkward position. *You* should know that, Professor Henderson."

"Ooh, it's been a while since I've heard that. Scold me more."

It looked like Liz was going to shout at Tom, but then her serious expression crumbled and she burst into fits of laughter. "That *so* isn't appropriate in front of Simon."

"The two of you are almost literally sickening," I despaired, as we got into the car. I huffed out a breath. "Why can't *I* have that? The two of you go all-out PDA almost the moment you step foot outside."

Tom glanced at me in the rear-view mirror as he revved up the engine. "Not *every* time. And I'll relent and say Liz has a point. That wasn't the time nor place to kiss Courtney, and you know it. I can tell from your face that you know it."

"I do, okay? But what else can I do to maintain her attention when she's obviously spiralling? I just..."

"Want to help her, and be there for her, and all that jazz," Liz finished for me. "I get that. But my god are you impatient, Si. Have you never thought that Courtney might just need some *time*?"

"Did *he* give you time to mull over things without meddling?" I fired back, pointing at Tom.

He winced. "Low blow."

"Each situation is individual," Liz said, "and need I remind you that Tom and I almost didn't get back together after I found out everything he did? And I was fucking with him, too. Has Courtney been messing you around?"

"No..."

"Then give her time, and space, and trust that if you're meant to be together then she'll reach that conclusion without you forcing your feelings on her."

It was the soundest advice I'd ever heard. But I could feel it in my gut that it would be the hardest advice in the world for me to follow. Give Courtney time and space so she could over-think us, and widen the distance between us until it was a chasm I could never cross? When Richard Blake was right there, on the other side of that chasm, with Courtney?

Following Liz's advice seemed damn near impossible.

Chapter Thirty-One

COURTNEY

I was fairly certain Becca did not need me, Peter *and* Ray to help her set up whatever was being set up at Cornstar Martini for our group night out. Since when did group nights out need this much organisation, anyway? And why were we having said night out at Becca's place of work? I'd asked these questions the moment I arrived at the swanky venue but my pleas had fallen on deaf ears.

"Can I *please* know what this is all about?" I begged, for the third time. Ray – Peter's flatmate (or soon-to-be-ex-flatmate, I guess) – handed me a freshly opened bottle of prosecco to continue filling up glasses to hand out to folk when they arrived. "Someone must have turned thirty or something, right? Who? If *I* don't know them then why am I here?"

Ray sniggered into his hand. "It'll be so obvious once everyone gets here. I swear it. So have some patience."

"Says the most impatient person I've ever known," Peter said from behind the bar. Cornstar Martini had two bars, one big and one small, and the venue had graciously allowed Becca to commandeer the smaller one and its attached function room for...whatever we were organising.

Peter was helping Becca cut and organise lemons, limes and orange slices into containers in a sickeningly coordinated fashion. He bumped his girlfriend's hip when they came within close enough proximity to each other; Becca responded by giggling and kissing him softly. Quite frankly I had never seen her so happy. So...loose. Peter was the best thing to have ever happened to Bex, and it was good they were moving in together.

I just wish it didn't hurt so much to be left alone.

"Courtney? Court? Earth to – oh for god's sake. Courtney, your phone!" Becca cried, good-natured but exasperated, nimbly reaching over the bar to extricate said device from where it was buzzing incessantly from inside my bag. She handed it to me. "Will you *please* answer it? It's been ringing all bloody day!"

"I don't want to." I was still kind of ignoring Simon. Well, not ignoring him *per se*, but I was only responding to one out of every three texts he sent me. It was Mum and Ailish I was ignoring, because they were trying to arrange coming up to Glasgow to see me, and I didn't have the bandwidth for it.

And Rich. Of course I was avoiding Rich.

I'd put on a good show at work that I was fine because that's what I always did, but outside of working hours I was falling apart. And of course Simon had chosen *this week* to visit the dog day care and witness with his own eyes the way Rich and I so easily bantered – not just with each other but with Liz and Tom. I was no fool; I knew how that must have looked to him.

And it hurt to think it was hurting him. Simon Saint was probably the most mature man I'd ever met, so I knew he'd never say anything. I was allowed to have male friends, after all. He wasn't the type of guy to feel jealous or threatened by such a thing. The difference here was that Simon knew Rich had deeper feelings for me, and had told me about them, which meant that Rich was no longer simply my best friend but someone Simon really was in direct competition with for my affections.

And I simply couldn't take it. I didn't want to hurt either of them, and I didn't want to hurt myself. But that didn't mean I actually knew what I wanted to do – or what I *wanted*, full stop.

So I was ignoring them like a silly, immature child.

"You can't just shut out the world every time you need a break," Becca chastised. She unlocked my phone, because she knew my password. "Not when you're...oh. Shit." I knew from her face what that meant, and also became horribly aware in that moment that Becca had been right that I couldn't afford to ignore my phone. I was waiting on an important call, after all: my third and final call to move from the wait list regarding an ADHD diagnosis to actually getting seen.

I took my phone from her and saw what I now already knew. I'd missed it.

Bex came around the bar to squeeze my hand. I barely even felt her touch. "I'm so sorry, Court. We can work this out."

"What's going on?" I couldn't tell if it was Ray or Peter talking; my head was full of dull buzzing. I'd missed it. I'd fucking missed it – this call that was so important to me, this call that I'd been waiting on for fucking years – all because of the damn condition I'd forced myself to get on the wait list *for*.

What was I supposed to do now? Where did I go from here? Going to the bottom of the list *again* was unfathomable to me. But I couldn't keep going the way that I was. With the way I currently was...

I didn't see a future. I only saw failure.

Becca must have explained what had gone on, which was fine because Peter and Ray already knew. Ray had even been in touch recently to send me articles about ADHD he thought I might be interested in, though I hadn't carved out a single spare ten minutes to read any of them. Another thing to blame on my own damn stupid self.

Ray clucked his tongue. "It isn't your fault, Court. I did the same thing."

"I thought you went private?" Becca asked, confused. "I thought—"

"Oh, Mum and Dad paid for me to go private *after* I had a mental breakdown regarding the wait list. It was either that or a psych ward." Ray shrugged as if this horrific piece of information was no big deal; going by the way Peter most definitely did not react I inferred that this was exactly the way Ray wanted people to handle his truth bomb.

"And you're..." I fished for the right words through the mess of my head. "How are you doing?"

"The meds really help," Ray said, eyes shining in a familiar maniacal way but without the edge of desperation I'd been seeing in myself more and more frequently, "but so does the therapy. If you can get the money together you should really consider going private. And by 'really consider' I mean that if it's a choice between your actual will to live and taking out a credit card then unfortunately the credit card is the only way to go. Or your parents, if they have the money."

I appreciated Ray's candour. So many people tried to skirt around my issues, or dismiss them, or try to make them out like everyone 'just had bad days sometimes', but he and I both knew better.

There was just one problem: I had no money. Okay, two: even if I was speaking to my mother she didn't believe there was anything wrong with me except being lazy and prone to over-drinking. She would never give me the money I'd need for private healthcare.

"Seems like folk are starting to arrive," Peter said, taking over the job of pouring prosecco into the last five glasses once it became clear that both Ray and I had abandoned our duties.

Becca squeezed my arm and offered me my most favourite smile. "We'll talk later, okay? You need my help, and I'm here for you. Don't spiral and cut me out or I'll cut *you*."

God, I loved her. Especially now, when I felt like I couldn't talk to Rich about anything important, having Rebecca Luton by my side was everything. But I couldn't hold her to my side forever. She couldn't be the person I leaned on every time I was falling apart. I needed...I needed...

I didn't know. I wasn't enough on my own; I'd never been.

The first few people to arrive were unfamiliar faces. Given what I knew about Harriet and Chloë, they were unlikely to show up exactly on time. I picked up a glass of prosecco and fiddled with it in my hands, though I didn't take a single sip; I knew I wasn't in the head space to drink, so in an act of uncharacteristic maturity I planned to fully avoid it for the night.

A few minutes later Harriet showed up with a few friends I recognised from social media as belonging to her old musical theatre group, along with, of course, her girlfriend. Everyone was dressed just about as eclectically as I imagined a group of musical theatre nerds could dress. For a moment I looked for Rich so we could laugh about it, but then I remembered he wasn't here yet and that I wasn't speaking to him outside of work. Then, finally, Liz, Tom, Simon, and a man I knew to be Tom's 'work wife', Daichi Ito, showed up.

Instead of going over to greet them, I melted into the background and pretended like I wasn't there, for barely a minute after they entered the bar Rich also showed up. He was wearing a faded blue fitted jumper that I knew from experience was soft as sin, paired with his favourite pair of dark jeans, his even more favourite pair of Doc Martens, and his hair in its usual messy scrawl across his forehead. It was a look I'd seen on him a million times. One that worked for him – that I'd literally told him was super cute. After that Rich had started wearing the ensemble every two weeks, at least.

Shit, I was not ready for this. Not at all.

I knew that if I went to speak to Rich first then Simon would take it personally. He wouldn't mean to, but he would. But the same didn't necessarily have to hold true about the opposite way around, since I'd told Rich that Simon was just fun to me.

The comment burned like acid in the back of my throat, even now. It had been a shitty thing to say then, and it was a shitty thing to even consider now.

I risked a glance in Simon's direction. He was drawing attention from all angles thanks to his excellent ensemble of a pale pink – *pink* – Henley, high-waisted charcoal grey trousers, leather boots, and that amazing trench coat he'd worn down in London. Simon had rough-styled his hair so it had more texture than usual; you could see the grey, but it added to the look. Did the guy even *know* how to dress poorly? I guess one could objectively see that Tom Henderson was the more handsome of the two – if this was a video game his stats would be higher overall – but Simon was a *really* snappy dresser. He honest-to-god look like he'd just walked off the pages of a runway magazine, like Ailish had thought. And I knew he smelled amazing, too, like something wintry and spicy and tantalising that I'd never quite been able to place.

"Why am I so obsessed with clothes today?" I asked my own reflection in the nearest window. But I knew I wasn't interested in the clothes so much as I was about the men; it was simply easier to focus on what Richard Blake and Simon Saint were wearing instead of anything else of even vague importance.

But Simon *held* himself so well, too. So elegantly. So effortlessly. I couldn't stop stealing glances of him. His relaxed posture belied the over-thinker I now knew him to be, hair-swiping nervous tic notwithstanding. I wondered if that had been drummed into him by his grandparents when he moved down to London to live with them. God, here I was, cowering in the corner afraid to face up to a situation I had put myself in, when Simon had been forced to spend his entire life moulding himself into someone he wasn't just to please the only family he had. He was doing a much better job than I was at showing his appreciation for being included in this night out. What's more: he'd been excited that we were both going to the same event. That much had been obvious at the day care.

I really, really didn't want to face Rich right now, even though I could see he was looking for me through the rapidly-growing crowd. Not when he was drinking and there was an audience and I still had no idea what to do or say to him. Our kiss was a chasm between us, heavy and oppressive.

I walked over to Simon with renewed purpose.

His face lit up when he saw me, and for a moment I forgot how terrible I felt. Simon's gaze scanned me from head to toe. "You look beautiful, Courtney," he said, bending low to kiss me on the cheek. My face flushed red, and I revelled in the fire that subsequently spread across Simon's cheeks.

"You, as usual, look far too fancy to be here, and seem to have caused most every guy, gal and non-binary pal in the room to fall for you," I replied, offering Simon a sly grin when he pretended to be scandalised. "Does anyone have any idea why we're here?" I directed the question at Liz, but it was Tom who provided an answer.

"No, but there are only so many objectively realistic options."

I gave him the finger. "Stop talking like a scientist and give it to me straight."

Daichi (whom I'd actually met once when he and his baby girl, Lily, came to pick up Ludo along with Tom) positively tittered. "Oh, things like this are always so exciting. The wait for the announcement – the not knowing – is part of the excitement!"

"I think we may be in for something very romantic," Simon murmured into my ear, pushing a strand of hair back as he did so. Aside from our impromptu kiss at the day care I'd avoided physical contact with Simon at all costs. Because when he was this close – when we were in each other's very small sphere of influence – I forgot all about the world outside. I forgot Rich, and my family, and my financial issues, and the damned missed call about my ADHD appointment.

But I couldn't keep cutting out the world. I was miserable

because of it.

"I don't think it will take long to find out what's going on," Liz said, before adding, "Do you want something stronger than prosecco, Court? I was thinking gin."

I shook my head. "I'm not drinking, actually."

Simon made to say something, but then Harry's voice cut over us all. "I'm sure you're wondering why you're here," she said, her smooth, lovely voice practised and loud from all her years in musical theatre. She addressed the crowd at large: "Well, I've never been one to keep people waiting."

Harriet's friends laughed, and Chloë yelled back at her girlfriend, "You're late for almost everything!"

Harry's eyes glittered. "I think for this event, at least, I can get to the point exactly on time." This time she directed her speech at her girlfriend. "Chloë. Four years ago I met you. Four years, and it took me six stupidly long months to ask you out. I was nervous. I thought for sure that the glorious – nay, bombshell – woman with the god-awful-atrocious singing voice would turn me down in a second. Turned out those six months had been the biggest waste of my life, because you jumped at the chance to go out with me. *Me.* So I vowed to never wait for anything after that. Eighteen months later we were living together – which we all know is, like, eight years in lesbian time." Everyone laughed once more. Of course they did. It was hilarious. "I guess by those standards, Liz beat us to the punch by living with her boyfriend when she was still convinced she hated him." An even bigger laugh. Beside me Tom kissed Liz's forehead so tenderly I actually thought I was going to cry. "But in any case," Harriet continued, "the last two years of living with you have been the happiest of my life. And I don't want that to end."

I worked out maybe two seconds into Harriet's speech what was about to happen and it was clear everyone else in the room did, too. Chloë, however, had been working on a blissfully oblivious, delayed cycle. But she realised the truth now. Her hand flew to her mouth, realisation hitting her like a ton of bricks.

Out of the corner of my eye I saw Rich was watching me instead of Harriet and Chloë, face unreadable. By contrast Simon stood on my left, completely engrossed in the romantic speech being laid before us. His bright eyes and quivering upper lip told me he was the kind of guy who cried at the sob stories on *X Factor* back in the day. It was endearing in a way I couldn't quite describe.

"Chloë," Harry said, when a hush fell over the crowd, "marry me. Just...marry me. I don't care what that looks like; I just want to see a ring on your finger and be able to tell everyone that you're my entire life."

We all knew what Chloë was going to say. We knew it, but still we waited with bated breath.

She sucked in a sob. "Yes!"

Chapter Thirty-Two

SIMON

The room erupted into euphoric applause.

The smaller function room of Cornstar Martini was filled wall-to-wall with happy, excited, laughing, crying people, all come together to witness and celebrate one thing and one thing only. God, Cornstar Martini. It was a great name for a vegetarian pizza and cocktail bar; as I absorbed the revelry around me I grew mad I'd never thought of it myself.

I'd had a feeling an engagement was on the cards tonight. After all, if it wasn't anybody's birthday than what was left but a proposal? The only question I still had was: why had I been invited, too? I only knew Harriet and Chloë through Tom and Liz, and not exactly well. Maybe they simply wanted to extend the invite because I'd come to Chloë's thirtieth birthday and I was still in Glasgow.

In any case, I was always one to celebrate romance.

"Well," Daichi said, clapping his hands together in earnest, "I'm glad I could be here to witness this! Was that not just *beautiful*? I hope someone recorded it so I can show it to May! Did you record it, Tom? Liz?"

"I'm sure someone will have recorded it," Tom said, handing Daichi a glass of prosecco in order to keep him quiet. Then he grabbed Liz's hand and pulled her along to the bar. "I'm thinking gin."

She grinned. "A man after my own heart."

"I'm just going to call May and tell her all about this!" Daichi said, giving me a nod to ensure I was fine with him abandoning me before heading out the door. He was a lovely man – I could see why he was Tom's work wife – but my god was he the epitome of an extrovert. I felt exhausted after having spent the last two hours in his company. How did Tom do it?

Regardless, that left me and Courtney alone.

My breath caught in my throat; suddenly I had no idea what to say to her. Why was I so nervous? Courtney had clearly been happy to see me, though it hadn't escaped my notice that it had taken her almost twenty minutes to come over and say hello. I don't think *she* had noticed that I was aware she was already here, skulking at the edge of the room as if Courtney had forgotten that the knee-length, backless satin dress she'd bought when we were in London made her quite literally impossible not to notice.

It was evident that Courtney was avoiding Rich, too, who had resigned himself to drinking at the bar with Becca and Peter. My brain was working overtime trying to conclude what had transpired between them for Courtney to avoid him so. They'd seemed a perfect pair when I'd dropped in at the day care, after all. Just what had happened between them?

It seemed serious.

I coughed softly. "Courtney," I began, "I–"

"Oh my God, Simon, I'm so glad you could make it!" Harriet exclaimed, dragging a love-drunk Chloë along with her. "I had something I wanted to ask you. Well, both of us."

I could only laugh; it wouldn't do to be annoyed that they'd interrupted me when in truth I'd had no idea what I was going to say to Courtney in the first place. "Ask me anything. That was a beautiful speech, Harriet. And congratulations."

She beamed at me. "Thanks. So...we know your restaurant is due to open soon, and Courtney and Liz haven't stopped gushing over how lovely it is."

I glanced at Courtney, who flushed pink beneath my gaze. "So you were complimenting me behind my back?"

"Be glad I wasn't bitching about you, instead," Courtney replied without missing a beat.

We returned our attention to Harriet and Chloë, who were waiting (im)patiently to ask their question. "So what do you need, ladies?" I asked, inclining my head politely.

It was Chloë who answered. "Well we were wondering...if it was at all possible – and you can say no, of course – but would it be possible to have an engagement party in your restaurant? Like, before you officially open?"

I pretended to consider it for a moment. In reality this was a great opportunity: I'd been planning to do a soft launch the week before opening, anyway, with the intention of inviting Joe and Rob Cooke to review the place. Given the fact they were also here to witness Harriet's proposal, I doubted she'd mind very much if they were at her engagement party. "Of course," I said, smiling broadly. "Anything you need, I'm happy to provide."

Harriet and Chloë squealed and jumped on me with obvious glee. "Thank you, thank you, *thank you*," Chloë cried. "I love Japanese food. Mum hates it, but she's a bitch so who cares?"

Courtney ugly snorted into her hand at the comment. After several more thank yous Harriet and Chloë retreated back into their crowd of adoring friends.

Once more leaving me and Courtney alone.

"Everyone here is completely and utterly bonkers," I said a long, drawn-out minute later, for lack of anything else to say.

"They're practically bouncing off the walls."

"That's what happens when you put musical theatre nerds together," Courtney chuckled. She placed her untouched glass of prosecco on the table next to us and turned to face me. The coloured lights danced across her skin, alluring and inviting. "That was really nice of you."

"What? Offering the restaurant?" I put a hand up to run it through my hair, but then remembered it would ruin the way I'd meticulously styled it. I dropped it impotently to my side. "It's the least I can do."

Courtney watched the movement with knowing eyes – like she was aware of all my quirks and what they meant. My heart hurt at the thought. "What will your grandparents say about an unofficial launch, though?" she asked, and that hurt stung for another reason entirely. "I figured they'd want to have some input as to how you use the restaurant. Doesn't the money for setting up the place come from their company?"

A pause. We were skirting dangerous, dangerous territory. I didn't want to talk about my grandparents and money and career aspirations *again*. Not now. But if not now then...when? Courtney and I couldn't keep having these circular discussions. I could see plain as day that they were already driving us apart. "No, the money used to set up *Seijin & Kei* came directly from my own savings. But in order to get time off approved to set it up I had to design the restaurant with my grandparents' tastes in mind. For the business plan, at the very least."

"Oh."

"Oh?" I parroted back, feeling a frown furrow my brow. Courtney's expression was unreadable. "What do you mean, *oh*?"

She avoided my eyes. "I was just thinking...it feels like everything you've done you've almost done behind their backs. Are you that afraid of them? Surely they can see that this is what you want to do, Simon. I know it's scary but—"

"Can we not talk about them *right* this second?" I replied, rubbing my forehead. Having a few gin and tonics back at Tom's before getting here was making my brain fuzzy. I didn't want to say the wrong thing, even though I knew it was almost certain that I probably would. I took Courtney's hand in mine before I could think better of it, gratified when she let me. "Can't we just celebrate? In any case, I was thinking I might travel for a bit after opening the restaurant."

Courtney's hand tensed in mine. "Travel?"

It was now or never to field my spontaneous, hopefully romantic idea to the woman I was wild about. I took Courtney's other hand and squeezed them both, keeping her tethered to me, begging for her to say yes to my question. "I've been working for so long without a break," I explained. Which was true, but not the reason I wanted to leave. "It's been a long time since I've been able to see the world for what it is, instead of because of a business trip." Also true. Also not the reason. "*You've* been working too long without a break, too."

That was also, most definitely, true.

"...me?" Courtney echoed. I could practically see the cogs in her brain processing what I was saying – what I meant.

I pulled her towards me in earnest desperation, until our hands were trapped between our bodies. When Courtney looked up at me I bowed my forehead to hers. "Travel with me. It will save you from having to think through Rich's offer. I know it's been hard for you, because you don't know what to do. The two of us travelling together—"

Courtney yanked away from my touch. "What do you mean it would save me from making a decision? You don't trust me to do what's right by myself? What are you trying to say to me, Simon?"

"No, that isn't what I meant. I—"

"I don't need saving," she spat out, disgusted. "I *need* to be able to make tough decisions, not run away from them."

"You know that's not what I meant, Courtney. You know

that. I just wanted—"

"*You* wanted to run away, but you don't want to do it alone. And you think I'll let you sweep me off my feet because the decisions that I'm agonising over mean nothing to you."

Her words stung like a slap to the face. When I made to take her hand once more Courtney backed off an inch, and that stung worse. "That isn't fair," I said. "You're putting words in my mouth. I never said that."

"You may as well have." Courtney waved emphatically at me. "You have *so many opportunities* in front of you yet you're lucky to know the one, true thing you actually want to do with your life. But you don't have the balls to do it!"

"Court—"

"Whereas I'm limited. Limited, and most every important decision paralyses me in place – and most of the trivial ones, too. But deciding what to do regarding Rich's feelings, and working with him...those are important to me, Simon. I can't just run away. It's not the answer to our problems that you think it is."

"You don't seem to actually *want* to make a decision, though, do you?" I bit out before I could stop myself. It was the worst thing I could have said. I wanted to punch myself for it. Desperately I scrambled for the words to fix the mess I'd made. "You've travelled before. You seemed to enjoy it. It isn't running away; it's giving you a chance to—"

"To what? Spend even *more* time not doing anything with my life that I want to do?" Courtney laughed bitterly. She spun around, surveying our surroundings, before shaking her head in dismay. "It's like you said, Simon. I've already travelled. And it left me with nothing. *Nothing.* I don't think I enjoyed it now I look back on it. And now...I don't know what I was thinking, blindly putting my faith in you. You're a coward. I don't think anything you're offering me can ever be what I want. No, what I *need.*"

Abruptly Courtney turned on her heel and left the bar.

"Courtney!" I yelled, following behind her after a beat of startled confusion. "Don't just walk away. You call me a coward then do the exact same thing right back at me!"

It was difficult tracking Courtney through the busy bar. To my dismay I realised Rich was a few steps ahead of me – just where had he been watching from? – and followed Courtney outside, which is how the three of us ended up facing off on the dark pavement.

Rich's face contorted into an angry snarl when he whirled around to face me. "Get lost. She doesn't want to talk to you."

"We weren't finished," I called out to Courtney. But then Rich was in my face, inches from me, shorter in stature than I was but fierce as a pit bull. And who was I to back off from a fight? I pushed him roughly in the chest. "You've never liked me because I had the balls to say hello to this amazing woman you see *every day.* You only made your feelings known after I stepped into the picture, like a kid realising he might lose his favourite toy. So get out my way."

"You son of a bitch," Rich snarled. "You think I needed *you* to show up just so I could see what I already had? Courtney doesn't need you! She doesn't need someone who'll push her to be something she isn't. She needs safety, and routine, and you've fucked all of that up."

"Don't speak for her like she doesn't have her own voice! Don't–"

"*Stop this,*" Courtney cut in, pushing Rich back when he prepared to shove me back. She offered him the kind of lovely, reassuring smile I wished she reserved only for me. "Call me a taxi?" Numbly Rich nodded, backing up from us, before reluctantly pulling out his phone and stalking away.

For the third time that night leaving me and Courtney alone.

She shoved me in Rich's place. "Where do you get off speaking to him like that?"

"I'm sorry," I said, because I was. I dragged a hand down my face, centring my breathing like Mum taught me how to do a million years ago to stop me being frightened when I had to spend the night alone, without her. But fighting the adrenaline in my system was tough. "I don't want to be a dick. He just—"

"Just what?" she countered, eyes glittering in the orange glow of the street lights. "Rich saw me in distress and decided to do something about it."

"Having a disagreement isn't the same as putting you in distress, Courtney. So we had *one* fight. I fucked up. Can't we talk about this properly?"

But Courtney shook her glorious mane of hair. "No. I think you've said enough. This was fun until it wasn't - I think you know that just as much as I did. You're too intense for me, Simon. You have too much baggage, when I already have so much to deal with."

Something inside me broke.

"Fine," I glowered. "*Fine.* If you can't see what we could be - if you don't *want* it - then I can't force you. So let's end things before they get uglier than this."

"Good."

We stood there, staring at each other, hackles raised and fiery. For one agonising moment I saw Courtney reach for me - to slap me, to kiss me, I didn't know. I leaned in for it regardless. But then she ran off. Before I could say another word - before I could retract every terrible thing I'd just said in the heat of the moment - she took that opportunity away from me by fleeing down the street.

Towards Rich, who had always been waiting for her, and a taxi ready to take Courtney Miller away from me forever.

Chapter Thirty-Three

COURTNEY

How had I found myself at Rich's flat? I couldn't even remember the taxi ride over. All I knew was that angry, defensive, betrayed tears were building up behind my eyes, burning my corneas and begging for me to rub away at them. I wouldn't let them fall.

I couldn't.

How had things gone so wrong, so quickly?

"What did he say to you?" Rich asked, handing me a mug of tea and throwing my favourite knitted purple blanket over my shoulders. His gran made it when she'd first met me, and I'd left it in Rich's flat so I always had something there that was definitely mine. Rich sat down beside me and folded his legs beneath him before adding, "I haven't seen you that angry in...well. A while."

I sniffed, fighting back tears. "I wasn't angry."

"Liar."

"We just wanted different things."

"Did you...lead him on?"

"No!" I leapt to my feet, outraged. "Why would you say that?"

"I'm asking because I wanted to know if this Saint guy had *reason* to believe you'd want the same things as him, Court," Rich said, gently but firmly, in that way that always calmed me down, "not because I'm criticising you. Sit down. I'll make us some toast."

I didn't have it in me to be combative; not anymore. So I sat down, obedient as a doll, and closed my eyes until the threat of tears subsided. In the background I heard Rich make the promised toast.

Simon had said some things. I had said some things. We had pushed each other too far, too quickly, because each of us viewed the other person's problems as easily solved. It was as simple as that.

But we were different people, and clearly our individual problems were too insurmountable for either of us to fix. Which meant, ultimately, that what I'd just told Rich was correct: Simon Saint and I wanted different things. Simon wanted to dream big but never actually commit to the final step that would make that dream a reality. Whereas I...

I was done running away. I was done chasing a dream – some reality of my life that was different than the one I had – with no idea of how to achieve that. I wanted to settle down and be content with what I had. I wanted to be able to wake up in the morning and tolerate being me, even if just barely. I wanted...

I wanted peace. No conflict. No challenges, or people challenging me.

Simon was better off without me.

"Sourdough toast and butter just the way you like it," Rich announced when he entered the living room once more, placing the buttery, carby goodness right in front of me. It smelled divine, but I had no appetite. When I made no move to touch the plate Rich urged, "Eat it," so I did.

Rich put on *The Lion King* even though I'd watched it last night for the millionth time simply to have enough background noise to block out my brain. I didn't mind; it was welcome. But after a few minutes I noticed my best friend fidgeting, shifting beside me with the kind of unsettled energy usually only witnessed in me.

"Out with it," I said.

"You don't want me to say it."

"Say it anyway."

"Is this things done for good with Simon?" Rich stopped fidgeting, his doe eyes earnest when I gave him my full attention.

Fuck. It hurt to hear it like that. Simon and I had collided so fast – too, fast – that in the blink of an eye things had gone from exciting and passionate and *different* to...

Well, not so different after all. Our fledging relationship had ended the same way all my others had. Even though Simon had been in a league of his own. If things couldn't work with him – couldn't be *better* with him – then I could only conclude one thing. Something I'd known all along, if I'd only been honest.

The problem was me. Only me. I was the constant in all my failed attempts at long-term, happy relationships.

"Court?" Rich pressed, concern colouring his face. Well, I guess I hadn't ruined *all* of my long-term relationships. Rich was still here and, what's more, was happy to be here. To support me, and care for me, and love me.

"How long?"

Rich blinked. "What do you mean?"

"I mean how long have you wanted things between us to be romantic? Don't avoid the question this time."

"Um..." He glanced at the ceiling as he thought about his answer. I followed his gaze, noticing that there was still a dent where we'd stupidly shaken a prosecco bottle until the cork flew out and almost took out my eye. We never recklessly opened a bottle of fizzy alcohol again. "A year, maybe?"

I all but choked on my toast. "A *year*? And you never said anything until now?!"

"That Simon guy riled me up, okay?" he admitted, sighing heavily. Rich slumped into the couch as if ashamed that another person could affect him so. "I could see that you thought things might be different with him. Your talk of it 'being fun' be damned, Court, I know *you*. You wanted to make a proper go of it with him. So I knew it was time to stop being a coward and tell you how I felt."

Stop being a coward. Simon and I had flung that at each other for entirely different reasons. Had they really been that different?

I guess it didn't matter now.

"Okay."

"Okay?" Rich shook his head in fond resignation. "I know your brain is probably going at a million words a minute, and you've played out at least twelve different scenarios in the last ten seconds, but you need to give me more than that."

I offered him a smile. I *think* it looked genuine. "Okay, let's give us a try. But...slow."

"I can do glacial."

There was nothing to do but laugh. Tonight had been a mess. Hell, the last few weeks had been a mess. A travesty of the highest highs and abyssal lows. I'd drank too much when I'd sworn I was done with that. I'd avoided facing up to my responsibilities – finding a flat, sorting out my love life, arranging an ADHD diagnosis – all to my own detriment.

But I was done. I couldn't be this version of myself anymore. I wanted, *needed,* to change.

Simon Saint did, too, but just as I couldn't be the one to help him do that, he couldn't do it for me, either. We owed it to ourselves to follow separate paths.

Rich took the plate from my hands to replace it with his own hands. My fingers were cold, but his were warm. After a few seconds I felt his heat warming me up, too.

Slowly.

I could do things slowly.

Chapter Thirty-four

SIMON

THE BAR TOP WAS ALL WRONG.

I'd royally fucked things up with Courtney Miller, past the point where I could ever fix things, and the bloody bar top for my restaurant was *wrong*.

"How is this onyx?!" I all but yelled at Kei, even though it wasn't his fault, or mine. I waved emphatically at it. "This is granite!"

"For the hundredth time, we'll fix it," Kei soothed, uncharacteristically calm. "I've already called the courier. It'll be fixed tomorrow."

"I won't be here tomorrow!"

"But you'll be back on Friday, right? *Right,* Simon?"

I didn't reply. It was Wednesday now. Wednesday. I'd avoided Courtney in the Plaza at the weekend after our horrendous fall out, and now I was going to London to see my parents. I'd booked the trip straight after Harriet and Chloë's engagement party, having drunkenly decided that I'd show my grandparents *and* Courtney just how determined I was to make it on my own. To stick to my word. To not be a coward.

In the cold light of the following morning I'd instead chosen to arrange early check-out from the Crowne Plaza and head back to London for good.

Courtney had been right, after all: if I hadn't said or done anything up until this point, at thirty-six years of age, then when was I really going to? The bakery and the ramen shop had been my way of rebelling against a path that had been set before me. A job I was good at, working for the company my grandparents had built from nothing. Making them proud was a grand, aspirational thing; they were my family. They loved me.

Who was I to disappoint them? I'd been acting like a child.

Kei extricated the pint glass of water from my hand when I clenched my fist dangerously tightly around it. "I don't like the look on your face," he said. "Tell me what's going on, Si."

"You don't need me here. Not after we open."

"Simon?"

"You said it yourself, before," I said, splaying my hands across the wrong bar top to stop myself from shaking. Damn it, I hated being this emotional in front of other people. Even Kei. "There's no reason I can't still oversee this place and the bakery whilst working with my grandparents. I just need to step back a lot more than you probably thought I would."

"Cut the crap," Kei said, tapping me on the shoulder until I blearily turned my head to face him. "What happened last Friday? What's going on?"

"Nothing happened."

"You're a terrible liar." A pause. "Something happened with Courtney, right?"

I grabbed the pint glass of water and smashed it against the wall. Kei flinched as shards of glass exploded all over the floor. Water drip, drip, dripped down the wall, darkening the pale green like a ghost.

"...I'll take that as a yes," Kei murmured, careful and on-edge. Because of me. Because I was a fucking mess. He deserved better than this version of me.

"I'm going to take over the firm from my grandparents," I said, grabbing my jacket and heading for the door. I forced a smile to my face. "I won't be back on Friday, but rest assured I'll be back in two weeks to help you with the soft launch and the hard launch. We'll make sure things go off without a hitch and then I'll hand over the reins. It's like you said with the bar top: you have things handled. You don't need me."

"You son of a bi—get back here! Simon. *Simon*!"

I fled the restaurant before Kei could finish his string of expletives. I'd find a way to make it up to him, of course. Just in a way that wouldn't involve me running the restaurant.

Our restaurant. My childish rebellion had one more victim. Just how selfish had I been?

When I reached the Plaza all of my belongings had been brought down, ready for my check-out ahead of my flight down to London. Courtney had to know I was leaving by now – her shift started half an hour ago, after all. So it came as no surprise to me that Courtney Miller was standing behind reception, as beautiful as the day I met her. That perfect blonde ponytail, not a hair out of place. Expertly painted red lips and just a hint of mascara on her curled lashes.

Her green eyes when they landed on mine had lost all their fire. She offered me the same wan smile she gave all her normal customers. Her 'service smile', Courtney had once told me.

So that was the way it would be.

"I hope you had a wonderful stay at the Crowne Plaza, Glasgow, Mr Saint," Courtney said, no trace of familiarity in her tone. I was a stranger to her. A guest.

I'd thought to apologise for the things I'd said. Or, rather, the way I'd said them. A screaming match out on the pavement was not the way for us to discuss our insecurities. But we'd been nipping at each other's seams for weeks now, slowly plucking out all the things we both ultimately knew we'd never aspire to.

Dreams were the realm of sleep. It was time to face the reality of our situation.

"I had a wonderful time," I said, finding the light in reception suddenly too bright for my eyes. I blinked it back. "Truly, this was the most meaningful trip to Glasgow I've had since...well, since I was a child. I mean that, Miss Miller."

God, that was too much. I'd tried to wrap things up as nicely and as genuinely as possible, but now I just sounded pathetic.

It almost looked like Courtney's mask slipped, and the ghost of a true and tortured smile tore through. But then she tossed her ponytail back with a laugh. "I'm glad. I wish you all the best, Mr Saint."

And that was that. I checked out of the Crowne Plaza and walked out the door, being mindful not to hit anyone with said door this time.

I doubted the sphere of my life would ever overlap with Courtney Miller's again. Maybe, one day, that thought wouldn't rip out my heart quite so much as it did right now.

Chapter Thirty-five

COURTNEY

WHEN I ARRIVED AT TOM AND LIZ's to house-sit whilst they went to Japan I was shocked to discover the house full of packing boxes.

"Just what...what is going on?" I asked between fits of giggles, when Jerry climbed all the way up my leg and into my arms. He had gotten so much bigger since I'd last seen him; at this rate, the cat would end up the size of a pug.

Liz looked harried and flyaway in that way only people who'd been packing up their life's belongings for days could be. "Did we never tell you? Shit, because you left Harry and Chloë's party ear—"

"We're moving," Tom cut in, giving Liz a very obviously knowing look as he hoisted their suitcases to the door. "Up into your neck of the woods, actually. Well, closer to Bearsden. I've been building a house out that way for the last year."

"You'll forgive me for saying this but...fucking rich people, right?"

"Fucking rich people," Liz agreed, but fondly. "It's not *quite* finished yet but enough of it's done that we can move in. At least that way we can get the townhouse sold."

"And you picked this moment to, uh, go to Japan?"

When it became clear I could offer Jerry no treats he clambered onto my shoulder and leapt over to Liz. She scratched him behind the ears until he purred. "The timing is a bit off," she admitted, "but when is the timing ever *right*? If you wait for the perfect time then nothing ever happens."

Tom nodded his agreement. "The timing right now, however, *is* perfect for catching our flight. The fridge is fully stocked but I've left a load of cash in the biscuit tin in the top left-hand cupboard in the kitchen."

"Forty going on eighty, Tom?" I asked, bemused. "Next you'll be telling me you have thirty towels upstairs, all colour-coordinated and perfectly folded in a gorgeously painted storage box."

A moment of silence. Then Liz exploded into fits of laughter, unsettling Jerry into nimbly leaping to the floor and stalking away. "He *does* have that, oh my god oh my god. He's like a granny!"

"Do you want to go to Japan or not, Doctor Maclean?" Tom muttered, thoroughly put out.

"Absolutely, Professor Henderson." Liz took a moment to collect herself, then closed the gap between us to smother me in a hug. I didn't realise how much I needed the comforting touch of a friend; I sagged against Liz and welcomed her crushing embrace. "We know about Simon," she whispered into my ear, "but I don't want to meddle. I'm your friend first, okay? So if you need to talk or cry or whatever—"

"Go fuck off to Japan," I said, giving her the finger when I pushed her away. But I matched Liz's grin, and when Tom roped me in for a bear hug I let him do so. "*No suggesting I fix things with Simon,*" I warned him, for good measure.

But Tom merely ruffled my hair like I was his hopeless little sister. "You've got to work that one out on your own, I'm afraid."

After giving Ludo and Jerry one final bout of hugs and kisses – Ludo whining to be brought with them, his tail pounding the floor with increasing fervour – Liz and Tom were off and out the door.

Leaving me alone, surrounded by a pile of moving boxes that were not mine.

They weren't mine, but they really were a physical manifestation of what I needed to do. Oddly that kind of helped. I'd viewed a flat the day before that I really, really liked. Unfurnished, because as I'd mentioned to Tom before any nice furnished flats were out of my price range. It was up by the canal just behind Maryhill, so a scant ten minute walk to my dad's place. A modern estate with private parking and everything, which part of me thought was pointless because I didn't drive but a very small part of me thought was nice because Mum and Ailish both did.

It was small – dinky, even – but it had an open-plan kitchen and living room with a balcony that overlooked the canal. Well, I could *just* about see the canal on my left when I stood out on it, but in Glasgow that definitely counted. The area was quiet and leafy, but because it wasn't the west end or the city centre or bloody Shawlands or Dennistoun the rent hadn't crept up at quite the same rate as the rest of the city, despite the gentrification of Maryhill in general.

And the landlord was happy for me to rent the place. All I needed to do was complete the paperwork, and pass the financial check, and I was good to go.

Good to go – me? Living all on my own, in a flat that lacked furniture, without the finances to *buy* said furniture?

But Tom had been right. One step at a time. Everything with Simon had fallen apart because we piled too much on each other, too fast. We'd both gotten nervous. We'd both gotten scared. Ultimately both because of the same things, or at least similar things. Yeah, I'd reacted differently to him, and pushed

Simon away when he instead chose to cling on to me like I'd save him from his situation, but at the end of the day we were kind of the same.

And I'd been *horrible* to him.

It didn't matter that I was going to try and make a proper go of things with Rich; I could still see that I had acted completely out of hand. Simon hadn't deserved having me say and do all those things to him when, in his own way, he'd been trying to help. He'd wanted us to have a future – just not a future I believe either of us actually wanted.

And then I'd completely blocked him out when he came to say goodbye at the Plaza.

God, I had to stop thinking about Simon. I had things to do, and we both owed it to each other to move on without hurting each other further.

With renewed vigour I gave Jerry a generous pile of treats, then took a heartbroken Ludo out on a walk (which brightened his mood considerably). It was a gorgeous day – a warmth to the sun that hinted at true spring – but unfortunately I wasn't walking Ludo with the aim to hang out in a park.

We reached my flat, and Ludo rolled around on my bed, and I set to finally packing up my own shit. I sent all the right paperwork to the letting agency, too, and was filled with a sense of both relief and euphoria when they told me everything was in order and that they'd have the financial check completed by tomorrow morning.

One thing at a time.

Once I had completed my packing I surveyed what earthly belongings I had. Most stuff was for the bin or destined for a charity shop – dozens of half-finished and abandoned projects, which I'd been convinced I'd go back to once I rediscovered my joy for said project. Knitting. Jigsaw puzzles. Watercolour paints. A box of magic tricks. But it was time to face the music: I wasn't going to return to these passing interests. I needed a clean slate.

In the end I had two boxes and four bin bags full of clothes, mostly all purchased in London with Simon. *Simon.* A pang hurt my heart. I wanted to treat the clothes more gently than unceremoniously tossing them into bin bags to move, but even packing them like that had been hard enough.

Unable to look at everything anymore I grabbed my laptop and a backpack stuffed with enough clothes to last me a few days and jogged back to Liz and Tom's, a very happy Ludo setting a punishing pace for the both of us. But I relished the burn in my muscles; my gasping for breath; the sweat trickling down my skin.

I was alive and I was functioning one step at a time.

After showering in the thus far much-envied but never-tried shower in the townhouse (Liz was leaving this? Really?) I settled onto the giant corner sofa in the living room and put trash TV on whilst mindlessly browsing the internet on my laptop. I don't know what possessed me to finally type 'Simon Saint' into Google for the first time, but before I knew it that was exactly what I was doing.

He was pretty private on social media, which was what I'd expected given that Simon *told* me he had his accounts set that way, but the third link on Google directed to what appeared to be his grandparents' investment firm. I found myself grimacing as I clicked it, expecting some dry as fuck announcement about him from when he first joined the firm.

What I got was entirely different.

Yeah, it *was* a dry as fuck article about Simon 'joining the empire Rupert and Maria Saint built from the ground up', but it wasn't the words that stood out to me: it was the photos.

There was no official, boring portrait of Simon but three family photos, including one of him as a young boy. I could see plain as day that these people loved him more than anything. The way Maria smiled down at the small, pale child like he was an angel. The way Rupert grinned with pride in Simon's graduation photo. The way Simon slung his arms around them both in the most recent photo, despite the more austere expressions on his grandparents' faces.

It was so at odds with the people I'd met in London. I'd taken Simon's appraisal at face value – that they were snobbish, and closed-off, and wanted Simon to fit a mould they had created for him.

But my god did they love him. I could see it now. Could understand the conflict Simon must have felt in trying to find the words to tell them he wouldn't follow in their footsteps. And I had trivialised all of that, because to me Simon's problem had *seemed* trivial in the face of my own.

I was a hypocrite.

But I didn't have to *remain* one. This was something I could fix. Who was I to say 'too late, the damage is done' and never look back? I had a voice and I had a phone and I had a will to reassure Simon his feelings were valid. That I still supported him no matter what he did.

No matter if we were together.

I picked up the phone.

Chapter Thirty-Six

SIMON

Saint Investments looked like every other building in the financial district of the City of London. Tall, slate grey, full of glass. It reflected a hundred other tall, grey, glass buildings in its large windows: an infinity of drab and boring.

And I was going to dive right back into it.

How had I ever managed to pretend I liked finance before? I had to remember. For my grandparents. For my family – what little I had of it. Taking over the firm would make them proud. They'd figuratively glow as they bragged about me to their friends, and tell me what a fine, upstanding man I'd grown into.

For them. It was for them.

My stomach lurched as I climbed to the top floor in the elevator. I was reminded, stark and sudden, about the last time my stomach had felt this sick in a lift. At the Plaza, when I'd had the flu.

But Courtney had looked after me, then all my fears washed away like sand beneath the waves on a shore. Like they'd never existed. Despite being sick, for the first time in a long time I'd felt invincible. And it had been true what I'd said to Courtney before we slept together: I liked who I was with her. But she had told me the same thing, and where were we now?

It had all been built upon fragile sand, and now it had all washed away.

God, I wasn't one for waxing poetic but clearly something inside me had fundamentally changed. "Get a hold of yourself," I chastised, straightening my tie and running a fretful hand through my hair before being let into my grandparents' shared office.

It was a beautiful office, to be fair, full of plants that my grandmother had painstakingly looked after over the years. Monsteras and ferns and orchids and lots and lots of calatheas. It brought a liveliness to the space which, when paired with the massive walnut desk my grandparents shared, had become my favourite room in the entire building.

But it wasn't my favourite room right now.

"It's about time," Rupert Saint grumbled, face like thunder when I closed the door behind me. Nan didn't look much happier.

"Are you done playing games now, Simon?" she asked. I flinched despite myself; I'd never been playing games. But I didn't have it in me to fight. Not anymore.

"You could say that," I relented, the words biting the inside of my mouth like acid. "I come here willing to fulfil all of my familial responsibilities."

Finally my granddad smiled. Sort of. I hadn't seen him truly smile in years; not at me, anyway. "It's taken you long enough to come to your senses. But I guess one must fly from the nest to learn these things on their own." He waved me over, riffling through a drawer with his other hand until he pulled out a sheaf of paper. "Come here, and we'll go over the con—"

A buzzing came from my bag, incessant and insistent.

"What have we told you about keeping your phone on silent during business meetings?" Nan demanded, exasperated with me like I was fifteen years old. "Turn it off, Simon."

I took out the offending device and fully intended to comply. Really, I did. But then I saw who was calling: Courtney. What was Courtney doing calling me?

I picked up the call before my wits could tell me to do otherwise, despite the outraged expression on both of my grandparents' faces. "...hello?"

A crackle of static. Then: "Are you free to talk? I just need five minutes. No, two." Courtney's voice was uncharacteristically hesitant. Like she was afraid I'd tell her to fuck off.

"You can have all the time in the world," I said, meaning it.

"Simon," Nan hissed, "get off the phone this instant."

"I wanted to say I'm sorry," Courtney said, cutting through my grandparents' protests like a knife through delicious, soft, golden butter. "I'm sorry about what I said, and how we left things."

"I'm sorry, too." And I *really* meant that. I held the phone closer to my ear, as if it would somehow bring Courtney herself just a little closer to me. "I tried to push my desires on you without thinking about what you really wanted. It wasn't fair, Courtney."

"I appreciate that." It truly sounded like she did. "But that wasn't the reason I called you."

"You didn't call to force an apology out of me? Colour me surprised!"

Courtney giggled, and it was the most beautiful sound in the world. "I called because I wanted to tell you that you can't give up on your dreams. You *can't*. But you just as equally shouldn't be afraid of what your grandparents might say. Bec—"

"This might be a bad time to say—"

"Because, Simon," Courtney cut in, "I don't think they'll react *at all* the way you're afraid they will. They love you, Simon. They really do."

"...how could you know that?" I stared at my (highly unamused) grandparents, watching me like hawks as I disappointed them with my dreadful etiquette for the millionth time in my life. Courtney couldn't possibly be right.

Right?

"Because look at how you turned out. Look how wonderful, and sensitive, and caring you are. That wasn't only your mum's doing; it was theirs, too. So tell them what you want from your life. Don't be afraid. And I...I won't be afraid, either. Okay?"

I found myself nodding. If Courtney said I could do it then it was possible, right? If she believed in me, and my grandparents, then it must be true. As easy as that, the knot that had been in my stomach for forever was cleaved in two.

"Thank you," I said, softly. "Truly, Courtney, thank you. You have no idea the impact you've had on me in such a short space of time."

"And you, Simon. *So* much. But look" – Courtney yelled into the distance – "I better go. Jerry is climbing the curtains again."

I barked out a laugh. "Okay. Give Ludo a head-scratch for me?"

"Will do. Be well, Simon. Goodbye."

"Bye, Courtney."

A beep, and the call was over. My grandparents sat behind their desk glaring at me, but I didn't care.

"I'm not taking over the firm," I announced, riding the high Courtney had granted me with her miraculous phone call. "I'm moving into the restaurant business full-time."

My grandfather got to his feet. "I dare you to say that again, Simon," he sputtered, incandescent with rage. "We give you *everything* and you—"

"You're my family, and I love you, and I know you love me in all the ways you can." I had to spew it all out before the adrenaline wore off, so I steamrollered on. "But I'm my own person, and you can't make up for the way you failed Mum by moulding me into your perfect son. I love working in the catering business, and I'm good at it. It isn't a passion project; it's my life."

A dark shadow crossed my grandmother's brow. "You're making a huge mistake."

"The mistake I made was not being honest with you sooner. If you want to talk to me about this properly then you know where to find me."

I turned and left the office, elated and giddy and a little bit terrified. They didn't call after me; I knew they never would. It wasn't classy. Maybe they'd prove Courtney right and they'd be okay with things. Supportive, even. More likely they wouldn't, but in the end it didn't matter.

I'd said what needed said at long, long last.

As I left the building and rushed to book a flight back to Glasgow I was struck by all that I had done wrong in the name of being a coward. Courtney and I had now cleared the air and apologised so we could start our lives on a blank slate once more, but someone *else* was still due a very sincere apology. Someone who had done nothing but support me through thick and thin – who had never doubted my dreams nor my ability to achieve those dreams for even a second.

"Kei, I'm so sorry about everything," I spat out the moment he picked up. "I'll be back in Glasgow tonight, so don't go crossing my name off the sign just yet."

I could practically hear the sound of him giving me the finger down the phone. "Fucking right you are. Get me a beer and you're forgiven."

"We own a bar."

"A lot of beer, then."

That was definitely a promise I'd have no trouble fulfilling.

Chapter Thirty-Seven

COURTNEY

Two weeks passed in a blur. Before I knew it, it was the night before Tom and Liz were due to arrive back in Glasgow. My new flat was ready to move into in a few days, I'd handed in my notice at the Plaza, and I had a coherent plan for how I was going to try and tackle my mental and physical health.

There was just one problem: having that plan didn't mean I *followed* it.

I knew I'd been spaced out the last two weeks. Too self-involved and not aware at all of what was going on around me. And as I sat beside Rich in Tom and Liz's living room, playing happy families with a dog and a cat to boot, I could tell he knew that.

"What do you want for dinner tonight?" Rich asked. I think it might have been the fourth time he'd asked me in an hour, because I hadn't given him an answer yet. It wasn't that I didn't *have* an answer, it was just that my answer was "I'm gonna have three bowls of cereal then go to bed" (I'd just done a food shop in Lidl and therefore had a fresh box of Choco Curls, the best cereal known to man) and I knew Rich wouldn't like this.

"I don't know," I lied, flicking through different film options on Amazon Prime. *The Lake House* came up, and I was suddenly reminded of London, and Simon, and Simon, and Simon.

"Oh, I love that film," Rich said, noticing what I was hovering over. "Do you want to watch it?"

When I clicked on the film I discovered it was rent-to-watch only. "It's not actually included with Prime." This filled me with a surge of relief I couldn't quite describe. Why was I glad to not watch *The Lake House* with Rich? It's hardly as if Simon and I owned the rights to watching it together. We didn't even watch it in London; we'd gone for *Speed.*

Was the entire back catalogue of Keanu Reeves films now banned from my mental watch-list?

"That's a shame," Rich said, sighing wistfully. "Watching a romance might not be a bad idea. Do you know which service has *The Notebook*?"

Abruptly I turned the TV off. "I think I might just go to bed."

Rich frowned at his phone. "It's barely seven. This is the third time this week you've gone to bed so early. What's wrong?"

"Nothing's *wrong*," I protested. And it wasn't; not really. But something didn't feel right. "I'm just tired out from all the extra shifts the Plaza are making me work while they find my replacement." I tried to snuggle against Rich's side but that didn't feel right, either. And when he tensed against me, and sat up straight on the couch, I knew he knew it, too.

"This isn't ever going to work, is it?"

"...what is?"

"The two of us as a couple." Rich's voice was small and faraway. He didn't look at me. "You're already bored of even trying, Courtney. Don't tell me that isn't true – I can practically see your eyes glazing over every night. You can't even last an hour without looking for something else to pay attention to. Anything but me."

For a long moment I couldn't speak. Rich's stinging evisceration came straight out of left field. Except...did it? I'd been so focused on anything *but* my love life the last two weeks that it was entirely possible I'd not given Rich enough attention.

He dragged a hand across his face. "The fact you're literally going over things in your head right now to see if I might be right or not says more than your words ever could. Gotta say, this stings like a bitch."

"That isn't fair!" I cried, cringing away from the couch to get to my feet. To go...where? This was Tom and Liz's house, and I was watching it. Rich was the one who could escape this situation, not me. "I haven't done anything wrong. I've just – I've just..."

"Not got the bandwidth to be in a romantic relationship with me whilst working on yourself." Rich turned from me, looking at anything *but* me, then bowed his head. "Which is fine. It's not something you've done *wrong*. But if this is how things start then I know we're doomed to ruin our friendship in the process. And I don't want that."

I bit my lip so hard I drew blood. I was trembling all over, though internally I felt an odd sort of calm. I didn't want to upset Rich – he was my best friend, damn it, and had been with me through everything – but there was relief intermingled with the anger, shame and upset. I'd agreed to go out with him on impulse, after all, and had only staved off feeling regret over that action by simply not thinking about it at all.

"Say something," Rich urged, when I didn't speak. Finally he turned his lovely brown eyes on mine, refusing to look away until I did indeed talk.

"You were the one who said you wanted this," I whispered. "You know exactly what I'm like, Rich, in my highest moments and in my lowest. I have things to focus on right now; I'm sorry I haven't been giving you the attention you want."

"It isn't" – Rich shook his head emphatically – "it isn't about that. It's that you're still finding the time to think about *him*, aren't you? Tell me I'm wrong and I'll let it go. But I think we both know the truth."

I could have lied. Could have told Rich a version of the truth, wherein it was natural for me to still be thinking about Simon because of the way we'd left things. Except Simon and I had made our peace with each other, and wished each other well, and genuinely meant it.

If we hadn't left things on bad terms then why couldn't I stop thinking about Simon Saint?

Rich let out a humourless chuckle, then got to his feet and made his way for the front door.

"Rich!" I exclaimed, running after him. "I just need some time." A lie, but I couldn't stop myself from saying it. "Don't walk out on me like this. Please."

"You accepted me as your boyfriend because I can give you a good routine, and make decisions for you, and won't judge you harshly when your mood gets low," Rich said, buttoning his jacket as he did so. "But here's the thing, Court: I can't keep making those decisions for you just so you don't have to. I don't *want* to; deep down I know you don't want that, either. But for this, at least, I'm happy to decide what to do. I'm not right for you. I probably never was – I was chasing a ghost that never existed."

"Rich—"

"And that isn't your fault!" Rich cut in. He forced a smile to his face that looked too stretched out – too thin – to be genuine. "It isn't mine, either. It's just...how it is. You need someone who can be more than I can be. I see that now. And maybe that's Simon bloody Saint, or maybe it's someone else, but it isn't me."

Neither of us said anything. We stood in the draughty hallway at a complete standstill, because we both knew Rich was right.

And that sucked.

"I don't want to lose you," I finally said, voice hollow and insubstantial. "You're my best friend. And I want to work with you to make your business a success. I *know* I want those things, Rich. I will never let that fall to the wayside."

This time, when Rich smiled, he looked far more like himself. "I know," he said, kissing my cheek. When I threw my arms around him he reciprocated. "I know those things will always be important to you. That *I'm* important to you. Just...not in that way."

"Not in that way," I echoed back. "But in every other way. And I always will."

He pinched my arm. "You fucking better. And when you make up with Simon—"

"Who said I'm making up with Simon?"

"Tell him Monday nights are still firmly *our* thing," Rich said. He wrinkled his nose. "Minus the kissing, I guess."

"Minus the kissing."

"I'll see you at work tomorrow." Rich let go of me and moved to the door, letting in a gust of cool air when he opened the main one and then the heavy storm door behind it. "Don't agonise yourself overthinking all of this, okay? I think you know what it is that you want – maybe more than you ever did before. And I'm proud of you for that, even if...even if that isn't me."

Rich left before I could say another word, which was just as well because I burst into tears. We'd barely even begun our romantic relationship, but I was happier now that it had ended than I'd ever felt *about* it. I guess that meant Rich had been correct: we weren't right for each other. Not in that way. And we probably never were.

When you make up with Simon...

How could I do that after impulsively embarking on a relationship with my best friend in direct retaliation to mine and Simon's fuck-up? I couldn't. I simply couldn't.

Right?

But one thing I knew with absolute certainty: my head was clearer now than it had been in a long time. I hadn't realised just how *cloudy* even pretending to be romantically interested in Rich had made me. It had been cruel to do that to him. Reprehensible, even. So if it took Rich some time to get over that, and me, then I was willing to take responsibility for that and to put in the work to make it up to him.

As for everything else...

I had a flat to move into first.

One step at a time.

Chapter Thirty-Eight

SIMON

"And with that, *Seijin & Kei* is finally ready for an audience!"

I surveyed the restaurant, complete with the correct onyx bar top; the amber colour offset the live bamboo behind it in a very aesthetically pleasing manner. There were no more boxes of glasses strewn across the floor. No paint dust, no holes in the walls or grotty spots on the windows. Everything was clean, classy and exactly as Kei and I had envisioned it.

In ten days we'd open for business. But before that we had the soft-soft-launch (where we triple-checked our entire menu) and the soft launch proper: Chloë and Harriet's engagement party.

Would Courtney be there? She would be, wouldn't she? After our phone call all I'd been able to think about, aside from work, was her. We didn't *have* to never see each other again. We were on good terms. We simply weren't...together.

Could I attempt to change that? Was I allowed to? Because god damn it, I wanted to.

Kei clinked a bottle of beer against my shoulder. "You should invite your grandparents to actually see this place. I'm sure they'll—"

"I said what needed to be said two weeks ago," I said, tone short. I didn't want to ruin this moment by thinking about my grandparents, who were yet to speak a single word to me. "If they want to have a relationship with me then it's up to them to reach out first."

"Real mature." I took the beer from Kei when he bumped my shoulder once more, and we both drank deeply. A comfortable, contemplative quiet spread around us, punctuated only by the sound of a gentle rain pattering the windows. This was peace, and joy, and what I wanted. Then Kei ruined it all when he said, "Though I guess they haven't been that mature, either. Clearly it runs in the family."

I snorted. "You're so funny."

"It's easy to be funny standing next to you." I gave him the finger; Kei reciprocated in kind. We stared out at the rain for another long moment. "So...once we open, what then? What's next for you?"

I could only sigh. "Can't we revel in the moment for a bit before stressing over the future?" Trust Kei, though, to be thinking about what came next. "I've only just had the balls to step away from the lordly Saint reputation; it might be nice to take it easy and focus on the here and now."

But Kei wasn't convinced. He put down his beer just so he could cross his arms judgementally over his chest. "Simon, don't fuck with me. I know you – this place and the bakery aren't the only projects rattling in your brain. There's something else in there you really, truly want to do. *Seijin & Kei* is just a step to reach that thing."

"You make it sound like I don't think this place is important."

"Don't put words in my mouth." He swore in Japanese, then said, "This place *is* important, but it isn't everything to you the way running my own kitchen is everything to *me*. And that's okay. The only reason I could fulfil this dream of mine is because of you, at the end of the day. So don't limit yourself, and for fuck's sake stop moping and just *call* that damn girl if you like her so much."

I felt like Kei had slapped me in the face with the change in direction his speech had taken. Though I supposed, from his point of view, my career dreams and the woman of my dreams were part of the same conversation.

"...what if she doesn't pick up?" I mumbled, averting my eyes. I felt like a damn teenager. Of course I'd been thinking about this in all the spare moments I had around getting the restaurant ready for business. "What if—"

"What if, what if, what if! Who cares about *what if* when you can find out *what will be*? And what *will* be if you're moving back to Glasgow for good is that you'll see Courtney again, and again, and again. You share friends, Si. She'll never be a stranger. Can you look at her as just a friend? Because I don't think you can do that at all."

He had a point. We both knew it. When I'd thought I was running back to London, never to see Courtney Miller again, it had been easier to handle the way we'd originally left things. But now we were on good terms, and I was in Glasgow for good, and Courtney was the reason all of that was possible.

"I need to go," I said, grabbing my jacket and practically slipping over the polished floor in my haste to leave.

Kei chuckled good-naturedly. "Good. Fuck off. Tell me how it goes when you're done screwing it o—"

"*Bye!*"

There was no time to lose. It was just after four in the afternoon; Courtney would be at home getting ready for her shift in the Crowne Plaza. If she was still working there – she might have quit already to work with Rich.

Richard Blake. Shit.

I skidded to a halt just outside Gregg's, because what would be more romantic than showing up at Courtney's door with four sausage rolls in tow? But the thought of Rich had me frozen in blind panic. Were they together now? Had Courtney accepted his advances? Would I be interfering where I wasn't wanted if I showed up now, after two weeks of zero contact?

I didn't know what to do.

My phone buzzing in my hand – I hadn't put it away since leaving the restaurant, in case I decided to ultimately call Courtney first – cut through my panic. Tom. Back from Japan yesterday and mad enough to move house *today*.

"If you ask me to help you move then you have another thing coming," I said the moment I picked up the call.

Tom hissed like a cat who'd had its tail stood on. "How'd you know I was going to ask that?"

"Your jetlagged arse doesn't want to move your furniture. *That's* how I know."

"Can you please help, even for an hour?" my pathetic best friend begged, pathetically. "I think I pulled something in my back on the flight to Glasgow. Damn seats—"

"You flew first class and we both know it."

"And yet despite that!" Tom cried, outraged. "There's a very nice bottle of Japanese whisky in the bargain for you."

Damn it, he knew the way to my heart. "Fine," I muttered. "Fine. You've convinced me."

"A true saint! I'll see you in a few."

Heading over to Tom and Liz's could work as a reconnaissance mission, anyway. Courtney had been watching the townhouse and their pets for the last fortnight, which meant there was a strong possibility that Liz would know if she'd accepted Rich's feelings or not.

I jumped into Gregg's and got those four sausage rolls, just in case.

Chapter Thirty-Nine

COURTNEY

"Courtney, thanks so much for coming back today!" Liz cried, crashing against me to pull me into a hug the moment she opened the door. "Lord knows why Tom wanted to pay you in cash but thanks for giving him a day to sleep before having to hit the bank."

"Something tells me he thought it would look *flashier* if he paid in banknotes," I said, not entirely joking. It seemed like the kind of stupid thing Thomas Henderson would want to do in lieu of simply paying me via bank transfer. But I didn't mind; I'd accidentally left my laptop on Liz's bed, anyway, because I'd basically lived in it for the fourteen days the pair of them had been gone. It was perhaps the most divine bed I had ever slept on, and I bitterly regretted the fact it was not mine.

I had to source a bed from a charity shop, pronto, so it wouldn't do to keep yearning for Liz's. For it wasn't just Tom and Liz moving house today: I'd received the keys for my new place this morning, and had already moved all my earthly belongings into it – minus my laptop and, you know, all the furniture I still didn't possess.

I could use a cardboard box as a coffee table for a bit, right?

A week, tops. Maybe three.

"Going by the fact both Jerry and Ludo hogged my bed last night I can assume you didn't sleep in the master bedroom?" Liz asked, as we made our way into the house and up the stairs.

I wrinkled my nose. "It would feel wrong to use the room you and Tom use for all your sinful exploits just for sleep."

Liz sniggered. "No, better you use the bed you were dry humping Simon on, I guess."

"*We do not speak of drunken antics in the broad light of day.*"

Another laugh, harder this time. "I can agree with that. But you liked the bed, right?"

Why were we still talking about the bed? It was weird because it was all I'd been able to think about, but that was because I needed to *buy* a bed. Why was Liz so interested in my opinion of her bed?

"It was the best sleep I've had in potentially forever."

"Then please," Tom said, sweeping into Liz's bedroom on disturbingly soft feet. He had dark shadows around his eyes from jetlag, and his hair was a manic mess, so he kind of looked completely bat shit insane. "Take the damn thing off our hands. Plus anything else in the house that you want – we've already moved everything we're taking to the new house."

I stared, open-mouthed, first at Tom and then at Liz. Maybe Tom *had* gone insane. "He's joking, right?" I asked, when I remembered how to speak. "You can't be serious."

"Au contraire, Courtney, we are," Tom said, smiling broadly. "Serious, I mean. Everything else is getting taken over to Mum's foster home in the country house—"

"A what in a what now?"

"Tom's Mum started a foster home in her gigantic Balloch mansion," Liz explained. "It only opened recently, but she realised she needs *way* more furniture at the rate the kids are already damaging things and demanding they want one of their own, well, everything. So please take *literally anything* you want out of this house, because you are definitely more in need of it than Mrs Henderson and her massive bank account."

"I still think she should have taken your dad's surname just to make things extra uncomfortable for you," Tom joked. Liz elbowed him in the ribs.

I didn't know what to say. What *could* I say?

The only thing that mattered: "Thank you."

Just at that moment a strangled meowing filled our ears, so Liz ran off to find out what Jerry was up to. When I was alone with Tom he pulled out a ridiculous stack of cash and threw it at my chest when I didn't take it from him.

"*Ow!*" I complained, because the money had hurt. How many notes had to be in the wad for it to hurt? "What was that for?"

"Because I know you'll never take it otherwise. I hope it's enough."

Dubiously I took off the elastic band securing the notes and riffled through them – then paused halfway through. "Tom," I began, slowly, "this is *way too much money.*"

"Says who?" He genuinely sounded affronted. "You looked after everything that's precious to me with as much love as Liz and I do. You take such good care of Ludo week in, week out, simply because you want to. Are you telling me that isn't *at least* worth what's in your hands? Because I put a rather high value on my pets, and my grandfather's house, and on you."

Okay, there weren't words. Stupid Tom had said something nice and genuine and sensitive that reminded me there were some horribly decent people in this world. But I was going to cry if I stood there and did nothing, so without another thought I flung myself at Tom and let him envelop me in a colossal hug. "Maybe you're one of the nice rich assholes," I murmured, blinking back tears.

"And maybe I'm not the *only* nice one, either."

"...what do you mean?" I asked, pulling away to raise a quizzical eyebrow at Tom.

"*Tom Henderson, you arsehole, why is the moving van outside completely empty*?!" a melodious, London-accented but rather pissed off voice cried up the stairs. The shit-eating grin on Tom's face told me everything I needed to know.

"Had to get this out the bank specifically today, did you?" I accused, holding up the cash. "Wouldn't have anything to do with you setting me up, would it?"

"Hey, I never got to *actually* set up the blind date in the first place," Tom countered, shrugging. "So let me and Liz have our meddling fun, just this once. Oh, and the moving van's for you."

"I don't drive!"

"Simon does, though." And with that Tom exited the room and rushed into his own, where I could hear Liz and Jerry and Ludo giggling, meowing and barking in cahoots.

"Jesus Christ on a fucking bike," I bit out, hastily checking my reflection to see that I looked just about as flyaway and unawares as I felt. I shoved the bank notes down the front of my dress, squashed against my bra, for lack of anywhere better to put them.

Was I ready for this? To see Simon again? My heart was racing. I felt sick. I was excited. I was nervous. He didn't sound like he knew I was here – that we were being set up. What if he rejected me? What if—

I bolted out into the corridor before I lost my nerve and collided with Simon on the stairs.

"Jesus Christ on a—*Courtney*?!"

It would have been hilarious that Simon had gone for the same cursed exclamation that I'd used if I wasn't so mortified. The cash I'd thrown down my dress went everywhere, flitting around us like snow in a Hallmark Christmas movie. For a moment neither of us did a thing.

Then Simon's lips quivered, and I was laughing, and he was laughing.

"Another job I didn't know about, or just the same old sex work?" he asked, helping me pick up the notes before handing them over. This time I far more sensibly put them in my bag.

I snorted. "Just Tom's idea of how much a house- and pet-sitter is worth. How much is a banana worth, Michael?"

"Ten dollars?" Simon said at the same time as me. His laughter softened. "It's so good to see you, Courtney."

I squeezed his arm like it was the most natural thing in the world. "I was just about to say the same thing. I...is that a Gregg's?" For Simon was holding a paper bag with the blue logo emblazoned on the front, the tell-tale delicious savoury smell of sausage rolls wafting into my nostrils now Simon and I were sharing the same air.

He ran his other hand awkwardly through his hair. "Yes, actually. I was going to – but it doesn't matter."

"You were going to *what*, exactly?"

His lovely grey eyes – I'd missed them so much my heart ached – flitted from me, to the bag, then back again. "I was going to bring them over to yours. But I didn't know if I'd be overstepping the mark. I didn't know if...well. If you'd want to see me."

"We only have that moving van until seven!" Tom yelled unhelpfully from above us. Liz sniggered like a fucking five year old. "So if you want to kiss and make up please do so with some expedience!"

"What's this about a moving van?" Simon asked, confused but completely ignoring Tom in order to direct the question at me.

"Oh, I moved into my new place today. Tom and Liz just

told me I can choose anything in this house to take to my new place, and very helpfully provided a van for me to do so. But unfortunately I cannot drive; I hear you can?"

Understanding dawned on Simon's face. "Would you let me help you move furniture into your new flat, Courtney? It would be my pleasure."

I pretended to consider things for a moment, simply to watch Simon grow flustered under my gaze. "Only if I can have one of those sausage rolls."

"You can have them all. Consider it interest incurred on my sausage roll theivery."

"How about half? Half for me, and half for you."

"Deal."

"Deal."

After we practically exhaled the baked goods whilst going around the townhouse picking out the bits and pieces I wanted for my flat – the square footage of my new place was basically the size of Tom's living room, after all; I had to be conservative – Simon's hand naturally found mine, and I found his.

It felt right. It felt *necessary.* How had I been scared of my feelings for Simon? For how serious I was about him? For how much he obviously cared for me? All I had within me was a longing for this man to be by my side. It was a different kind of safe than I felt with Rich. Than I had ever felt with anyone else. But that wasn't at the forefront of my brain right now.

Simon Saint was a gorgeous man, and the sight of him standing beside me fully clothed when he should be naked and horizontal was quite frankly a mortal sin.

He caught the change in mood delightfully quickly. Pausing from unlocking the moving van he raised my hand to his lips and grazed my knuckles, slowly, one by one. "What do you say to getting your furniture moved over as quickly as physically possible and then—"

"Christening the bed?"

"I was going to say 'grab some dinner and see where the night goes', but I like your version better."

"We just had, like, one thousand calories of sausage rolls ea —*ahh*!" For Simon had swept me up into his arms, and began spinning the two of us around on the pavement like an idiot. My idiot.

"I missed you," he said, kissing my forehead. "More than I could possibly put into words."

"It's not fair that you get to say that first," I pouted. "Now if I say I felt the same way it sounds cheap."

"Nothing about you is cheap, Courtney Miller."

God, that did it. I was crying. Simon swept my tears away, but more followed them. "Get us to my fucking flat so I can cry for another reason, you bastard," I said, horny even when I was overwhelmed with emotion.

Finally Simon kissed my lips. His arms tightened around me, and I wrapped myself around him, but our lips were soft and gentle against each other. Chaste, even, despite the torrent of not-so-chaste emotions I could tell Simon shared with me – if the fiery look in his eyes was anything to go by.

"I've never been so happy to follow an order than that one."

Chapter forty

SIMON

We did not, in fact, manage to build the bed in Courtney's new flat before we started tearing our clothes off.

"The mattress will do," Courtney pointed out, breathless, as she wrenched off my turtleneck. Said mattress was lying on the floor in her bedroom, surrounded by planks of wood and a carved headboard leaning against the wall waiting to be constructed. But Courtney was very much correct: making the bed could wait until later.

I threw her on top of the mattress, glad for its high quality, cloud-like surface. You couldn't even feel the floor beneath it. "This is the bed we first kissed on, isn't it?" I murmured against Courtney's mouth. We couldn't stop kissing for even a moment; we'd wasted too much time already.

"And dry-humped on, as Liz kindly reminded me today." Courtney whimpered when I dragged my nails up her stomach during the process of pulling off her dress. God, I'd missed this. Courtney was wearing mismatched underwear from two different sets I knew she'd bought in London – that she wasn't wearing a complete set of either endeared her to me more than I could ever vocalise.

I trailed kisses down her navel, and Courtney giggled. "You stubble, Si, it tickles," she said, running her hands through my hair until she found decent purchase. "I thought you preferred being clean-shaven."

"I've been busy with the restaurant. And mentally... preoccupied."

"Preoccupied?"

"Yeah. I couldn't get this super hot hotel receptionist off my mind. She's also great with dogs."

"Oh?" Courtney quirked an eyebrow when I looked up at her. "Who is she? I'm jealous."

I was about to fire back an equally silly retort, but mention of dogs and jealousy pulled out a question I couldn't stop myself from asking. "What happened with Rich?"

For a moment it looked like Courtney wouldn't respond. Then she directed me back up with a tug on my hair until the two of us were lying on the mattress, facing each other.

"I kind of said I'd be with him" – a knot twisted my stomach – "but my heart wasn't in it and we both knew it. I'm still going to work with him, though. For a year."

"A year?"

"Long enough for me to really get my shit together." Courtney stroked my face, softly, slowly. "Obviously it sucked to mess Rich around like that, but we'll be okay. He knows me better than anyone, after all. Even he knew we made better friends."

"So does this mean it's *Rich* I'm going to have to convince that I'm a good guy, not your family?" I sighed dramatically. "Because your mum and sister love me already. Is you dad tough to impress?"

"He's a teddy bear. But Rich is basically his surrogate son, so..."

I grinned. "Challenge accepted."

We kissed with absolutely no haste. Our mouths were lazy and deliberate and affectionate, for the frenzy that had gotten us to this point thus far – half-naked and lying on a bare mattress – had passed. Now we were both content to lie together surrounded by boxes and furniture and a million other things both Courtney and I had to organise in our lives.

From the pocket of my jeans my phone buzzed, shocking us both out of our dreamy little reverie.

"You should check it," Courtney urged. "It might be important." I couldn't think of anything more important than existing in this moment for all of eternity, but because Courtney said I should do it, I did it.

But when I unlocked my phone and saw what the notification was about, I frowned at the screen. "This is...an email. From my grandfather."

"Is that unusual behaviour for him?"

"No, but we haven't spoken in two weeks. Not since you called me and I told him and Nan that I wasn't taking over the firm and if they didn't like that then they could leave me alone."

"You *didn't!*" Courtney gasped, sitting bolt upright.

I rose more slowly. "I did. You gave me the courage to say what needed said. Admittedly I didn't give my grandparents a chance to reply but they've been silent ever since, so..." I shrugged my shoulders.

"Read it out," Courtney said, leaning over my shoulder to read the screen as she did so. It wasn't an invasion of privacy: it was the most natural thing in the world. For what would I ever hide from her? What would I *want* to hide from Courtney?

Nothing.

"It reads," I began, opening up the email. It had no subject title, which was very odd behaviour for Rupert Saint. "Simon, we hope you are well."

"Your grandmother and I are quite frankly shocked at the way we all left things when last you were in London. Perhaps the most shocking part, however, was the fact that it never should have come to that in the first place, and we know that the fault in this matter lies with us, not you. We have known for quite some time that your heart did not belong to finance and investments, but you were so talented – and made us so proud – that we kept pushing our wishes onto you. In this we have been beyond unreasonable; you had every right to lash out the way you did. That you felt you couldn't speak to us regarding the matter for years on end saddens us more than we can put into words. We hope it is not too late to mend the bridge between us. If you could give us the opportunity to support and love and cherish you the way we should have done your mother, we will spend the rest of our lives proving that we deserve such a chance."

"Our love always, Rupert and Maria Saint." I barked out a laugh. "All of that just to be so formal at the end. Everyone talks about meetings that could have been an email, but this is the complete opposite." My mouth was too dry, my eyes absurdly wet. Courtney was stroking tears off my cheeks, but I had no idea for how long she'd been doing it.

"See," she said, voice low and soothing, "I told you. They love you, Simon. You could be a stripper and they'd still love you."

"I think that might be taking it too far."

"But then my third job as a hooker would make more sense. The stripper and the prostitute – what a pair!" Courtney took my phone from me to place it on the floor, then held our hands together between us. "Are you okay?"

"I just...yeah. I am. I need some time to process, but I'll be okay."

"You just have to do things one step at a time." When I flinched Courtney added, "That's what Tom told me when I was getting overwhelmed! It's such a simple thing but – I don't know. It's been helping me a lot."

I clucked my tongue. "The *bastard*."

"...excuse me?"

"Tom was a neurotic mess during his PhD – when I met him," I explained. The tears had dried up, thankfully, but I still felt like a mess. Courtney didn't seem to care. "He tried to do too many things all at once, all the time. See, his undergrad was not at all challenging to him. Too gifted or whatever."

"The bastard."

"Exactly. So I told him what Mum always used to tell me, when she was stressed over paying the bills and looking after me and working three jobs at once. Because all those things, in turn, stressed *me* out. 'We just have to do things one step at a time, Si,' she'd tell me. 'We get *one* bill sorted, then we'll have a nice dinner. I'll do my next shift at *one* job, and you can get *one* night of homework done, then we can go get ice cream to celebrate!'"

Courtney looked like she was going to cry – good, because I was done being the crybaby – but then she squeezed my hands, gave me my favourite crooked smile, and said, "She was...well, I wish I could have met her. I wish you'd had your entire life to know her."

"I had all the time I was ever going to get. I've made my peace with that. After all, I got more time with her than loads of kids ever do with their mother. Oh, god, that wasn't a dig," I added on, when Courtney's face contorted like a gargoyle. "You relationship with your mum is totally different, Court. I didn't —"

"I called her. Yesterday. It went okay, I think."

"So...why the grimace?"

"Reflex reaction." Courtney shook out her hair and laughed softly. "I'll have to fix that."

"I'm proud of you."

"I'm proud of me, too."

With a contented sigh I laid back down onto the mattress, taking Courtney with me. "So what next? For this evening, I mean. The van is due back at seven."

She frowned. "What time is it now?"

"Six."

Something filthy crossed Courtney's face, but then she groaned. "Let's be adults for once."

"Having sex is pretty adult if you as—"

She swatted my arm. "Let's get the van returned early, then order some take-out and actually, you know, make the bed."

"Who are you and where is Courtney Miller?" She kissed my nose in response, and I pulled her in close to my chest. "That sounds good to me. Although we seem to be making a habit of lying in bed together, half-naked, but not having sex."

"Oh, there's a whole lot of sex in your future, Simon. A disgusting amount. Soon you'll be *begging* for the nights where we lay together, half-naked, but not having sex."

"You had to ruin it."

"I had to ruin it."

"I like who I am with you, Courtney," I said, kissing the crown of her hair, kissing her forehead, kissing her lips. "And I like who I can see myself becoming with you by my side."

Courtney's tongue darted out to just barely graze my teeth. I could feel the smile that curled her lips before I saw it. "I like who I am with you, too, Simon. I like who I am with you *a lot.*"

"I'd say that's a pretty great place for us to start."

Chapter Forty-One

COURTNEY

We were due to meet Simon at his restaurant to try out the entire menu ahead of the soft launch tomorrow night, and Dad was late. Of course he was late; if the roles were reversed I'd have been late, too.

"I don't understand where he is," I grumbled, checking my reflection as I spoke. My hair was overdue a trim; the ends had gone scraggly whilst my roots were unbearably long. Especially when paired with the beautiful clothes Simon had bought me in London, I looked a bit mismatched. Although...I kind of liked that. Mismatched.

In any case, thanks to Tom, I now had the money to get a haircut. A very nice one, in fact – a cut and colour at that fancy hairdresser one of my old Plaza clients had been harping on at me to go to for literal years on end now.

I'd been thinking a lot about what to do with the money Tom had given me. Well, actually, when it came down to it, the decision over what to do hadn't taken a whole lot of thinking. I'd been given the oddest fairy godmother one might ever hope to have, but I wasn't going to look a gift horse in the mouth by using the money I now found myself in possession of on something frivolously expensive.

No, I had something far more important to spend the money on. A celebrity-style hair cut could come later. For now I made do with spritzing salt spray all over my hair so it hung in easy, messy waves around my face. That way my overly long dark blonde roots and split ends were far less noticeable.

When I heard a knock on the door I just about had a heart attack. I'd expected a buzz to come through the alarm from the front door into the flat building before someone actually came knocking. Shaking some sense back into me I padded over to the door and peeped through the spyglass. It was Dad, finally, sheepishly shuffling his feet in that way where he knew fine well he was late.

"And what time do you call this?" I demanded when I swung the door open, though the foolish grin on my face told him that I was joking. He handed over a bouquet of flowers that he'd obviously been hiding behind his back. And not the cheap kind from the supermarket; the really nice ones that you had to order online. The flowers were every shade of pink: my favourite colour. I didn't know what any of them were called, since I wasn't a flower person, but god did I appreciate the effort.

"I had to wait for these to arrive in the post," Dad apologised after giving me a hug. "And the downstairs door was open. You should look into that – it's a security risk!" I rolled my eyes until he said, "Show me around the new pad, then."

"I don't have everything in the right place yet," I explained as I showed him around the small flat. Small, but my own. "I think it'll take a while to work out where everything Tom and Liz gave me can comfortably go."

"It was so kind of them to help you out like this. You have good friends, dove. Still can't believe you didn't ask your old man to help you move in though!"

"With *your* back?" I turned from him to put the kettle on, then went through the motions of making two cups of Earl Grey tea. "Besides," I continued, "Tom hired a van for me. Pretty sure it was part of his 'get Courtney and Simon back together' plan but it was a useful and appreciated gesture nonetheless." Dad chuckled, then accepted a cup of tea when I handed it over.

We wandered over to the balcony, both of us revelling in the feeling of fresh air on our faces when we stepped outside. "So what do you think?" I asked, nervous for some reason. I'd never lived on my own: what did *I* know about furnishing or picking a good location or any of the other things people had to think about?

The glow of pride emanating off my dad told me he didn't need to say a thing. I could tell he loved the place. But I appreciated it nonetheless when he said, "It's perfect, Courtney. Your sister will be so jealous – it's bigger than her place in London!"

"Oh, I don't doubt it." I checked the time on my phone. If we left in five minutes we would only just barely be late to meet Simon at his restaurant. But before we left I had something important to discuss with my dad. Something that could be put off no longer. "Before we stuff our faces..."

"Which I sincerely cannot wait for."

"I wanted to run an idea by you."

Dad stilled in a way I knew I often did, too. We both hated open-ended statements like that, for who knew what was coming next? For all we knew someone was going to ask us to sell our soul or join an MLM.

"Um," I began, not quite sure where to start. But if I didn't jump right in I'd never say anything, so I took a deep breath and said, "Tom gave me quite a lot of money for house- and pet-sitting. Like, way more than he should have, but he insisted. And...well...I want to go for a private ADHD diagnosis."

The relief on Dad's face was palpable. "I'm so happy to hear that, dove. I really think that's the best thing for you."

"I'm not done. I want you to get one, too. But I'll pay for it!" I amended quickly. "I can afford to pay for us both. I've looked up a few clinics in Glasgow and—"

"Hold up, hold up." Dad scrutinized me from beneath his brows. "You want me to let you pay for *my* diagnosis? Have I gone mental or am I hearing you right?"

I took a disgruntled sip of tea. "You were already mental."

"Very funny. But I don't need you to do that for me. Really, I don't. You've already done more than a daughter should ever have to do for her Dad, Courtney."

"Dad—"

"And besides," he continued, steamrollering right through me the way I always did to other people, "I may have already booked myself in for a consultation. With my *own* money, that I've been saving up for a while. I was going to tell you about it next week."

I could only stare at my Dad, dumbfounded. He'd...what? Made the same decision I'd made, but separately, independently, from me? Was that...progress?

A knock on the door interrupted us. "Strange," I murmured, frowning back into my flat before leading my dad inside. I closed the balcony door behind us to keep the heat in, then walked over to the front door. "I think you have the wrong number!" I called out.

Only for Simon's muffled voice to respond, "I bloody well hope not."

"Dad and I are going to meet *you*," I said, still not opening the door. I glanced back at Dad and realised that his sheepishness from earlier was not, in fact, sheepishness, but was instead suspicion. "Dad, what's going on?"

He waved uselessly behind me. "Just open the door."

So I did. Simon stood there, of course, dashing as high hell in the suit he wore the day we first met, his hair styled back, his grey eyes twinkling in mischief. But he wasn't alone.

Behind him stood Ailish and Mum.

"Surprise," everyone said in unison, kind of weakly.

"It didn't feel right to have only your dad come to sample the menu," Simon said, which was the worst excuse I'd ever heard. When I said nothing he added on, hastily, "Please don't hate me. We've only just made up."

I let him stew for a couple more agonising seconds. It was worth it, to see the panic on his face. But I must have smiled or twitched or in some other way betrayed myself, for Simon sighed in relief. "You're yanking my chain."

"I am indeed yanking your chain. Come in, everyone! Excuse the language but how the fuck are you here, Ailish? Mum...?"

Mum happily barged in once I moved out of the way, feverish with excitement. Excitement? To visit my new flat? "Simon called us a couple of days ago asking if he could fly us up for his new restaurant's grand opening!" she gushed.

Simon chuckled. "The soft-soft launch."

"He flew us first class, Courtney! I knew he was a keeper the moment you introduced us to him."

"Introduced is a bit—"

"Just let her have this, Court," Ailish said, pausing a moment before we both swept each other into a back-breaking hug. "I missed you."

"I know," I whispered, feeling just a little (a lot) overwhelmed. "I missed you, too."

"She hasn't stopped talking about you since you came down to London. I really think...well, can't you see she's trying?"

It was a difficult thing, to hold so much anger and resentment and sorrow towards someone you were supposed to love unconditionally; it was a harder thing to let that all go. But since meeting Simon I'd learned a lot of things about myself –

good, bad, truly heinous – and had also learned what I wanted to *be.*

Alone was not one of them.

"She gets one shot," I said, noticing Simon watching me and my sister talking as if he were eavesdropping on a vital war meeting. Behind him Mum was flitting about all over the place. She'd dyed her hair peroxide blonde, so sharp and drastic from her natural colour that it drew the eye wherever she went.

"You dyed your hair," Dad said, before I could, when Mum made it into the living room.

Mum stopped short in front of him, as taken aback as he was. "Graham," she stage whispered, as if shocked that Dad was here even though it was obvious he'd been in on this surprise from the start. "You look...well. You've been taking care of yourself."

Dad pointed in my direction. "All Courtney's work. I'd never have gotten out of bed for all those early morning jogs if she didn't keep me on schedule."

"She was always much better at looking after others than herself." Mum swung around to face me, immediately stricken by what she'd said, and quickly added, "I don't mean that as a criticism. You've always put others before yourself. I'm sorry I never saw you for who you really were, Courtney. I know things have been hard between us, and I know a lot of that is on me. But if you gave me the chance then I'd love to get to know who you've grown up to be."

Just like that. Just like that Mum said everything I'd ever hoped she'd say. How much introspection had that taken? How much effort? How much work? Suddenly all that resentment that had built up over the years simply washed away.

"I think I'd like to get to know you too, Mum."

As we made our way to the restaurant – we were *all* late now, which an irate Kei Nakamura was only too happy to remind Simon of via a barrage of expletive-filled texts – I found myself enjoying listening to Mum and Dad and Ailish bicker over the most banal of topics. *Masterchef.* The overuse of autotune. The Tories.

"Seems like you're not the only one who's been doing some self-improvement," Simon murmured over the din, side-eyeing me with such genuine affection I felt my poor dead heart grow two sizes.

"Careful," I warned, though my hand shadowed over his on the gearstick, "you're still in the doghouse for surprising me like this."

"Will I like the doghouse?"

"Maybe. Do you like being tied up?"

"We can hear you!" Ailish cried, disgusted. "Get a room or buy a hotel or something, Simon. Jesus."

We could only laugh. If this was what it meant to have your family by your side – to feel hopeful for where you could all go, together – then I couldn't wait to see what happened next.

So long as Simon was part of that family, too.

Epilogue

TWO YEARS LATER

COURTNEY

"Courtney, a kid brought a goat in through the front door again!"

"A goat brought a goat in?"

"Hilarious. Can you sort it, please?"

Abandoning the paperwork I was finishing up I ran out to front-of-house, where a boy around the age of ten was laughing his fucking arse off as he ran around the café with a goat that stood at the height of his shoulders. The speckled tan fur and the way she gleefully bleated as she chased the boy told me exactly which goat it was.

"You know better than to be in here, Carrie!" I chastised the goat, making a show of corralling her back outside to the general sounds of joy and merriment from the entire café. Sneaking the animals inside had been the number one most common 'crime' children had been committing ever since Simon and I opened the place three months ago. Well, I say children, but a fair few of the perpetrators had been full-grown adults.

I didn't care. I thrived on the chaos.

Once Carrie was safely back outside – a group of kids cheered, and behind me the boy responsible for letting her into the café bowed deeply – I returned to find Ailish chugging down a large cup of coffee she'd made for herself thirty minutes ago but had since forgotten about.

"And to think I *want* kids," she exhaled between gulps.

I patted her on the shoulder. "Sucks to be you. Haven't you given up yet?"

"Fu – god, no," Ailish said, quick to correct her language when a very judgemental mother and her toddler walked by on their way to the toilets. "I'd take this any day over medical writing, easy." This was still something I was struggling to comprehend – Ailish quitting her job and moving back to Glasgow to help me run The Mill.

The Mill. A café with an attached petting zoo, with wholesome, affordable, global food available from 8am to 7pm every day. On Wednesdays Rich brought the dogs down for the afternoon so the kids could play with them – with their owners' permission, of course. Even Mrs Campbell's spoiled labradoodle got in on the fun, and he had never been a Wednesday dog before.

At the weekends we opened up the bar and ran adult-only evenings. There was something incredibly wholesome about watching folk drink wine and beer and cry over how cute Carrie and Mr Big were. The goats, not the TV show characters.

In the end I had to remove the 'farmer' part of my dream, but honestly?

This version was the dream.

"Will the two of you stop nattering and take some orders?" Mum cried, making a show of being overwhelmed behind the till when in fact she was having the time of her life. No, of course she hadn't quit her job to make this a family affair; she merely wanted to 'spend a day in our shoes' to see what we got up to. Mum *had* moved back to Glasgow alongside Ailish, though, and was very much enjoying living back in her precious Hyndland ("Everyone in London was so rude, and so *bougie*!" she'd decried, the moment she knew she was coming back).

She and Dad were going on a date later. A date. Ugh, I didn't know if I could take it.

"You're supposed to be taking orders so I can finish up my paperwork, Mum!" I reminded her, though I bumped her out of the way to take over nonetheless. A harassed father with three kids – regulars; his name was David – breathed an audible sigh of relief when I took over.

"Courtney, thank god," he murmured, quiet enough that Mum didn't hear. "I don't think your mum knows how to input 'beans and sausages' into the till."

"You'd need to add *sourdough toast* and *gluten free* to your order for her to understand anything. Don't worry, anyway; I put in your order the moment you walked through the door. Take the table in the corner; Ailish is just about to clean it for you."

David's expression of gratitude spoke volumes more than words could. I could see, in that moment, why Simon's dream and mine were so perfectly aligned. To be the haven, the solace, for parents and toddlers and teenagers and nannies and poor students alike was a dream *worth* having, after all. We were bringing joy to these people. Safety. Routine.

I hoped The Mill would be open forever.

After David and his kids headed over to the newly-cleaned table I had Ailish take over the tills so Mum could serve food, silently thanking the gods that two of my part-timers were due to start in five minutes.

"I think I saw Simon coming round the back, by the way," Ailish said. "I thought he wasn't due back until fo—"

I rushed out of the café before she could finish her sentence, checking in with the kitchen staff on my way in case they needed anything (eggs, as usual). So I made a pit-stop at the barn to grab some, only to find Simon already fulfilling their request.

It was funny, watching a man in a full, tailored suit bending low over a chicken coop to collect eggs. But it was hotter more than funny, because Simon's ass was exceptional. When I snuck over and squeezed said ass he let out a strangled cry of surprise.

"Hey, stranger," I giggled, moving an inch backwards so Simon could right himself and turn to face me.

"I almost cracked these!" he exclaimed, indicating towards the eggs in his hands. I placed them into the box I'd brought out with me, then placed the box on the floor to jump up and sling my arms around his neck; Simon eagerly wrapped his arms around my waist.

I bit the end of his nose. "I missed you. Two weeks is too long."

"It would have been three if Nan had anything to do with it."

I searched Simon's warm grey eyes for a sign anything was amiss, but all I saw was long-suffering patience and affection. "Has she stopped asking us to move down to London yet?"

He grimaced. "Not yet, but get this."

"Get what?"

"Papa wants to move to Glasgow."

"You're *shitting me*," I said, slapping Simon's shoulders until he put me back down on the ground. "The mighty Rupert Saint, rolling around with us commoners?"

"He says there are a few businesses up here he's interested in as his retirement projects."

"Ah, because everyone knows you retire simply to take on more work. How's the bakery?"

"Busy as usual." Simon peered over my head towards the café. "Though I'd say it's busier here."

"It's *always* busy here."

"And that's just the way you love it." Simon smiled, and it was the warmest, fondest smile one could ever hope to witness. It was a smile just for me.

"That's just the way I love it, yeah, though I could handle the *man* I love being a little less busy."

Simon's eyes twinkled, then in one fell swoop he dipped me low and kissed me, hard. "Then you'll be happy to know I have fully handed the reins for *Saintly Pastries* over to Nicola; she made an offer on the place I simply couldn't refuse."

I couldn't believe what I was hearing. "You...you sold the bakery? Just how much did she offer?" I wasn't aware Nicola had ever been wealthy enough to outright *buy* the bakery.

But Simon sniggered into my mouth. "She offered well below market value, but that was more than enough for me. I just want to spend more time with the woman I love."

We needed to get the eggs back to the kitchen, and I knew Mum was probably driving Ailish up the wall with her incompetence, but for one precious moment Simon and I indulged our desire to stand together, in the quiet, just the two of us.

Where we went from here was anyone's guess, but I knew with a certainty I'd never felt before that I was going to enjoy the adventure no matter how it looked, or where it took us.

COMING SUMMER 2024

THE SKIP-ME GIRL

Jessica Carpenter is a 30-year-old with a PhD in genetics, a great business idea, and zero money to make her dream a reality. Cue her sister, Cassie, so obsessed with dating shows that she enters Jess into one. It's a great opportunity for Jess: she can finally let loose for a summer and get the money to kick-start her business if she wins the entire show! It can't be that hard, right?

Wrong.

Because Jess is a classic 'skip-me' girl. She's got no time for men, her work comes first, she puts no effort into her appearance, and she rolls her eyes whenever a woman tries to please a man. In a show filled with fake tans, excessive drinking and himbos galore, can Jess ever clinch that number one spot and the prize money that goes with it?

Or will an unexpected love affair ruin it all?

Coming 2025

Recipe for Disaster

The last thing timid Danielle Fisher expected was to break up with her long-term boyfriend at his sister's engagement party, but when she's pressured about having kids and criticised for her food anxiety just one time too many that's exactly what she does. Tired and fed up with being treated like a proverbial doormat, and dying to expand her very restricted diet, Dani knows she has to find the will to change.

Enter Joseph Cooke, one half of the prominent food review blog Two Many Cookes and close friend of the bride-to-be. He needs inspiration for his blog...and Dani seems to be exactly what he needs. So Joe offers Dani a partnership she cannot refuse: she'll be the subject of his new food anxiety series, and in turn he'll help her overcome it.

As things heat up in the kitchen *and* outside it, will meddling exes, hidden agendas and massive over-thinking spoil the broth? Or are Dani and Joe as perfect for each other as bread and butter?

Acknowledgements

This was a tough one to write. It was personal, and it was a slog, and there were many tears to be had. But I did it!

Courtney Can't Decide was a lesson in how to write a romantic comedy about two fundamentally very sad people. Which was probably why it was so tough *cries*. Anyway...

This book could not have existed without my beautiful sister, Cara, to whom this book is dedicated. It also couldn't have existed without the other C in my life, Chloë, who was the inspiration for her named counterpart in the *Hot Mess* trilogy and just got engaged to her beautiful girlfriend. I outlined this book well before their engagement so let's just say I predicted it would happen. I love you both more than words can ever say. Your absolutely batshit bonkers personalities are why Courtney is who she is.

To my readers: another day, another rom-com. Another year, maybe? I'm sorry I've been so slow at getting my books out the last couple of years. Burn-out is hard but I'm finding ways to get over it.

Here's to the next one!

About the Author

Hayley Louise Macfarlane hails from the very tiny hamlet of Balmaha on the shores of Loch Lomond in Scotland. After graduating with a PhD in molecular genetics she did a complete 180 and moved into writing fiction. Though she loves writing multiple genres (fantasy, romance, sci-fi, psychological fiction and horror so far!) she is most widely known for her Gothic, Scottish fairy tale, Prince of Foxes – book one of the Bright Spear trilogy.

You can follow her on Twitter at @HLMacfarlane or TikTok, also at @HLMacfarlane.

Also by H. L. Macfarlane

FAIRY TALE SHARED UNIVERSE:
BRIGHT SPEAR TRILOGY
PRINCE OF FOXES
LORD OF HORSES
KING OF FOREVER

DARK SPEAR DUOLOGY
SON OF SILVER (COMING SOON)
HEIR OF GOLD (COMING SOON)

ALL I WANT FOR CHRISTMAS IS A FAERIE ASSASSIN?!

CHRONICLES OF CURSES
BIG, BAD MISTER WOLFE
SNOWSTORM KING
THE TOWER WITHOUT A DOOR

OTHER BOOKS:

ROMANTIC FANTASY
INTENDED

MONSTERS TRILOGY
INVISIBLE MONSTERS
INSATIABLE MONSTERS
INVINCIBLE MONSTERS

Thrillers
The Boy from the Sea

Rom-coms
The Unbalanced Equation
Courtney Can't Decide

Short Stories
The Snowdrop (part of Once Upon a Winter: A Folk and
Fairy Tale Anthology)
The Goat
The Boy Who Did Not Fit